The Body Under the Bridge

Nick Louth is a best-selling thriller writer, award-winning financial journalist and an investment commentator. He self-published his first novel, Bite, in 2007, which was a No. 1 Kindle best-seller in 2014. It has sold a third of a million copies, and been translated into six languages. Freelance since 1998, he has been a regular contributor to the Financial Times, Investors Chronicle and Money Observer, and has published seven other books. Nick Louth is married and lives in Lincolnshire.

Also by Nick Louth

Trapped
Heartbreaker

DCI Craig Gillard Crime Thrillers

NICK LOUTH

THE BODY UNDER THE BRIDGE

CANELOCRIME

First published in the United Kingdom in 2020 by Canelo

This edition published in the United Kingdom in 2020 by

Canelo Digital Publishing Limited
31 Helen Road
Oxford OX2 0DF
United Kingdom

A CIP catalogue record for this book is available from the British Library.

Print ISBN 978 1 78863 995 8
Ebook ISBN 978 1 78863 698 8

Look for more great books at www.canelo.co

Printed and bound in Great Britain by Clays Ltd, Elcograf S.p.A.

For Louise, as always

Chapter One

Unforgettable days often start in normal ways. Detective Chief Inspector Craig Gillard slid his unmarked grey Vauxhall into the last available space in Epsom Police Station car park. Shrugging up his raincoat against the squally wind, he made his way inside. He was not in a great mood. Chief Constable Alison Rigby had called him away from a colleague's cremation service to take charge of a missing person case. It had irked him. There had been a phone call from Rigby's secretary, then a text from the woman herself. No apology, no explanation. The murder of an officer was rare, and the death of DC Colin Hodges a month ago had been a shock to the entire team. Senior officers normally respected the close-knit nature of detective work, and it was unheard of for an officer to be dragged away from a funeral.

Particularly for a new case as apparently trivial as this.

Beatrice Ulbricht, a twenty-five-year-old German-born student at London's Royal College of Music, had been due to perform as a member of a string quartet at the church of St Martin-in-the-Fields last night. She didn't turn up, and hadn't been seen since.

Big deal.

I

That had been Gillard's initial reaction. A quarter of a million people go missing every year, for all sorts of reasons. Most of them turn up again, given enough time. The woman had been missing for less than twenty-four hours. In the case of a young child it would be significant, as it could be in the case of someone who had learning difficulties or was in some other way vulnerable. But an adult in these circumstances could have any number of reasons for not wanting to show up: illness, performance anxiety, nervous breakdown, falling out with another musician. There was also suicide to consider.

He knew that Rigby always had reasons for intervening in day-to-day policing, and didn't always share them with those concerned. She didn't micromanage lightly. He guessed there was something important he wasn't being told. He hoped that it might become obvious once he spoke to the witness.

Gillard barged open the big double doors of the station, nodded to the desk sergeant, and was pointed towards the interview suite where PC Lynne Fairbanks was interviewing a young woman. Gillard apologised for missing the start. Introductions were made. Karen Ellsworth, a fellow member of the Lysander String Quartet, had reported Beatrice missing. Ellsworth had short dark hair, large dangly earrings and was wearing a charcoal grey trouser suit.

'As I told the officer here, Beatrice said she was on her way to London, but never showed up. It would have been our big break, and I'm not sure we will get another chance.' She seemed furious that her colleague had let her fellow musicians down.

'Do you have fears for her safety?'

'Yes, that's why I came in to report it.'

'Has she ever done anything like this before?' Gillard asked.

'Never. It's completely out of character. I got a text from her yesterday afternoon to say she was on her way into Waterloo—'

'Where from?'

'From Guildford, on the train. Well, Clandon actually.'

Clandon's small station, a few miles east of the city, served a semi-rural hinterland. On a good day its well-heeled commuters could reach central London in less than an hour. 'Can you show me the message?' Gillard asked.

Karen nodded and passed him the phone.

Bea, where are u? All set for tonite?

On the train now. I'll be there. X

The reply was timed at 15.58 on the Tuesday.

'Is that the entire thread?'

'Yes.'

'And Beatrice lives with you?'

'Yes, we share a flat at the Royal College's student accommodation in West London. She's not been home.'

'How can you be sure?'

'None of her stuff has been touched. The music stand has still got the music for the previous concert on it. And her violin is missing.'

'Have you been in contact with her other friends?'

'Yes, two of them are the other members of the quartet. I think all her London friends are musical. No one has heard from her since late yesterday afternoon.'

'When did you actually last see her?' Gillard asked.

'On Sunday. The quartet played at a wedding at Clandon Spa Hotel, near Guildford' Gillard knew the place, it was one of the grandest hotels in the area.

'Are you aware of any change in her personal circumstances, such as a death in the family, breaking up with a boyfriend, anything that would make her particularly unhappy?'

'No. She's got a steady boyfriend in Germany.'

'Does she have a tendency for mood swings—'

Karen shook her head until her earrings jangled. 'I'm not getting this across to you. She's steady as a rock. She's the leader of our quartet. I mean she's the one who makes sure that *we* turn up.'

Gillard nodded, and rolled a pencil between his fingers. 'I know it's a big thing for you, missing the concert and all, but people go missing for all kinds of reasons, and after such a short time there's no fundamental reason to believe anything untoward has happened.'

'She would *never* have missed that concert,' Karen said. 'You don't know her.'

'Okay. We'll need a description. What was she wearing?'

'When I saw her on Sunday, she was in her typical uniform. A mid-calf-length navy blue overcoat, with a long rainbow scarf. She had this lovely mauve fedora, too.'

'She should stand out then,' Gillard replied. 'Do you have a photo?'

Karen dug into her bag and produced an iPad. 'I picked this from her YouTube channel,' she said, selecting a video and turning it around so the officers could see it. Beatrice was wearing a sparkly black dress, standing in front of a full orchestra, with her eyes half closed and a beatific smile.

4

The detective tried to concentrate on the woman's elfin face, framed by wavy chestnut hair, but the power of the music and its overwhelming melancholy kept intruding. It was almost as if the soundtrack for the case was getting ahead of itself, the woman's musical epitaph appearing before they knew whether she was dead or alive.

Lynne's jaw was almost hanging open in admiration. 'She's really good,' she gasped.

Karen nodded. 'That's *Zigeunerweisen*, Pablo Sarasate's masterpiece, one of the hardest pieces in the repertoire.'

Lynne was entranced. 'I got up to grade six violin, but couldn't begin to tackle that. All that double and treble-stopping, and glissando.'

Karen turned to Lynne, clearly surprised to find such knowledge in a PC. 'Beatrice has such enormous talent.' There was a catch in her throat as she said: 'I have a really bad feeling about this.'

Gillard excused himself and beckoned for Lynne to join him outside the interview room. Once he was outside he said to her: 'I don't quite get why the Met Police aren't investigating this. She disappeared on their patch.'

Lynne shrugged. 'All I know is that it was passed back to us because the woman was last seen in Surrey. And I suppose because Ms Ellsworth first reported her missing to this station. Her parents live just up the road apparently and she was visiting them.'

Gillard blew a heavy sigh and made his way back into the interview room, followed by Lynne.

'Ms Ellsworth, you say that your quartet played at a wedding reception in Surrey on Sunday evening? And that was when you last saw her?'

'Yes.'

'And you went back to London after that?'

'Yes, three of us went back by train from Clandon on the Sunday evening.'

'Why did she not accompany you?'

'As I told the PC, after the recital she was picked up by a friend, Adrian Singer.'

'Aha. Have you contacted him?'

'Yes. I rang him. He said Beatrice left his home late on the Sunday to catch the last train to Waterloo.'

'So we already have a disconnect, don't we? Mr Singer told you she headed up to London on the Sunday, but two days later she replies to a text from you saying she is only *that* afternoon on her way up from Clandon.'

Karen nodded. Gillard saw that Lynne already had various phone numbers and addresses noted, including that of Mr Singer. He was beginning to see why the Met had passed it back.

After the interviewee had left, Lynne turned to the detective with a face full of respect. She asked: 'What do you think?'

He pursed his lips. 'Well, normally eighteen hours since the last phone contact is no time at all, except perhaps for a child. But the crucial thing here is that she missed an important concert. I'm no musician, but clearly it's out of character.' He was about to continue when his mobile rang. A glance at the screen confirmed the call was from the chief constable.

'Yes, ma'am?' he answered.

'I was sorry to drag you away from the funeral earlier, Craig, but this is a very important case and I want you on it.'

'Yes, ma'am.'

'The missing woman is the daughter of Germany's Minister of Justice, Karl-Otto Ulbricht.'

'I see.' Suddenly it all made sense.

'Exactly. I've had enquiries, via the Home Secretary, that is *our* Home Secretary. I tried to pass it back to the Metropolitan Police, because that is where the young woman lives, and as far as we can establish where she was last in contact with anybody, but unsurprisingly, because she was last seen here in Surrey, they don't want to touch it with a barge pole. So it's our baby. Your baby.'

'Thank you, ma'am.' Gillard tried his damnedest to keep every trace of sarcasm from that response.

'I'm sure you'll do a fine job, Craig. I'm counting on you. I'm allocating DI Claire Mulholland to help you.'

The line went dead.

–

Gillard had originally entertained hopes of being able to make it for the funeral reception at the Red Lion, Colin Hodges' local. His wife Joan would have ordered a great spread, and he had been looking forward to munching his way through a great stack of sandwiches. The magnitude and urgency of the case now dumped upon him made that impossible. He texted Joan his apologies.

Before driving back to Surrey Police headquarters in Guildford he emailed Research Intelligence Officer DC Rob Townsend, appended the missing woman's mobile number and told him to get cell tower traces done in time for an incident room meeting in Mount Browne at four o'clock. Three hours should be enough. He also put in an urgent email request to the Met to get some basic interviews undertaken at the Royal College of Music in South

Kensington with the missing woman's teachers, friends and fellow students. He wanted her medical records, and any electronic devices at her student digs too. Years of experience led him to copy in the chief constable to ensure that his resource-grabbing request to the Met was treated with the appropriate respect, rather than the virtual two fingers that a nobody like him would normally get from the capital's police service. Finally, he rang Mr Singer and left a message.

With the ball now rolling, Gillard began to consider the student's movements. Lynne's detailed notes showed that the Lysander Quartet had the week before taken a last-minute booking for the Clandon Spa Hotel wedding reception. Their set was over by eight, and all the musicians bar Beatrice went back to London. No one had seen her since that time, but there were two text messages from Beatrice's phone on Tuesday afternoon. The one he had seen was to Karen Ellsworth, confirming that she would be at the concert in London. According to Karen, Beatrice's second text was an hour later to another member of the quartet, saying she was fine and would be there on time.

The hands-free phone disturbed his thoughts as he was motoring on the A3. It was the control room patching through a call from an Adrian Singer. Perhaps the last person to see Beatrice Ulbricht.

'Hello Mr Singer.'

'I'm returning your call, detective chief inspector. I had a message earlier from PC Fairbanks. I'm really worried to hear about Beatrice. It's quite unlike her.'

'Yes, that's what everybody says. I'd like to get you in to make a detailed statement, but perhaps I can just ask you a couple of questions.'

'Of course.'

'I understand that you had picked up Ms Ulbricht from Clandon Spa Hotel after the concert.'

'I did, yes. I brought her back to my place in Westmeare for dinner, and after that I dropped her at the bus stop.'

'So she was heading back to London?'

'Yes.'

'You went to fetch her from Clandon Spa Hotel five miles away, but you only dropped her back at the local bus stop. That's four or five miles away from Clandon station.'

He was silent for a moment. 'Actually, I didn't drop her. She walked out to the main road where the bus stop is. It's only two hundred yards.'

'What time was that?'

'Just before eleven.'

'Are there bus services at that time of night on a Sunday?'

'I don't know.'

Gillard didn't want to press too hard at this point. There were obvious question marks over Singer's account, but he would rather apply pressure when he was in a position to make notes.

'Did you contact her to make sure that she had got home all right?'

'Not until the next day. And she didn't reply. I think she's upset with me.'

'Why would that be?'

'We had an argument. I think she misunderstood my intentions.'

Or understood them too well, Gillard thought.

'Do you have any idea where she might have gone?'

'None whatever.'

He arranged to visit Singer in the evening, and then hung up.

The man had volunteered a great deal of information, including some that did not put him in a great light. But it was equally likely he hadn't told the complete truth.

–

Rob Townsend was waiting by Gillard's desk, like a dog expecting dinner. The officer, whose fresh face and short gingery hair made him look younger than his twenty-six years, could never hide his excitement when he thought he had made a case breakthrough.

'Sir, we've got a good clear trace on Beatrice's phone. It shows her in Clandon, then later in Westmeare until eleven, when it was turned off. It remained off for all of Monday and a bit of Tuesday. On Tuesday afternoon she headed up to London, according to the cell site analysis. She lights up all the towers from Clandon to Waterloo. The speed and path fits with a train journey, with further traces within London during the evening. There's another trip, seemingly by road, towards Brentford this morning.'

Gillard blew a sigh of relief. 'Hopefully she's not missing at all then. What about texts and emails?'

'There's dozens incoming, only a few in the other direction. I've just sent an electronic copy of the warrant to the service provider, so we should be able to see the full contents today.'

'Did you call in any CCTV?'

'Well, I thought maybe we didn't need to. It would be hard to know where to start.'

'Not Waterloo obviously, unless you want to send Carl Hoskins mad scanning a million people emerging from trains. You obviously start at the quietest place, where she would be easy to spot. Clandon station, I suppose. Does that fit the trace?'

'Yes, that seems to be where she got on.'

'Did you ring Network Rail to check whether it has CCTV there?'

Townsend looked flustered. 'Not yet, sir.' It was easy to see what he was thinking. *She's obviously alive and kicking, so why would we bother?*

Gillard sighed. 'Have you tried ringing her?'

'Yes, but not for several hours. There was no reply.'

'Let's have another go.' Gillard reached across for the paperwork, tapped out the number on his desk phone and heard it ring out. It then went to a message service which said the mailbox was full. He shrugged, waited a minute, then tried again. This time the phone was answered.

'Hello, is that Beatrice Ulbricht?'

It clearly wasn't. There was a lot of background noise, but Gillard could just about make out the words being spoken to him. He repeated Beatrice's name, then loudly spelled it out. 'Can you hold it all for me?' Gillard asked, and then read out his police credentials. 'Yes, the entire container.'

Gillard hung up, offering Townsend a dour expression.

'Who was that?' Townsend asked.

'Someone called Gladys at the Brentford waste transfer station. She's got Beatrice's phone. Found in a consignment of rubbish.'

'Oh shit,' Townsend said. 'That's not good news.'

'They just found the phone, Rob,' Gillard said. 'They haven't found a body so far.' Gladys had told him that the device had been picked up out of the container of unsorted rubbish this morning. It joined a dozen other phones recovered over the last week, along with fountain pens, spectacles and various other metallic items through which the overhead magnet earned its keep.

'She told me that if they hadn't spotted it, or if the magnet hadn't grabbed hold of it, it would be on its way to Bristol this evening to be burned at the Severnside Energy Recovery Centre.'

'So Beatrice is still missing?'

'Yep. They're taking a look through the hopper for her, but in the meantime, Rob...'

'I'll get right back on the CCTV, sir.'

'Thank you, Rob. I'm a lot more worried now than I was an hour ago. Millennials are inseparable from their phones. I can't think of a good reason why it should be at a rubbish dump.'

'Unless she's there too,' Townsend said.

Gillard nodded grimly as he reached for the phone. Alison Rigby would want to know. He punched out her direct line. As so often, it fell to him to be the bearer of bad news.

Chapter Two

Adrian Singer lived in the village of Westmeare, population 280, in a quiet rural corner of Surrey. His home was a small whitewashed cottage with a neat well-tended garden surrounded by a white picket fence. There was a wooden sculpture by the door and a rustic wagon wheel leaning against a wall. Gillard parked his car behind the aged Honda Civic already there, and turned to PC Lynne Fairbanks.

'Nice place he's got.' Gillard was sure that the climbing roses over the front door would look lovely in the summer. Even in the steady rain it looked delightful.

'It makes me think of the gingerbread house in Grimm's fairy tales,' Lynne replied. 'And we know how that turned out.' They both peered in at the warmly lit house, then got out of the car shrugging up their raincoats against the weather. Singer met them at the door. He was a balding fellow in his early forties, slightly unkempt, with bright eyes and a limp handshake. Gillard and Fairbanks were offered coffee and biscuits, and sat at a rustic table in front of a roaring open fire while it was prepared. The low-ceilinged lounge boasted an upright piano, an expensive-looking Bose stereo and a series of three brass instruments balanced on stands.

'Trombone, alto sax and trumpet,' Fairbanks said. 'Can't play any of them, though I can bang out a few tunes on the piano.' She then leaned in to her boss and whispered. 'I'd expected him to be a bit younger.'

'Me too. He's more like a teacher than a friend.'

Singer appeared, and once they were all seated, the interview began. Singer said that he first met Beatrice Ulbricht in France when she was a promising sixteen-year-old and he was playing in the orchestra that accompanied her. 'We had a relationship back then,' he said. 'There's no point trying to hide that. But since then we've really just been friends.'

The remark sat steaming between them, very much like Gillard's raincoat in front of the fire.

'You said that you picked her up from the wedding reception, which is five miles away, but then left her to get the bus back last thing at night on a Sunday,' Lynne said. 'That's not very kind, is it?'

'Well, you've got things the wrong way round. We had an argument, and she stormed out. I was going to give her a lift, but she said not to bother.' His eyebrows were high and arched, as if in permanent surprise.

'What was the argument about?'

He exhaled, his mouth spread wide in discomfort. 'Well, there was a misunderstanding, let's say that. I thought she was planning to stay here and go back in the morning.'

'And she thought you were trying to seduce her?' Gillard asked.

Singer recoiled, as if the idea was repugnant. 'It really wasn't like that.'

'Wasn't it?' Fairbanks asked, with a sceptical smile.

'Look. I knew the wedding organiser, and he rang me to try to get him out of a hole. The previous quartet he had booked cancelled at short notice because of illness. He only had a few days to find another, and asked me to help because of my Royal College links, so I rang Beatrice. The rest of Beatrice's group are frankly not quite in the same league as the Stanislavsky Ensemble who had cancelled, but beggars can't be choosers. The Lysander Quartet were happy to play an undemanding ninety-minute set for a few hundred pounds plus travelling expenses and a free meal. I offered overnight accommodation if any of them needed it. Purely to keep their costs down. It's perfectly normal for these low-key events. And Beatrice accepted, initially.'

'I see,' said Lynne, giving him a level stare.

'You can choose what to believe, but it is true. Anyway, once we'd had supper she seemed to change her mind. I was baffled, and a little offended.'

Gillard said: 'We'll need to take a cheek swab of your DNA to eliminate you from our enquiries.'

'That's perfectly all right,' he sighed. 'I'd expected it.'

The sample taken, the two detectives left. They had arranged to meet Eric Sargent, the wedding organiser, to verify the details that Singer had given them. Gillard drove to the end of the road and found the bus stop. He'd seen worse. It was a fairly typical rural bus shelter, a pitched wooden roof over a rudimentary brick enclosure, a single rusting metal bench within. Getting out to inspect it more closely, there was no legible information about the services or their frequency. A damaged Perspex display, scratched and defaced with marker pen, held the tattered remnants of what might have been a timetable. He crouched down and shone a torch over the flagstones.

Chewing gum, cigarette ends, silver paper and cellophane cigarette wrapping. Nothing unexpected.

–

Detective Constable Carl Hoskins smiled to himself as he opened the first file of CCTV footage. Cell site analysis put Beatrice Ulbricht at Clandon railway station at a quarter to four on the Tuesday afternoon. That would be exactly right to catch the South Western Railway 15.48 service to Waterloo. There were two CCTV cameras car park side at Clandon, covering the station apron and the ticket machine. Right on cue, Ms Ulbricht appeared at 15.45, right below the left-hand camera, hurrying through the rain and dodging puddles. She was wearing the navy coat, mauve fedora and scarf, and carrying a violin. There were no platform cameras, so it took a while for Hoskins to establish which carriage she had boarded. Each coach had had one internal camera at each end. He had already been sent a link to the footage from the 15.48 which was stored on the South Western Railway database.

She had got on right at the back, carriage eight. She sat roughly in the middle, reading a magazine. There were a few other passengers, only one having got on with her at Clandon. After five dull minutes trying to ignore a businessman picking his nose right opposite the camera, Hoskins fast-forwarded right to the end, the final two minutes before arrival at Waterloo. By then the carriage was packed. Almost everybody had stood up and crowded the doorways for a fast escape upon arrival. He couldn't see her, not even the hat. As the doors opened, the detective watched the raincoated commuters squeezing off, laden with briefcases, umbrellas and phones.

Once half of them were gone, Hoskins did a double take.

The woman had completely vanished.

He rewound three minutes and tried again. No sign of her. 'Christ, I bet she's moved to a different carriage,' Carl muttered. He looked through the data files. Eight carriages, sixteen cameras. Assuming they all worked. There were often one or two out of action. He put his head in his hands. Gillard was not going to be happy with this. He'd lost her somewhere. But he knew from the cell site analysis that she had made it as far as Waterloo.

Thursday

The Brentford waste transfer station is an old landfill site in West London, squeezed between clusters of railway lines. High razor wire fences, a variety of elderly cranes, eight-wheel quarry lorries and lots and lots of noise. DCI Gillard and DC Carl Hoskins were given fluorescent red high-vis jackets on arrival, and shown the main activities of the site, which were not highly sophisticated. Essentially, tipper trucks dumped vast quantities of mixed waste on the concrete floor of the five-acre facility, and a variety of machines, including a crane with suspended magnet, went through it looking for recyclables. Forget plastic, glass, paper. The only stuff worth retrieving at this stage was ferrous metals, thanks to the magnet, and copper, much of which was retrieved by hand from cables, old televisions and so forth.

Manager Tony Lowgreave brought them into the office, the higher of two stacked Portakabins, reached by a rickety ladder. He offered them scalding hot instant coffee in flimsy plastic cups.

'We like to think we are doing our bit,' Lowgreave said, as he risked a sip of the coffee. 'It's not glamorous work, but we save thousands of tonnes of valuable product from going to waste. The stuff we can't make use of goes in sealed railway containers across to the Bristol Channel. It's burned to produce electricity. So it's pretty green.'

Gillard set aside his less-than-single-use coffee, probably the only drink worse than any police beverage, and asked to be shown the retrieved mobile. It was on Lowgreave's desk, in a clear polythene bag. A standard Samsung model, clearly contaminated by some sticky substance.

'Is that how it was?' Gillard asked.

Lowgreave nodded and brought in Gladys Olewando, who had answered the phone when Gillard had rung it. A very large black woman, on whom three square yards of hi-vis was utterly redundant, she said she had retrieved the phone from the magnet.

'Do you get many phones in the rubbish?'

'Maybe half a dozen a week,' she said. 'The magnet doesn't do them any good, but this one was on a long streamer of metal cans and coat hangers dangling beneath.'

'And you're quite sure there is isn't a body?' Hoskins asked.

'We dumped the entire container out onto a big plastic sheet,' Lowgreave said. 'That is what we always do on these occasions. In the old days, I would have just sent the guard dog in there. He'd have found a body in no time. Anyway, Gladys and Mick went through it. No body, no body parts.'

'Where did that hopper come from?'

'Ah, now. Most of what we take in here is household waste from the Borough of Brent. But we have a contract with Network Rail to take their mixed consumer train waste from Waterloo and Paddington, two consignments per day. This came from the Waterloo truck.'

'That makes some sense,' Hoskins said.

Lowgreave passed across a business card. 'That's the bloke you need to talk to at Waterloo.'

–

An hour later, the two detectives were standing looking out from a high window over the enormous concourse of Waterloo Station. With them was Phil Perkins, the Network Rail recycling manager. He pointed to an arriving train on platform six. 'There you go. That's the slow Guildford service, come in via Cobham. The fast ones go via Woking. The procedure is that the mixed waste from on-train bins is picked up by contractors and then goes into a hopper, which is wheeled out to the waste trucks.'

'Does anyone go through it at this point?'

'No, not really. There's always a security check, because of the possibility of explosive devices being residual in bins, which used to happen in the old IRA days. So our operatives always take a visual glance in the bin bags, especially if they feel anything unusually heavy: batteries, wires, stuff like that. Unfortunately, although we have plans to ban concessionaire use of single-use plastics in-station by 2020, and are already providing refill points for plastic water bottles, the issue of mixed waste in litter bins, whether on-concourse or on-train, is still moot,' he said, sucking his teeth. 'The problem is that coffee cups, carton lids, straws, drinks bottles and so on can be recycled in some cases, if they are clean. In practice, approximately 38.4 per cent of bins are dreg-contaminated and consequently recycling non-compliant. It's simply not cost-effective to deal with it.'

'So, in short, it goes to the tip?' Hoskins asked, clearly exasperated by the bureaucratic lingo.

'In short, yes.'

'Do you ever get mobile phones turn up in the rubbish?' Gillard asked.

Perkins laughed. 'Last year there were over 7,600 mobiles left on trains coming into Waterloo. But generally not in the waste receptacles. They tend to be left on seats or in luggage, coats or jackets. That makes commuters look like a very careless bunch, but actually it's simply a result of the enormous numbers of people that use the railway. In 2018 there were 94.4 million passenger journeys. We are Britain's busiest railway station,' he said proudly.

–

Within twenty-four hours of her being reported missing, the search for Beatrice Ulbricht had been ramped up into a major investigation, using the Holmes-2 major inquiry database. As senior investigating officer, Gillard had a team of eight officers drafted in purely to look through CCTV, while another twelve detective constables dealt with the calls received from the public on the information line. The Metropolitan Police had allocated two officers to interview fellow students and friends in London, while the British Transport Police had offered a liaison officer. A press conference was due to take place at six that evening with a formal public appeal, but already the early editions of the free London papers, widely distributed across Surrey's commuter network, were carrying the story. The front pages carried glamorous pictures of Beatrice in evening dress, embracing her violin, wavy hair cascading over one shoulder. The inside pages showed a series of hazy stills from the railway's CCTV cameras, of her carrying a violin case and wearing the distinctive fedora.

Gillard had set up an incident room meeting for one p.m. as a working lunch, with sandwiches provided from the chief constable's personal budget. There was no surer sign of a high priority case than bought-in food.

He was under no illusions. The major effort was being made to coincide with the arrival from Germany of Karl-Otto Ulbricht, Germany's Minister of Justice and father of the missing woman. He would be accompanied in his brief trip to Mount Browne by the British Home Secretary. They would arrive around six o'clock.

No pressure, then.

–

Gillard's first port of call on return was the surveillance suite. This was part of Mount Browne's forensic centre, and was set up to provide the equipment needed to review CCTV. This was the first time they'd ever had the staff to fill every desk. They were led by DC Carrie Macintosh, who had just transferred over from Police Scotland. Ms Macintosh, inevitably known as Rainy, had abandoned her seven-year career as a junior doctor because of the stress and long hours. With spiky hair, a no-nonsense demeanour and an earthy Glaswegian sense of humour, she fitted in well with the largely male CID. One of the lads, all agreed.

'Have you managed to trace her?' Gillard asked.

'Nope, she's vanished, sir.'

Hoskins had managed to establish that Ms Ulbricht had got up from her seat in carriage eight and, taking her violin, had moved through into carriage seven. After that the trail went cold and Rainy's team had made little progress 'The CCTV in number seven didnae work,' she said. 'One camera produced nae image at all, and the other image was snowier than a blizzard.'

'What about carriage six?'

'Perfect CCTV, enough to show she never went in there. So we've bitten the bullet and downloaded all the network rail footage from platform four at Waterloo, which is where the service terminated. There are two exits, one out onto the station concourse and one down into the Northern Line, and nine cameras, so it will take a while to be sure.'

'Okay.'

–

There was a big team on the case, but there were even more detectives in the incident room for the meeting than Gillard had expected. You didn't need to be a senior officer in CID to guess that the presence of large piles of generously filled baguettes and sandwiches was strongly correlated to attendance. As well as the CCTV and information line teams, DI Claire Mulholland and DCs Michelle Tsu and Carl Hoskins were there along with DC Townsend, who seemed to be busy with his phone. The one guest was Nigel Duffy, a grey-haired inspector from the British Transport Police who looked to be in his sixties.

They were just about to start when the door opened and Chief Constable Alison Rigby strode in, power dressed in a houndstooth jacket, black slacks and court shoes. Her arrival chilled the atmosphere faster than the arrival of the Salvation Army at a lap dance joint. Rigby took a seat at the back, as if pretending that would in some way make her more incognito.

Gillard called the meeting to order, and after a few introductory remarks summarised what they knew so far. 'Beatrice Ulbricht, twenty-five, an accomplished violinist studying at the Royal College of Music for an MSc in musical performance, has been missing since Tuesday afternoon when she boarded the 15.48 Waterloo-bound train at Clandon just east of Guildford. Had she remained aboard, she would have arrived in London about an hour later. And we know for a fact that her phone did arrive in London. It was finally found at the Brentford waste transfer station, and the cell site analysis corresponds with the movement of the contractor's waste consignment from Waterloo. We are assuming it had been deposited in a waste bin somewhere on that train.'

Gillard dimmed the lights, set up his laptop projector and activated the video screen. 'This is Ms Ulbricht getting on coach eight at Clandon. As you can see she is hard to miss. Not only the mauve fedora, but that distinctive rainbow scarf, the navy blue overcoat and the violin. We've already had a half-dozen calls to the information line from people who saw her during the early part of the journey, and we should get more after this afternoon's press conference. As is typical with eyewitnesses, they notice her getting on and taking a seat, and when she moves to a new carriage. We've nothing firm on where she got off.'

The CCTV footage showed her taking a seat right under the camera at the rear of the coach. Gillard paused the video and clicked on another, edited from the coach footage. This showed her getting up and walking the length of the carriage, and through to the next coach. 'This is carriage seven, where the CCTV doesn't work. We must assume she continued her journey in this coach because there is no sign of her on carriage six, where both cameras were working.'

He brought the lights back up, then walked over to the whiteboard on which the train's movements were detailed from top to bottom. 'This is the fact that I want everybody to concentrate on. At some point on this fairly busy commuter journey, Ms Ulbricht and her phone parted company. Now it's conceivable that she left her phone behind, and that somebody else may have dropped it in a bin. There aren't really any other obvious reasons why her phone would have found its way into a rubbish container.'

Rob Townsend had raised his hand. 'Sir, just had the phone contents relayed to us by the service provider. The last text message Ms Ulbricht sent was at 16.39.' He looked down at his phone. 'The message was: "On the train now. Just arriving at Clapham Junction".'

'Okay Rob, so she was nearly into central London. I want to know who that message was sent to, and the thread of any conversation,' Gillard said. 'Cross check the time with when the service really did pass Clapham. That could well be the breakthrough we're looking for.'

He turned to the others. 'All right, CCTV people, I want you to concentrate on any platform footage from Clapham Junction and Vauxhall, and leave Waterloo to British Transport Police. Discarding the first dozen stations should save us all some time.'

'What are we saying to the press?' Claire asked.

'The indication so far is that we're talking about a missing person. We are worried for her safety, because it would not be normal for her to miss an important concert engagement, but at this stage we don't have an indication that anyone else is involved.'

'Have we got any good pictures of her wearing the hat?' This question was from press officer Christine McCafferty. 'I think it would help to have good pictures of her, with what she was actually wearing, rather than this glamorous publicity pic with evening dress and her hair—'

Claire interrupted. 'Before we get to the point of considering her safe, you should know that our Mr Singer, who had offered to put Ms Ulbricht up for the night, was interviewed by Sussex police in 2007 over an incident at the private school where he was head of music. He left the job shortly afterwards.'

'Was he ever cautioned?'

'No. There were allegations but no evidence, a least no evidence the school was willing to put forward. But after eleven years there he left within a week.'

'Okay,' Gillard said. 'That's useful information. But we must stick to the evidence. She seems to have been alive and kicking long after leaving his clutches on Sunday.'

At this point the chief constable stood up, the full six foot two, and made her way to the front. 'Thank you for this, Craig, you sound like you are fully on top of it. While it would obviously be a huge relief if Beatrice Ulbricht is found unharmed, I think we should make sure we are not missing any avenues here. If you need more resources, just let me know.'

Claire Mulholland munched a tandoori chicken and lettuce sandwich as she watched the chief constable depart. Once Rigby had gone, and most of the other officers dispersed, she closed the door and turned to Craig. 'How many of us are working on this bloody case?'

'Fifty, give or take, if you count the civilians.'

She nodded and swallowed the last of the sandwich. 'Do you remember Yvonne Fairfield?'

'Name's familiar.'

'A nineteen-year-old mixed race woman from Staines. Okay, she'd done drugs, and been cautioned for soliciting. But she's been missing three years and nine months. She'd been beaten up in the past but wouldn't identify the assailant, who was probably either a boyfriend or a pimp. We don't even have a single cop working on her case. I've been trying to make enough time to get another look at it. Her mother emails me every single day asking if we've made any progress.'

Carl Hoskins, eavesdropping from another desk, nodded in agreement. 'I've got a case of a bloke injured trying to stop some toe-rag stealing his car on Monday night. Uniforms took a statement but I haven't had a moment to go and see him in hospital and get a follow-up.'

Gillard sighed. 'It's the Madeleine McCann effect. I've had this discussion with Rigby a few times. Press priorities inevitably trump policing priorities because our bosses are politicians.'

'Ah yes, and you have got to curtsy to two of them tonight, haven't you?' Claire said, with a laugh.

'Don't remind me.' He looked down at his phone, on which an email had just come in from the surveillance team. 'Hell, I don't believe this,' he said.

'What's happened?'

'Latest from the surveillance team. Initial checks on platform CCTV show no sign of Beatrice getting off at Clapham Junction or Vauxhall. BTP says she didn't get off at Waterloo either.'

'That's the last three stations. So where did she go?'

'It seems she just vanished into thin air.'

Chapter Three

The team's first attempt to track Beatrice was a skimpy one, hours of CCTV footage scanned on fast-forward, relying solely on cameras covering platform exits. To be certain it required looking in detail at the recordings from many dozens of platform cameras. By four o'clock, the CCTV team and their counterparts at BTP were sure: nobody resembling Beatrice Ulbricht had left the train at Waterloo, nor at the two immediately preceding stops.

Gillard called in Research Intelligence Officer DC Rob Townsend to get some clarification, and asked Claire to sit in too. Townsend came to the conference room with DI Nigel Duffy from the British Transport Police.

'Rob, you've had the chance to examine the detailed cell site timeline, I believe. What can you tell me?'

'Between the time Beatrice got on the train and the final text from her at 16.39 she received fourteen phone calls, none of which she answered. By this time the voicemail was full in any case. There were also eleven text messages received. Only two were answered, both from fellow members of her quartet. The first was Karen Ellsworth's, sent at 14.46 and answered at 15.58, and the second was responding to a message sent at 13.42, from Teus Zukowski, another member of the quartet.'

'What time did the train arrive at Clapham Junction?'

'It was on time, arriving at 16.40.'

'So just one minute after the last text was sent, saying she was just arriving.' Gillard looked around the table. 'The thing that baffles me is that we have two completely different narratives for Beatrice Ulbricht's movements. We have the one we can see, where she travels for forty-odd minutes on the train and then, poof, disappears. Then we have the electronic story, which has an utterly consistent cell site record seemingly for the entire trip. That includes two texts definitely sent from the train, and then an autonomous trip in a rubbish container to Brentford.'

They all sat for a minute pondering this conundrum.

Claire spoke up. 'Is it conceivable she could have been murdered on the train and someone else took over her phone?'

'There were lots of people around,' Gillard said.

Duffy nodded. 'There is almost no chance. This isn't like the old days with slam door carriages, when you could conceivably throw a body off the train. On some of the older intercity coaches with droplight windows, where you reach out to externally open the door, you could still do it. But modern commuter train doors will not open while the train is moving.'

'What about the interconnecting corridors between carriages?' Townsend asked.

Duffy shook his head. 'The concertina sections are bordered by glass doors, so someone would have seen. There are no gaps to get a body onto the track. Besides which, if she was on the track we would have found her by now. As I mentioned in my email, the entire train was searched as soon as we were notified, though it would have undertaken six or seven further journeys in that time.

Nonetheless, we also stripped the cover from the seat she was identified to have been sitting at, and have supplied that to you in case you want to do any forensic analysis.'

Gillard picked up the DI's defensive tone. 'Thank you for that, Nigel. We appreciate what you and everybody at BTP have done. Of course, we still haven't finished going through the miles of CCTV footage on each and every platform for the ten stations between Clandon and Clapham Junction. That might provide us with some answers.'

'Logically, there is only one possibility,' Rob said, counting off on his fingers. 'If the phone says she was on the train approaching Clapham Junction, and if the cameras showed she never got off after Clapham Junction, *and* Nigel here says she couldn't have been murdered on the train, then—'

'She stayed on at Waterloo and waited to be whisked back towards Guildford!' Claire said.

'Exactly, but dumped the phone in the bin,' Townsend added.

'If she stayed on, there will surely be witnesses,' Gillard said.

'Why on earth would she stay on?' Duffy asked.

Gillard shrugged. 'No idea, maybe she forgot something. We'll deal with that later. But if she did, then there is a good chance she is still alive, somewhere.'

–

They were still discussing possibilities in the meeting room when a young female PC came in to tell them that Gillard was urgently required back in the incident room. 'The German minister is here, sir.'

Gillard looked at his watch. It was only just after five. He hadn't expected him until six. DI Duffy smirked and said: 'Very punctual, the Germans.'

'His daughter is missing!' Claire retorted. 'No wonder he's here early. If it was one of my kids I'd set up camp in the car park, and not shift until she was found. He's probably beside himself with worry.'

'Fair point,' Duffy said, hands raised in mock surrender.

Gillard and Claire Mulholland made their way to the incident room. There was clearly something important going on inside, because an enormous personal protection officer was posted outside, identified by his lanyard as being from the *Bundesministerium der Justiz und für Verbraucherschutz*. Another PPO was inside the room. Through the glass door the chief constable could be seen conducting a guided tour for a tall and rather imposing silver-haired man in a grey suit and red tie, and two officials that he guessed were from the Home Office. Rigby was pointing out the whiteboards where pictures of his daughter were pinned by magnets, and the detail of the train journey to Waterloo were noted in marker pen. Rigby turned round as Gillard opened the door, and introduced him to Karl-Otto Ulbricht, finishing with: 'DCI Gillard is one of our most experienced detectives, and I have faith in him.' She then turned to Craig: 'I've already told Herr Ulbricht that we have made significant progress, and established that his daughter travelled back to London from Surrey, confirmed by cell site analysis of her mobile phone.'

That wasn't quite true, but Gillard wasn't about to contradict the chief constable in front of Beatrice's father. There would hopefully be opportunities to put the more nuanced reality to him. Ulbricht shook the detective's hand firmly, grasping his elbow with the other hand.

'I'd like you to know, sir, that we are doing absolutely everything possible to find your daughter,' Gillard said.

'I am so grateful,' Ulbricht said, in barely accented English. 'For my wife and me, this is the most terrible experience. But we have an enormous depth of respect for the thoroughness, efficiency and expertise of the British police.'

Gillard wondered if he would be quite equal to that exalted level of expectation. 'I understand that the Home Secretary will be here shortly, so I was hoping to grab a few minutes before so I might be able to ask you a few questions which would help us get some insight into Beatrice's state of mind.'

'Yes of course. I believe you have some CCTV footage of her, and I would like to see that too if possible.'

'Certainly.' Gillard steered the minister back to the conference room he had previously occupied, and brushed down a seat which had somehow accumulated crumbs. The two personal protection officers followed, one staying inside and the other out.

'Forgive me if you've been asked this before, but can you think of any reason why your daughter would miss such an important concert?'

'None whatever. This was, as I'm sure you know, at St Martin-in-the-Fields, raising money for refugees. It was probably the most high-profile event she had been involved with to date. I know the entire quartet had been practising very hard for it, because Beatrice told me so.'

'Does she suffer from stage fright or nerves? Had she just broken up with a boyfriend? Anything like that?'

The minister shook his head. 'No, she is very focused in front of an audience, and has a steady relationship with a young man she has known for many years in Germany.'

'Has she ever suffered from depression or any other mental health issues?'

He licked his lips. 'Well, when she was a teenager she went through a difficult time. She tried to cut her wrists because of some bullying at school, but that was a long time ago. Of course no parent, particularly a father, can ever pretend to know the secret life of their own daughter, but as far as I'm aware she has been incredibly happy to be doing what she loves doing, and by all accounts doing it exceedingly well. Beatrice has such a bright future ahead of her.' He paused and wiped a paw of a hand across his eye, as if there was a speck there. He blinked a few times, and reached for a handkerchief. The word *entschuldigung* was muttered as he did so. Excuse me.

Gillard averted his gaze. The tears of a minister, particularly a minister of justice, must be some of the most rarefied and precious fluids on earth. But then family is in a different galaxy to affairs of state, however heart-wrenching they may be. The detective glanced up at the security man, and saw contrast. A meat-wrapped package of invincibility, expressionless as a wall.

'When did you last speak to her?' Gillard asked the minister.

'Not for two weeks, to my shame. I have a few week-old text messages from her, which I did not get round to replying to, but answered at length only yesterday. Much too late, of course.' He looked up, drenched in regrets.

'What did she ask?'

'She wanted me to come to the concert. And then she reminded me in the next message, saying how important it was to her. I was too busy of course. I'm always too busy.'

Gillard wasn't going to ask him about those late replies, but the minister's confessional was not completed. 'I told her I loved her. I told her that if she ever had any problems we would always be there for her, her mother and I. Always. I asked her to ring me as soon as possible.'

The two men stared at each other for a moment. Gillard spoke. 'I take it you have not received any messages which could be construed—'

'No. I am not rich. It would make no sense.'

'It may not be money. A political hostage taker might seek a subtle change in policy, the removal of a clause in a piece of legislation, even the approval of a citizenship request. Or the barring of one. We've all read about the strength of the far right in Germany.'

Ulbricht had clearly not considered all of these possibilities. 'I will think about this.'

'I don't want to alarm you,' Gillard said. 'It's entirely possible that your daughter has had some kind of breakdown and does not want to be near anybody at the moment. But it's very important that if someone has abducted her, you must scour not only your own official and private emails, landlines and mobiles, but ask your family and close friends. A ransom demand could come by post, it could be spray-painted on your garage, it could be placed as a coded advertisement in a newspaper.'

The minister nodded, clearly impressed by the detective's lateral thinking. He consulted the mobile phone which had sat with discreet silence throughout the meeting. 'Ah, my time has evaporated. I have to catch a flight to Brussels for a conference on refugees. So many of them have daughters too, in as great a danger as my own, if not more. And I haven't finished writing my speech.' His briefly raised eyebrows spoke volumes. 'I will have my meeting with the Home Secretary during the flight.'

'Do you have just one minute for me to show you the footage of Beatrice?' Gillard asked.

He hesitated for a moment, but then said, 'I'm told my officials are waiting outside. Please email it to me.' He dropped a business card on the desk as he stood, his shoulders groaning under the weight of responsibility. Gillard stood too, and they shook hands firmly and with feeling.

'I will do everything I can,' the detective said, passing across his own business card. 'Ring me, any time.'

The minister nodded. 'She is our only child. Precious beyond dreams. Our world dangles by a thread.'

–

Spurred by the exhibition of guilt and shame, Gillard texted his own long-suffering wife, Sam, to tell her that he would not be in until eight or nine o'clock. He had only just finished when the young female PC who had summoned him earlier arrived with a laden silver tea tray, of all things.

'Where's he gone?' she asked.

'To Brussels on the plane.' The tray contained two expensive bought-in designer coffees and an entire box of artisan biscuits.

'Oh shit, I've just driven in to get them from the deli in the centre of Guildford.'

'They won't be wasted. Take a seat.'

'Where's Her Royal Highness?' she said, looking around as if Alison Rigby could be lurking around any corner. 'She told me to get them and give her the bill.'

'Schmoozing with the Home Secretary if she's got any sense,' Gillard said. 'She'll have her hand out for budget. So have a biscuit with me. Take a moment's peace, because you never know when the next one will be.'

The PC, whose name was Andrea Kirkland, sat down and unlidded one of the coffees. Gillard took the other, which turned out to be a rather velvety macchiato. For five tranquil minutes they sat and ate, discussing family, friends and hobbies. He offered her the last biscuit, which she declined. Mount Browne is a land of no second chances, so Gillard popped the morsel into his mouth. The moment he'd done so, Rainy Macintosh wandered in.

'Ah, workshy corner,' she announced. 'And no bickies left.'

Gillard had heard of Rainy's good-natured insubordination, and smiled it away. 'Any progress on the CCTV?'

'Aye, sir. But not of the kind you would like.'

'Did she stay on the train at Waterloo and go back towards Guildford?'

She shook her head. 'No, we checked that first. Unless she stayed in coach seven, with the non-working CCTV. In which case she could be fucking anywhere, pardon my French, sir. So we're being methodical. She got on at Clandon and we're doing each station in turn on the way up to London, just in case she got off. We've split the work with the BTP. We've done Horsley, Effingham Junction, Cobham, Oxshott, Claygate. BTP's working on the stations heading down from London.'

'I just do not understand how she could have vanished into thin air.'

'Personally I think she's trying to disappear. Maybe she slipped into the toilet to change into a hoodie and jeans,' Rainy said.

'She'd still have had the violin with her,' Gillard reminded her. 'It's her most valuable possession, apparently.'

'Maybe it was just an empty violin case, which she stuffed her clothes in.' Rainy shrugged her shoulders. 'I don't know, maybe she's a magician. She's got the hat, after all.'

–

The press conference at six o'clock and the attendant publicity brought forth dozens of fresh sightings of a young woman who was by all accounts striking as well as distinctively dressed. Gillard read through the notes on the clipboard which summarised titbits of information gained so far. While a couple of dozen witnesses had called the information line to say they had seen her get on the train, there were only five who had seen her come in to their coach from the adjacent one. These all agreed that she had taken a seat right at the back. Witnesses generally had a hazy idea of which coach they were in, but from their accounts some could be presumed to be in the carriage with the defective CCTV, number seven. They all described the woman squeezing into the corner, and leaving her violin and a small rucksack on the aisle seat next to her.

Frustratingly, there was a considerable difference of opinion over where she got off. Three said they had no idea, one suggested Effingham Junction, which was only two stops from where she got on, another said Clapham Junction, while the final one was certain she had not passed him to exit before he left at Waterloo. The discrepancy between the journey of the phone and the journey of the woman seemed if anything to be getting wider.

Gillard sighed and made his way to the surveillance suite in the forensic unit. Near the back there was the wave of an arm from DC Carrie Macintosh, like a schoolgirl trying to attract the teacher's attention.

'Sir, I've got her. She got off at Earlsfield, the stop before Clapham Junction. Come and have a look.'

Gillard looked over her shoulder and watched the young woman leaving the train. The timestamp on the CCTV said 16.37. Beatrice made her way along the island platform, and down a flight of stairs towards the exit. 'I've got her coming out through the barriers onto the street, too, if you'd like to see that?'

'Fantastic work, Rainy,' he said. 'There's only one problem. Two minutes later, someone else who was still on the train sent a text from her phone to say she was arriving at Clapham Junction.'

'Och, she's a wee witch and no mistake. Vanishes into thin air one minute, but later manages to be in two places at once. I wonder what else she can do?'

When Gillard got home, just before ten p.m., Sam was on the phone but blew him a kiss. She wordlessly guided him back into the kitchen, and indicated to him the moussaka leftovers which just needed reheating. She was clearly in listening mode to one of her large circle of female friends. The exclamations of excitement and approval she interjected as she wandered around with the cordless were an intriguing little detective puzzle in their own right. Gillard often tried to figure out who his wife was talking to based on her tone of voice and the subject matter. To her parents it would be matter-of-fact, flat tones, interspersed with eye-rolling for his benefit. Her mother's health issues generated the most extreme of these reactions. By contrast her closest friends merited a glass of wine, sips alternating with chuckles and squeals of delight, while she sprawled on the settee, snuggling down for a long session.

This was different. The tone was more surprised, more formal, yet still gushing. 'No! Really? Oh that's wonderful. Did he?' Gillard gave her a mute query, and she mouthed a reply. He didn't recognise the name. Helen, was it or Ellen? Summoned by the microwave ping, he waved his fingers and blew her a kiss as he retreated back into the kitchen. He left Sam and her friend to their own devices for the next half an hour, suddenly feeling overworked and friendless, eating alone, staring at the oven whose digital clock announced that there were less than ten hours before he had to return to work.

'So sorry, Craig,' Sam said, while her husband was stacking the dishwasher. 'That was Ellen.'

'Do I know her?'

'You met her once, at Georgia's party a couple of years ago. Big glasses, big hips, a bit loud?'

Gillard nodded, though he could only vaguely recall the woman.

'She's met a new man, who sounds amazing, and she is utterly in love. She's dropped two dress sizes. She has always struggled with her weight.'

'How do you know her?'

'I trained with her. She's not a PCSO anymore, she's a receptionist at a vet's in Bedford. We're good friends on Facebook.'

Gillard wilted under the blizzard of factoids, but tried to store them away in case he was tested on them later. Sam continued Ellen's tale of being wooed: the surprise bunch of roses, the surprise holiday in Morocco, the makeover and spa weekend and so on.

Later, when they were in bed, Sam told him she had invited Ellen and her new beau over for dinner on Saturday. She smiled sweetly at him, an unspoken request for the workaholic detective inspector to take an evening off.

'I'm sure it'll be fine if we find the violinist alive,' Gillard said. He summarised the case for her. 'Anyway, it's looking increasingly likely that she is just playing silly buggers. For what reason I have no idea.'

She put her arms around him, and the warmth of her body and their cosiness together culminated in a bout of gentle, unhurried lovemaking. He fell asleep with her hair fanned across his face, his arm around her shoulder.

He was awoken by his mobile on the bedside table. It was 1.47 a.m. He levered himself upright to glance at the caller. A withheld number. Something made him feel this was important, so he took the call anyway.

A woman with a pronounced German accent requested that he hold the line for the Minister of Justice. *Shit.* Gillard slipped out of bed as Karl-Otto Ulbricht came on the line. 'Mr Gillard, I have only just had the chance to look at the CCTV you sent me.' His voice was stern, with a tremble of upset or possibly anger. 'You didn't tell me that you had undertaken a reconstruction of my daughter's travel.'

'I'm sorry, I don't understand,' Gillard replied as he walked out onto the darkened landing, stark naked, and gently closed the bedroom door behind him. 'We haven't reconstructed her movements.'

'So how do you explain these falsified videos?'

Gillard suddenly imagined the chief constable right in front of him here on the landing inspecting his naked scrotum prior to removal, if he had by some error sent the wrong video clip to Germany's justice minister. 'Sir, what I thought I sent you was a series of clips of your daughter entering Clandon station, boarding the train, and her departure from the platform at Earlsfield.'

'Yes, but who is it? She is wearing my daughter's coat and hat and carrying her violin.'

'I'm sorry, are you saying that the woman on the train is not your daughter?'

'Of course that's what I'm saying. It's not her.'

'But, sir—'

'It's not her, do you hear me? It's not her! I had expected better from the British police.' He hung up.

Shit shit shit.

Sam called out to him. 'What is it?'

'That was the German Minister of Justice Karl-Otto Ulbricht.'

'Calling you? Oh my God!'

'He claims the woman on the train is not his daughter.'

'Huh? Who is she then?' Sam asked.

'That's a very good question.'

Chapter Four

Friday

'Didn't *any* of you morons check?' Alison Rigby was roasting the entire incident room team, more than twenty people. It was 6.30 a.m. Each and every one of them had been summoned for an early meeting at Mount Browne, so that the chief constable would herself have an answer to offer the minister at the start of the German working day, which was seven a.m. British time.

'Ma'am, with all due respect, we did check,' Gillard said. 'We have three pictures of Beatrice Ulbricht from her friends, one of them wearing the same distinctive hat and coat. What we don't have, precisely because she is wearing this broad brimmed hat and had her collar turned up, are any good facial images from the CCTV to check them against.'

'You are clearly all bewitched by the hat, coat and violin, aren't you?'

'Ma'am, to be fair,' said Carrie Macintosh, 'this person, whoever she is, has not only the clothes and the possessions, but the phone of the missing woman. It's a very elaborate and pointless exercise, surely, to impersonate her?'

'Elaborate, yes. Pointless, maybe not. You are supposed to be detectives,' Rigby said, lasering the entire room with her blue stare of death. 'And detection is built on evidence. You made assumptions, and then built on those assumptions. Surrey Police has already squandered a thousand man hours on this case. Add to that British Transport Police, the Met and God knows who else. Everyone has been deployed to crawl all over footage from the railways, footage that we now know is not of the missing girl.'

'It will still be relevant, because—' Macintosh interjected.

'Shut up, detective constable. The valuable first few hours and days of the hunt for a missing person have been wasted because we have been looking in the wrong place. Yes, whoever is impersonating her will be relevant eventually. But whoever did this must have intended to waste an awful lot of police time and energy and, because of your incompetence and failure to make basic checks, they have succeeded beyond their wildest dreams. You should all hang your heads in shame.'

Rigby, casually dressed in sweatshirt, jeans and trainers, stalked around the room staring at each detective in turn. Very few could meet her gaze. 'Herr Ulbricht told me that his daughter is a little shorter than this woman, and she walks in a different way. Her hands are different. The minister rang to tell me this at three o'clock this morning.'

Gillard raised his hand to speak. 'Ma'am, we have the seat cover where the impostor sat. We haven't done anything with it yet, because we didn't think we needed to, but I shall get it sent off to see if we can get a DNA trace.'

'That's a good start,' Rigby said. 'The Met have interviewed her fellow quartet members, but I'm unsure whether they have seen any of the CCTV. Let's make sure that we can get the father's impressions corroborated.'

'Yes, ma'am,' Gillard said.

–

There was a collective sigh of relief as the chief constable walked out. Eye-rolling stares were exchanged, early morning yawns that had been kept stifled groaned out, eyes rubbed, coffee – even the vile police issue substance – urgently sought. Rob Townsend sprawled on his chair, his arms and legs splayed out. He looked utterly rogered. Gillard knew that the young research intelligence officer was still more than a little distracted by his relationship with the much-fancied crime scene investigator Kirsty Mockett. His self-confidence had grown, even as the quality of his work had deteriorated. What he was now about to be told would hopefully wake him up.

'I've been having a think about this phone of Beatrice Ulbricht's that travelled up to Brentford without her.'

'That's right,' Townsend said, stifling a yawn. 'Doesn't make sense. Someone was on the train with her phone after she left at Earlsfield.'

'No, Rob. I don't think there was anybody using her phone by the time the train approached Clapham Junction.'

'What about the text sent then? The cell site analysis showed it was sent in the vicinity of Clapham Junction, at about the time the train was pulling in.'

'You're forgetting one thing, Rob,' Gillard said. 'Something that you as our chief geek should know. When I looked at my own phone today, I found there was a setting to pre-set a text to go at a particular time. The

46

message that was being responded to was received before Beatrice even got on the train. So the text could have been prepared, by her or someone else, before our mystery woman boarded the train.'

Townsend pursed his lips. 'I suppose that's possible, but why?'

'False trail, Rob. As Rigby said, someone wants us to think that Beatrice got as far as London, and if she is missing, *that* is where they want us to look. Both the carefully placed phone, and our mystery woman's journey are designed to build that piece of fiction. That would only make sense if Beatrice actually disappeared *before* she got on the train. And if that's true, she's in the middle of our patch. In Surrey.'

Townsend stroked his chin thoughtfully. 'Deductive reasoning, yes.' He yawned, and then realised something. 'Forgot to mention that forensics finished with Beatrice's phone late last night, so we can now have a look on the SIM card.' He rubbed his hands together in anticipation. 'We might be able to prove your point about the delayed texts.'

'Did forensics find any dabs?'

'The phone was smeared in Coke and coffee, probably from being in the bin, so not much survived. Still, they managed to lift a few. There's nothing that obviously matches any criminal records, except for the lady at the waste transfer station, she's got a bit of form from twenty years ago. Anyway, all the partials are now being looked at in Lewes to see if we've got anything else, which could take a few days, but they tell me not to raise our hopes.'

Gillard nodded. 'Someone going to this trouble is not going to leave their dabs on the phone, are they?'

'Well, the impostor girl wasn't wearing gloves.'

'True, but we've never seen her handling the phone.'

'Someone was.'

'Rob, there was an incredible level of preparation for this. That's why I am now much more worried about the young lady.'

—

The Royal College of Music allocated Gillard a practice room for him to interview the other three members of the Lysander String Quartet. The large airy chamber had a high window which illuminated a beautiful old harpsichord as its centrepiece. But what the detective wanted from them required their eyes rather than their ears. Do you recognise this woman? That was the simple question he put to them. Karen Ellsworth, Ignacio Vacelar and Teus Zukowski, all in their twenties, sat together at a couple of folding tables, watching CCTV footage that the detective played on his laptop. The two male musicians looked up as soon as they saw the woman walking across the rainy car park at Clandon railway station. 'That's her,' said Ignacio, a slightly built Spaniard with a morose expression.

'Are you sure?' Gillard asked.

'Well, the hat, the coat and scarf are hers—' Teus said.

'They are, but this woman is slimmer, maybe younger than Beatrice,' said Karen.

The three musicians then discussed elements of their friend's hair and clothing, without coming to a firm conclusion. Gillard switched to the footage on the train, which was a little clearer because the angle was lower. He froze at a frame in which part of the woman's cheek and eye could briefly be seen.

'My God,' Teus said. 'It *is* someone else.'

Ignacio nodded his agreement. 'She's stolen Beatrice's Politi.'

'Her what?' Gillard asked.

'Her violin. It's a 1932 Enrico Politi, made in Italy, worth many thousands. I recognise the case. This woman is swinging it about like it's a cheap handbag. See, there! She just dumped it on the seat next to her.' He shook his head as if this was the biggest part of the crime.

The other two nodded their agreement. 'We do not know who this woman is.' Karen pointed accusingly at the screen. 'But she is not our Beatrice, and she is not a musician.'

Only then did Gillard tell them that Beatrice's own father had agreed with their conclusion. The detective fast-forwarded through most of the rest of the CCTV footage, showing them a few salient moments of her movement through the carriage and ending with her departure from Earlsfield station.

'Anything else you can tell me about her?' Gillard asked. 'I mean, are you sure none of you have seen this woman before?'

'It's difficult to tell,' Ignacio said. 'But no one at the college comes to mind.' He looked to his colleagues for confirmation, and they nodded.

The detective spotted Teus feeling for Karen's hand beneath the table, and giving it a squeeze. They exchanged wan smiles. Emotional preparation for bad news.

'So this woman robbed Beatrice of her clothing?' Karen asked.

'She may have come across it by other means. It's clean and undamaged, which we have to see as a good sign.'

'There is one other thing,' Karen said. 'Beatrice knew how to look after herself. She was mugged once in Germany, years ago, and went on some kind of self-defence course, I don't know what type. I know she sometimes carries a pepper spray.'

Gillard looked at the notes that the Met had provided. There was no mention of a spray having been found in her room. 'That's interesting,' he said. Most types of pepper spray were illegal in the UK.

'Is there any hope, detective?' Ignacio asked.

Gillard shrugged. 'If this was an abduction, yes. I think you can see this woman has gone to extraordinary lengths to create a fictitious journey for Beatrice. She had her phone, her precious violin and her clothes. Your friend would not voluntarily have parted with any of them, so the best hope we have is a kidnap.'

–

Gillard was back at Mount Browne by noon, and arranged an informal incident room meeting for one o'clock. In the meantime details had come by email via the Met Police about Beatrice's bank accounts. For a supposedly struggling music student, Beatrice was not poor. There were several thousands spread over a current account, a savings account, and a separate euro account with a German bank. A solid monthly deposit was made into this from her parents' account. But the balances were unchanged since Friday. Only the credit card had been used in the last four days, to buy a return rail ticket from Waterloo to Clandon on Sunday. That fitted with her journey to play at the wedding.

The biggest news was hiding at the end of the email. An asterisked section of the letter noted there had been an attempted withdrawal on Beatrice's cash card on Tuesday afternoon at a cash machine in Earlsfield, where the impostor had got off the train. Gillard cross-checked the time and his jaw dropped. He double-checked the platform footage, and the last sight of the imposter leaving Earlsfield railway station. He swore softly to himself. It confirmed a growing suspicion, one that had been growing like a cancer in his gut ever since they had discovered the woman on the train was not Beatrice.

He gathered up his papers and walked into the incident room. It was nearly time. A whiteboard had been set vertically with marker pen notes to cover each aspect of the rail journey from Clandon to Earlsfield, with a parallel trace for the phone.

'Okay, let's get this meeting under way,' he said. 'I've got some fresh news for everybody.'

They all gathered together: DCs Hoskins and Macintosh, DI Claire Mulholland and DC Rob Townsend plus Christine McCafferty from the press office.

'Let's start with the evidence. Beatrice Ulbricht was last seen on Sunday leaving a wedding reception in Clandon, Surrey. That was five days ago, and is the last cast-iron evidence of her movements. She was given a lift by a friend called Adrian Singer and, according to him, intended to return to the station by bus from the stop near his house. There is no bus at that time. From eleven p.m. on Sunday to three p.m. on Tuesday she disappears, phone off.' He tapped the whiteboard. 'Then we have two ghosts, both elaborately conceived in an attempt to deflect the search for her. One, we have the movement of her phone from the time it was turned on at around three p.m. on Tuesday, via a journey by train up to Waterloo, being consigned to a waste receptacle on the train at some stage, before turning up at the Brentford waste transfer station. Pre-prepared texts were set on this phone to be sent at various points along the journey. That is ghost number one. The second phantom, and an equally impressive feat of organisation, is a young woman, taking the same train as the phone, wearing Beatrice's distinctive fedora, overcoat and scarf, and carrying her violin. This young woman was very careful to hide her face from CCTV. We know nothing whatever about this impostor, but will be focusing more on her later.'

He turned back to a whiteboard on which was pinned an Ordnance Survey map of the area around Clandon. 'What I want to do, belatedly, is focus the inquiry closely around the area from Clandon to Westmeare. Someone has been working very hard to distract us from this location, but I think it is crucial to our inquiry.'

Christine put up her hand. 'I'm having to deal with a lot of pet theories from members of the press, sir. *The Sunday Times* insight team is working on some big piece, and I've had numerous calls from the German dailies which have asked us to comment on various political or kidnapping ideas. I've just had to say "no comment." Is there anything you can tell me?'

'Not at this stage, Christine. We are still treating her as a missing person, although I think many of you know that I'm increasingly worried about her safety. I am hoping it is an abduction, because the alternative is worse.'

Carl Hoskins interrupted. 'Are you thinking she was kidnapped by that other woman, sir, the bird on the train?'

Gillard smiled at the detective constable's slang, though he was aware it grated on many nerves within the department. 'No, Carl, I have another theory, and in a few minutes I shall show you the proof. First let's deal with the eyewitnesses to the impostor.'

He handed over to Claire, who ran through a fat clipboard full of summarised statements from those who had rung the helpline or sent in emails. 'Sadly, we have no one who saw our impostor arrive at Clandon, and only a couple who noted her departure from Earlsfield railway station,' she said. 'We do have one witness, in a vehicle, who claims to have seen Beatrice at the bus stop in Westmeare at around eleven on Sunday night. I want to emphasise that we think this may be the real Beatrice Ulbricht. If so, it might mean that Adrian Singer is in the clear.'

Hoskins muttered: 'Unless he came out all furious from home after the row, found her at the bus stop and clouted her one.'

'We'll check all that out when we re-interview him,' Gillard said. He then detailed the fact that Beatrice's bank accounts had not been touched.

'I have got one very clear and significant piece of evidence that has come to light in the last hour,' he said. 'The banking audit trail shows an attempted cash withdrawal from her current account at a Spar supermarket in Earlsfield on Tuesday afternoon. Two attempts were made on the pin code, neither successful. Obviously not a third attempt because failure would have blocked the card.'

'So maybe it is a robbery,' Rainy said.

'I'm thinking that it's actually an attempt to communicate with us,' Gillard said.

Everyone looked confused.

'I don't get it, sir,' Hoskins said. 'What is she trying to tell us?'

Gillard smiled. 'The attempted withdrawal took place at 4.35 p.m. on Tuesday. At that time our impostor had not yet arrived at Earlsfield. She didn't arrive until 4.37 p.m., according to platform CCTV.'

'Jesus, sir, this is doing my nut in,' Hoskins said, holding the shaven-headed article for emphasis. 'How did she manage that?'

'She's a witch, told yers,' Rainy said. 'First she manages to be invisible, then two places at once, now time-shifting.'

The detective chief inspector shook his head. 'Without seeming to be too misogynistic about it, I'd like to suggest that our impostor is simply a clever distraction. The purpose of the attempted cash withdrawal was simply to demonstrate to us that a second person is involved. This person, let's assume a male, has a significant job to do. He drops the Beatrice double off at Clandon for her train journey, then drives up to London to pick her up again at Earlsfield, while the phone she abandons in the bin makes its merry way onwards to Brentford.'

'Wow,' Townsend muttered to Christine. 'All stitched together so it makes sense.'

'Any CCTV at the cash machine?' Claire asked.

'Surprise, surprise, no. It's one of the few in the area without a camera,' Gillard said. 'I've already asked the Met Police to forward any street CCTV to us, but I'm not holding out my hopes. I think this particular location was picked very precisely, by someone who knows how to plan.'

'What's the next stage?' Townsend asked.

'ANPR. I want the nearest number plate recognition cameras to Earlsfield around that time matched to any we can drag up from around Clandon or Westmeare an hour earlier. There's a fighting chance we'll get a match. I also want to drag in Adrian Singer and turn the screws a bit. I've already obtained the search warrant. Any questions?'

'So definitely no ransom demand here or in Germany?' Hoskins asked.

'Nope. Not a thing. In six days there should have been something. I'm particularly concerned because of the twice failed bank card transaction.'

There was a short pause while the implications of that sank in to the assembled detectives.

'She's dead, isn't she?' Rainy asked quietly. 'Otherwise she would have given them the pin code to save her life, wouldn't she?'

Gillard bit his lip, and nodded. 'It seems quite likely.'

'Och, the poor wee lassie.'

–

Adrian Singer was arrested in London on Friday afternoon and brought to Epsom Police Station for questioning. Meanwhile, CSI crawled all over his charming cottage in Westmeare, then bagged up his computer and other devices to be analysed.

The man himself, fairly peeved to have been dragged out of a Royal College of Music brass tutorial in front of two students, sat in a baggy jacket and cargo trousers with his arms folded while Gillard and Claire Mulholland went over his account of the evening spent with Beatrice Ulbricht.

After two hours of going backwards and forwards over his story Gillard said: 'So just to be clear, you offered her the spare bedroom, and made no move on her. I can't understand why she suddenly became so upset that she would leave immediately, especially given how uncertain the bus services were.'

Singer gave a long sigh, and said: 'Look. I might have given her a hint that if she wanted to come to my room, that wouldn't be a problem. I imagine that's why she got upset.'

'What kind of hint?' Claire asked.

'Honestly, it was nothing. She could just have ignored it.'

'Can you remember what words you used?'

'No, not really. We'd both had a bit to drink But I do recall thinking it was absurd that she should decide to leave at that point.'

'What time was this?' Gillard asked.

'At 10.45 p.m., I think.'

'Beatrice has money. I'm wondering why she didn't just ring a taxi,' Claire said.

'I told her that there weren't any nearby, which isn't quite true. She couldn't get a signal on her mobile either, typical for Westmeare.' He paused and then said, 'I told her there was a bus at eleven o'clock which stopped at Clandon station.'

'That was a lie, wasn't it?' Gillard said.

Singer nodded. 'I was really hoping she would stay. I thought that I would leave her at the bus stop for half an hour, to cool down, and then go and fetch her and bring her back.'

Claire folded her arms. 'I don't think you're a very good judge of a woman's character, if you expected leaving her to stew at a rainswept bus stop where the promised service never arrived would improve her mood.'

Singer shrugged. 'I feel terrible about what happened, really I do. But I didn't have anything to do with her disappearance. I promise you that.'

'Sadly, we're not in the position to take your word.' Gillard looked down at his notes. It would take a few hours more for forensics to finish with the samples taken from Singer's home. Going through his computer would probably take days. His gut instinct was that Singer was telling the truth, more or less. He had one gambit left to take.

'Mr Singer, I just have one more question. It's about the reason you left Meadowfields School in Dorking at such short notice.'

Singer went pale, and scowled at the worn floor tiles of the interview suite. 'Some allegations were made about me.'

The detective looked down again at his notes, made a couple of small marks with his ballpoint pen on a random document, trying to give the impression that he had a detailed account of those allegations, even though he had no idea what the music teacher had been accused of. 'Well, perhaps you'd like to give me your version.'

'I didn't think the police had ever been brought in. The school said it didn't want a fuss. Did they report me?'

Gillard shrugged.

'All right. A year eleven student who had been in my clarinet class accused me of inappropriately touching her.'

'Did you touch her?'

'I adjusted the position of the instrument, and corrected the fingering. Nothing more. I expect she has made some lurid allegation.'

'Were you alone with the girl?'

'Yes, for a minute, but only because the other tutee had left the room to get a new reed for her mouthpiece from the storeroom.'

The two detectives stared at Singer without saying anything.

He suddenly became animated. 'The girl didn't even *want* to be in the bloody class. Her ambitious parents had bought her a clarinet. She hated it. She hardly practised, had no gift or interest in music and probably felt trapped. An unwarranted complaint against me to her parents was the easiest way of getting her out of music. She probably had no idea of the collateral damage it would cause to *me*.'

It was a plausible story, and he relayed it with full eye contact. 'If a whisper of this reaches the Royal College, I will be ruined,' he said.

'We're just trying to get to the truth,' Gillard said. He had no plans to pass on what he had heard.

'Self-pity is never attractive,' Claire told Singer. 'You're worrying about your career. You should be worried about Beatrice Ulbricht. You put her in harm's way.'

Singer barked a sarcastic laugh. 'If a woman waiting at a bus stop is considered to be in harm's way, then millions of women are at risk every single day.'

'It was in a lonely rural spot, at eleven at night,' Claire said.

Singer looked heavenward. 'Beatrice has a blue belt in Aikido. She can look after herself.'

'Well, at the very least you were not very kind to her,' Gillard said.

'God, don't you think I know that? If I could have the time again, of course I would have done things differently. I mean it was only twenty minutes after I watched her storm out that I went out to fetch her.'

'You went to the bus stop?' Claire asked.

'Yes, on foot. I'd had too much to drink to take the car and it was only a short distance.'

'And she wasn't there?'

He shook his head. 'Gone. Just vanished.'

Chapter Five

Alison Rigby had pulled in Gillard every day for updates. Friday afternoon's summons came at around four o'clock, and the detective chief inspector found himself facing his boss across her desk. She listened intently as he laid out what they had discovered, and the intention to refocus the case around the village of Westmeare where the missing woman was last seen.

'Mr and Mrs Ulbricht arrive tonight from Berlin,' she said. 'They'll be staying at the Fynton Park Hotel in Guildford until we have a conclusion in the case. I've promised them all reasonable access to the latest developments in the inquiry. I'm sure the minister will want to speak to you from time to time.'

'Yes, ma'am.' Gillard felt his throat go dry at the prospect of being so closely scrutinised in his work.

Her blue eyes locked on to him. 'Special Branch has already begun a preliminary investigation into Beatrice's past, and found nothing untoward. But if you have the slightest feeling that the family is connected to her disappearance, the time to tell me is now,' she said.

'There is nothing to indicate it, ma'am.'

'So what's your best guess?' she asked.

The detective chief inspector took a deep breath. 'She could still be alive, I suppose. Our abductor, who I have a hunch is male, is extremely well organised, well-resourced with a vehicle, forensically aware as regards mobile phone and CCTV usage, and had access to a confederate who was willing to impersonate the missing woman. The good news is that the chance of catching a criminal increases at the square of the number of people involved in the crime.'

'So you think this was planned in advance?'

'It has to be.'

'But who could have predicted she would walk out from Singer's house to that particular bus stop at that time of night?'

Gillard shrugged. 'We only have Singer's word for that sequence of events. We'll get the DNA tests back from his home tomorrow morning. Then we'll know more.'

'I'm relying on you to crack this quickly. I don't think I've ever had so many phone calls from Whitehall, offering extra officers, checking that we've got the latest forensic equipment, suggesting that they would fund an expanded training budget. It's like austerity in reverse, so I'm not knocking it. Politically, of course, the Home Office is simply covering its back. They don't want to risk me standing up and saying that we were too poorly resourced to investigate this crime properly. While it's all very well us raking in extra cash, we need a result and we need it quickly. We are being watched.'

Dismissed, Gillard turned and retreated from his boss's office. He certainly felt he was being watched.

–

DC Carrie 'Rainy' Macintosh had the unenviable task of assessing the helpline calls, social media postings and emails that flooded in about the case. She had a team of five, who winnowed out the cranks, the weirdos and the plainly abusive, of whom there were a lot. The fact that Beatrice Ulbricht was the daughter of a German minister seem to antagonise a small but vociferous section of the population who referenced the war, Nazis, or the World Cup final of 1966 in a variety of tasteless jokes. There were dozens of informants who suggested that the Beatrice Ulbricht imposter was actually their ex-wife, or estranged daughter, or in one case, dead daughter. Chasing up anything plausible was extremely time-consuming, particularly because only a minority of informants were willing to leave an address or phone number. After eliminating the absurd and abusive, Friday's haul of possibles included a man in Inverness who reckoned the impostor was a girl that he taught in a music class in Edinburgh two years ago, a charity shop worker from Cheshire who recalled selling an identical hat to a young woman last Christmas, and, finally, someone who had emailed a link to one of Beatrice's own videos, along with a short message.

Hey there Craig, here's a clue! IC

Rainy flicked through the video, which was of Beatrice playing the Sibelius violin concerto at a church hall in Streatham, South London, last November. There was nothing obviously different about it, except the unusual personalisation of the message. She would forward it for his attention.

-

The back roads around Westmeare led to some of the most rural areas of the county. Craig Gillard and Claire

Mulholland sat in his unmarked Vauxhall, parked in the bus stop from which Beatrice Ulbricht may well have disappeared, raking over what little evidence they had. They had been driving around for an hour, looking for any clues to what an angry young woman might have decided to do after leaving a nearby house.

'All right,' Claire said, looking down at her list. 'Mobile reception is pretty poor just here, I've only got one bar on mine. There is a taxi firm in the village, a one-man band who was on an airport run on the evening in question. He claims not to have received any calls from Beatrice, and of course that checks out with her own mobile. The next nearest firms are in Guildford, ten to fifteen minutes away.'

Gillard nodded, his fingers gripping and ungripping the steering wheel. 'We've got thousands of hits on the ANPR cameras around Earlsfield, not surprisingly, but the nearest camera to here is four miles away on the A25. We haven't had any number plates that crop up on both. There are only three CCTV cameras in the village, one covering the pub car park and two at private homes. Uniforms are checking to see if they picked up any passing traffic.'

She leafed through the various sheets. 'Mr Edward Lightfoot, seventy-seven, driving his van, said he saw a young woman with a hat, scarf and violin standing at the bus stop in Shere Road in the pouring rain a bit before eleven p.m. He guessed that there wouldn't be any more buses that day, and had considered stopping to give her a lift, but decided not to.'

'Why?'

'He didn't want any accusations, that's what the state-ment says. "I felt guilty even considering it. But after what happened I feel even worse." He says he's got a granddaughter of Beatrice's age.' She looked up at Gillard.

'Do we have the number plate of his van?'

Claire shook her head. 'Not on here.'

'What idiot did the interview?' He looked across at the uniformed officer's name, but didn't recognise it. 'Okay, let's get it and find out if the van flashed up on any ANPR in Earlsfield on Tuesday afternoon.'

'Not got much, have we?' Claire asked.

'Let's pray for forensics first thing tomorrow.'

-

Gillard drove Claire back to her home at Staines that evening. It was raining heavily yet again, and while stuck in heavy traffic they listened to the Lysander Quartet's first and only CD, which he had bought for ten pounds from Karen Ellsworth when he last interviewed her. He was no expert on Bach string quartets, but he found himself enraptured by the beauty of the playing.

'Mind if we have the weather forecast on?' Claire said, eyeing her boss suspiciously. 'There is supposed to be a warning over the next couple of days.'

He nodded and switched to the radio. The outlook was every bit as bad as she had predicted, with an unusually deep depression sweeping in from the Atlantic. High winds with localised flooding was inevitable, the forecaster said.

'A bit more than April showers,' Claire said.

'I hope it stays dry Sunday morning,' he said. 'I'm teaching Sam to rock climb. She's done indoor ascents with me a few times, but I wanted to get her used to the feel of real rocks under her fingertips.'

Craig Gillard had rarely played the car park game, sucking up to your boss by having your vehicle seen prominently at work at some unearthly hour. But arriving at 6.15 a.m. inevitably made him look like he wanted to impress. It was almost two hours before his shift was due to start, but he wanted to get an early look at the forensic tests that had been run overnight at Mount Browne's own lab. As he slid the Vauxhall into a nicely prominent slot near the entrance, he couldn't help noticing the chief constable's car was already in her reserved space.

Perhaps she'd been there overnight?

He made his way over to her vehicle, and pressed his ear to the bonnet. He heard the characteristic ticking of a cooling engine. Arrived within the last few minutes, then.

Gillard walked into reception to find the chief constable and four other people standing with mugs of coffee. He immediately recognised the sleek patrician features of Karl-Otto Ulbricht. A handsome and well-coiffed woman next to him he assumed must be Mrs Ulbricht. The other two were multi-lanyarded young men with the alert keenness of officialdom: one seemingly from the German justice ministry, the other from Whitehall.

'Ah, Craig,' Rigby said. 'Just the person to guide us around the forensic centre, where I believe we are expecting results, am I right?'

Utterly blindsided by this early arrival of heavies, Gillard asked for a minute to make preparations. He walked calmly until he was through the first double doors and out of sight, and then sprinted to the forensic centre.

It took him three hasty attempts to punch in the correct code. Senior forensic officer Petra Amin looked up at his arrival. 'Ah, Craig. We do have some results—'

'Thank God. The parents of the missing girl are in reception right now, I need some progress to offer.'

Petra spread her hands and widened her eyes. 'Okay, what have we? Yes, not too much from Adrian Singer's home, I'm afraid. No blood, no semen, no signs of struggle. We got plenty of DNA which is being tested at the outside lab, and we should get results by mid-morning. A couple of the techies worked overnight on Singer's computers. Nothing incriminating so far, I gather. The satnav on his car shows only local use in recent days.' She looked up. 'Does that help?'

'Not a whole lot.'

He noticed Petra looking over his shoulder. 'Incoming, watch out,' she said.

He turned, and saw the chief constable leading in the missing girl's family.

From somewhere, he dragged together a one-minute presentation of the evidence he had just been told about. He hoped it would sound like he was familiar with every aspect of it. He watched as Beatrice's father translated his words for the benefit of Mrs Ulbricht.

'We are doing everything we can,' Gillard said. It sounded like an apology.

'Who was it who was impersonating my daughter, wearing her clothes and carrying her violin?' Mr Ulbricht asked. It was an entirely reasonable question. Gillard just wished he had an answer.

'We're still working on that.'

Mrs Ulbricht looked directly at him. She had pale blue eyes and quite chiselled cheekbones beneath her silvery blonde hair.

'Do you think our daughter is still alive?' she asked in accented English.

'There is hope,' he said. But in truth there wasn't much.

–

It was a disconsolate DCI Gillard who returned to the incident room, looking for something – anything – to distract him from his gloom over the case. DC Carl Hoskins looked to be afflicted by the same miasma. He was sitting slumped over his terminal, playing and replaying some very dark CCTV footage.

'What've you got there, Carl?'

'Probably nothing. This is a camera from a residential address in Westmeare, on a side road not far from the bus stop where we think Beatrice was waiting. There are only two vehicle movements on the side road during that time, one of which is from the drive where the camera is located. But look at this,' he said, pointing the tip of the pen at something in the top left-hand corner of the fisheye lens image. 'That is a concave blind spot mirror, for the householder to be able to pull out and see traffic coming from the left.'

'The left would be towards the main road?' Gillard asked.

Hoskins nodded. 'You can see the passing of vehicles on Shere Road as kind of dark dots preceded by the halo of headlamps. They are absolutely tiny. If we were in the original *Blade Runner* then I'd just be able to zoom right in, and identify every vehicle that passed.'

'Yeah, but at least we're not forced to have sex with robots.'

'Huh, you've clearly not tried to get my Brenda going before an early shift,' Hoskins muttered.

'Too much information, Carl,' Gillard replied, then added, 'Unlike almost every other part of this bloody case.' He sighed heavily. 'I think we've got some image enhancement software in-house now, I'll check with Rob Townsend.'

Gillard found the research intelligence officer slouched in the surveillance suite, yawning extravagantly, sipping some posh bought-in coffee. 'Yes, I've got a 2019 version of Close Focus,' he said. 'It's supposed to be the best there is.' He had huge bags under his eyes.

'Well, we've got a real challenge for it.' Gillard rang back to the incident room, and got Hoskins to email the CCTV link to Townsend. The young detective constable used the largest, most high-definition screen in the room, and pulled up the half-hour footage. Even on this screen, the blind spot mirror was no bigger than a thumbnail at the edge of the image.

'I'm not sure we'll get anything,' Townsend said. Using his cursor he outlined an enhancement focus box around the mirror, clicked on maximum magnification, and blew it up until it filled most of the screen. At this magnification it looked like a jumble of grey circles. 'The CCTV is from a pretty good domestic system, but there's not much more than a hundred pixels for the mirror. You won't see anything.' He clicked to let the sequence run, which simply illuminated the occasional lateral passage of brighter then darker blobs.

'It's not entirely useless,' Gillard said. 'We can distinguish between left-to-right and right-to-left movement, and each pairing of light and then darker blobs indicates a vehicle passing. So we can still count the passage of traffic past the Shere Road bus stop, which is just up thirty yards or so to the left.'

'I'm not sure how much that is going to help,' Townsend said, looking up at his boss.

'It might do. Let's go back to basics. I'm assuming we believe Singer's account of Beatrice leaving his home, because we have an independent witness who saw her at the bus stop just before eleven p.m. This elderly man, Edward Lightfoot, says he didn't stop, but presumably somebody else did shortly afterwards. I don't believe Beatrice would have waited more than an hour when it was clear the bus wasn't going to come and she was unable to get a taxi. So she might have hitched a lift. So between eleven and midnight, we can count the vehicle movements in each direction. That in itself is useful. But given that the bus stop is only thirty yards out of shot, we should also be able to detect whether vehicles were slowing down to stop, by measuring the passage of the dark and light blobs across the screen. Does that make sense?'

Townsend was nodding in agreement, wide-eyed with appreciation for cold, hard logic.

'I'll send in Hoskins to assist. Take an hour and see what you can manage,' Gillard said, patting the young detective on the shoulder. 'And do try to get some more sleep, young man. I need you fully awake and on the ball.'

–

It was only half an hour later when Rob Townsend messaged Gillard to say he'd managed to make some progress. When the detective chief inspector arrived at the surveillance suite, Townsend proudly displayed a much clearer picture of the blind spot mirror. Though vehicles still moved across as blobs of light and dark, it took much less imagination to see them for what they were.

'How did you do that?' Gillard asked.

'The enhancement focus box has a probability sampler, which allows the subdivision of individual pixels. Though the camera never recorded this kind of detail, the processor can do a statistical likelihood of what the picture was trying to show. It's a bit like predictive texting, where the computer suggests what to say.'

'That's great.'

'I also think I know when Beatrice was picked up at the bus stop.' He pointed at the screen, as he ran a five-second segment of the footage. 'You can see this dark blob which slows down, and there's even a light grey blob behind which could be brake lights. The time is 11.17 p.m. There is no other vehicle on her side of the road which shows the same characteristics.'

'Fantastic. You now think we can distinguish between large blobs which could be a van or truck and smaller ones?'

Townsend blew a sigh. 'I'll give it a go, boss.'

—

Gillard sat with Claire in the Mount Browne canteen at noon, him with a rather chewy Saturday special of lasagne, she with a dry chicken salad. These were good culinary reasons why it was the one place they wouldn't be ambushed by the chief constable or her VIP visitors. The two detectives had shared all the latest snippets on the Beatrice Ulbricht case, and felt they were running out of evidence to examine.

'Only one eyewitness to seeing her at the bus stop,' Gillard said. 'Given the distinctive hat and violin case, that indicates she may not have been there for very long. We think we have a vehicle slowing down for her, caught in the blind spot mirror, at 11.17 p.m. But we haven't got any idea of make or registration number. Rob's newly inaugurated "blob-size analysis" says it certainly wasn't a small saloon, and could possibly have been an SUV, people carrier or van. But that still doesn't get us very far.'

'I can't tie any of that up with the door-to-door enquiries,' Claire said. 'The team has visited every house in the village, as well as the pub. She wasn't seen, full stop, anywhere except at the bus stop, and then just by the one witness.'

'Do we agree that she is dead?' Gillard asked.

Claire nodded. 'I'd love to be wrong, and we mustn't exclude the possibility, but there's been no ransom approach to the family.'

'We've had all the DNA tests back now, and as we suspected there is nothing that matches anyone on the national database.' Gillard described how he had been present when CSI sprayed a reactive substance called BlueStar all over Adrian Singer's house, garage and shed. This product, the modern successor to Luminol, was designed to react with even the slightest dilute trace of blood to give a luminescence that can be detected by the naked eye. 'If there had been even a speck, we would have found it.'

'Maybe he just strangled her,' Claire said. 'No blood.'

'It's possible, though Beatrice wouldn't have been a pushover with her Aikido skills. Singer looks more the cerebral type. Besides, that thesis leaves our witness to Beatrice at the bus stop as an anomaly. Singer could only be the perpetrator if somehow she returned or was brought back to his house later on.' Gillard shook his head. 'I think Singer is in the clear, and short of digging up his garden and emptying the septic tank there's not much more we can do. I am now moving more towards the idea that she was picked up at the bus stop shortly after arriving there. I do think we can sketch in some things about our abductor.'

'Go on then.'

'Male, driving a van or SUV, physically capable, with a close confidante or girlfriend who would be willing to act as his stooge for the train charade. He has a good understanding of how the police work, a particularly good knowledge of mobile phones, including delayed texts, and at least the rudiments of cell site analysis. Those things I'm confident of, but here's where I get to guessing: I think he may be a local man, otherwise why create the false trail to London? My gut feel is that he is a sexually-driven attacker, who has the confidence to make an opportunistic assault, knowing he has places nearby to either hide or dispose of a body.'

He looked at Claire to assess her response.

'I've a simpler idea,' she said. 'Our killer is a woman – the very same woman we saw on the train.'

Chapter Six

Gillard spent Saturday afternoon with Claire driving around the leafy vicinity of Westmeare looking for locations where a body may have been disposed of. They had visited a couple of dairy farms, a trout hatchery, a builder's yard, and many streams and rivers, all swollen by the recent rain. Meanwhile, Claire had fleshed out her theory. A woman had stopped at the bus stop, given Beatrice a lift and taken her home to kill her. Gillard had listened patiently, but then answered with statistics: female on female stranger killings were almost unheard of. If a woman had killed or abducted Beatrice, then she would have to have had a much stronger motive. To the usual emotions of love and jealousy could perhaps be added musical rivalry. But nothing on any of the interview notes, either their own or those conducted by the Met Police, had given even a hint of this. All they were left with was conjecture.

The life of a detective is full of hours and days which seem pointless, until suddenly a clue appears. But on this weekend afternoon, fate had not cooperated. Gillard had dropped Claire back at Mount Browne to pick up her own car, then headed home. He'd been aiming for seven, but it was nearly nine p.m. when he finally arrived.

Sam had earlier sent him a couple of texts to remind him about that evening's dinner party, but once she revealed that Ellen's boyfriend had been forced to cry off too, he knew the pressure on him was off. It was now a girls' night in, and his attendance he knew from experience could only detract from the quality of the conversation, and inhibit revelations. That didn't stop Sam from glaring at him as he opened the door and let himself in. 'At least home-made pâté doesn't spoil,' she said, as she gave him a perfunctory kiss. 'The main course is a different matter. Halibut doesn't like to be kept waiting.' *And neither do I*, was the not-very-hidden subtext.

'That's a lovely dress,' Gillard said, admiring the low-cut satin number he hadn't recalled seeing before. Sam's flicked eyebrow dismissed the conversational gambit. Ellen emerged into the kitchen holding a still-full glass of white. He was surprised he hadn't remembered her. Dirty blonde hair, trim figure and dressed to kill in a lacy black top, dark hose and high heel sandals. They batted a bit of small talk around for a few minutes, until Gillard put his foot in it.

'I understand your boyfriend couldn't come?'

Sam sighed, passed behind her husband and jabbed him sharply in the ribs with a fork. Ellen might not have seen the weapon, but Gillard's jump could not be disguised. Their guest's eyelashes flickered for a few seconds, before the obviously well-prepared statement: 'Gabriel travels a lot, often at short notice,' she said. 'I'm really sorry he's not able to meet you both, he did say he was looking forward to it.'

'Gabriel bought Ellen a pair of Jimmy Choos,' Sam said, her eyes flicking towards their guest's elegantly shod feet. He welcomed this hint. He'd heard of the luxury brand, but hadn't known whether it applied to handbags, wristwatches or lingerie.

'Very nice,' Gillard said, reaching towards the open bottle of wine. It soon became apparent that Ellen was in no state to drive, and he hoped that he wasn't going to be asked to give her a lift to the station. As he went upstairs to change he popped his head into the spare room, and was relieved to discover it had been made up for a guest.

The curtains were open, and he went to close them. The guest bedroom looked out over the front of the house. He glanced out and could see no signs of life in the bungalow opposite. Good. Sam had complained about Gillard's aunt Trish staring in at them.

The detective was off duty. So he paid no attention to the aged red Fiat parked a little further down the cul-de-sac. But someone inside was paying attention to him. After fifteen minutes, the car engine started, slid into gear and drove quietly away.

Sunday

Britain's weather seemed to be at its worst that April Sunday. Craig and Sam Gillard had given up the outdoor rock climb in favour of half a day spent indoor bouldering near Southampton. The mountain biking they had planned for the afternoon was a washout, with a thunderstorm so intense they were soaked in seconds. Lightning continued to arc across the sky as they departed, and they were stuck in a jam trying to get on the M27 because of power cuts to traffic lights. Now, having reached the motorway early on Sunday evening, the weather hadn't yet finished with them. The eastbound M3 motorway was closed from Winchester because of an accident, the A31 was flooded at Alton, the A3 closed at Godalming. They had reset the satnav to go cross-country, and finally re-entered Surrey at eight p.m. on the B2139, heading east, south of Godalming. They were just outside the delightful riverside village of Lacey Dutton, waiting at traffic lights to cross the sixteenth-century single-lane Loxcombe Bridge over the River Wey. As they edged along the leafy road in crawling traffic, the rain began to hammer down on the roof of the Toyota RAV4. There was no traffic coming from the other direction.

'That's not a good sign,' Gillard said, trying to make himself heard above the pounding on the roof. 'Maybe the traffic lights are out here too.'

'That's all we need,' Sam said. It took another ten minutes for them to get within sight of the bridge. The road was two inches deep in water, and began to resemble a stream. A couple of cars ahead were making U-turns, giving up on the wait. The lights seemed to be working, but traffic was stationary. Gillard reached over into the back seat for his waterproof jacket. He wriggled into it, slid on waterproof trousers, and pulled the cuffs down over his boots. 'I'm going to take a look ahead. There's an unmarked road to the right we could take if the bridge is out of action.'

'Okay. Don't get wet!'

Gillard gave his wife a sarcastic look as he pulled up his jacket hood, opened the door and stepped out into the deluge. Numerous car alarms sounded in the distance as he made his way along the edge of the lane past the traffic lights and onto the narrow footway over the bridge.

The first view of the water staggered him.

Normally this was a beautiful riverside scene, with pastures on either side and the Jolly Boatman pub at the far end of the bridge. Now the pub car park was a lake, the riverside decking submerged, most of the picnic tables floating in a leisurely circle. The Wey itself was four times its normal width and sweeping debris of all sorts towards the bridge.

It was only when Gillard spotted the first floating car that he realised how serious this was. A black BMW saloon, its rear above the water, four-way flashers and alarm still going, swept along the nearside bank of the river, bashing into the lower branches of riverside trees. Further across, the bridge itself was under siege. Peering over the parapet, he saw the water level was within a few inches of the top of the arches. A large uprooted tree had wedged itself underneath the central span, with a thick bough arching over the bridge, blocking access to traffic from both directions. A small crowd had gathered on the left-hand side of the bridge, looking over into the water at the base of the tree. From the shouting and gesticulation he could tell something serious was going on. As he joined them, Gillard could see there were two more cars in the water. One, a small Peugeot saloon, was being rammed repeatedly underneath the central arch of the bridge, next to the tree. Its roof and crazed windscreen were already partially flattened, but there was a waving arm protruding from the driver-side window. A second, larger vehicle was rolling over and over laterally against the next arch towards the Lacey Dutton side. A young man in soaked jeans and T-shirt was trying to climb down the bough of the tree to reach the occupied car, but the tree was rolling left and right in the water threatening to throw him off.

The policeman knew what he had to do. He ran back to the RAV4 and pulled open the driver-side door. 'Sam, there is someone trapped in a car in the river. We need the ropes, helmets and head torches right away.' He went round to the hatchback, pulled it open and grabbed the equipment he needed. When Sam joined him, he placed a yellow helmet and head torch on her already-drenched hair. Without hesitation she shrugged on her jacket, fixed the helmet strap, and looked up at him. The rain had already made her eye make-up run down her face in long streaks, but determination was set there. He gave her a very quick hug, and kissed her damp face.

'I love you,' he said, and ran ahead with two coils of rope on his shoulder back towards the bridge. Sam followed behind.

The young man, still visible in the Victorian street lights from the bridge, had edged down to within three or four feet of the car. A couple of powerful torches were being trained from the parapet onto his intended target. 'There is a child in there with her, but I can't get any closer,' he shouted. The water level inside the car was already at the top of the steering wheel, and a woman was trying to get out from the driver-side window. But her biggest problem was that the car was trapped driver-side against the pier that held up the bridge, and was being repeatedly smashed against the stonework by the force of the water and the uprooted trees within it.

The downpour was almost biblical. The gutters on the bridge were overflowing, silvery cords pouring into the river. Gillard tied one end of his climbing rope to the nearest lamp post, and clipped a loop to his harness. It was many years since the detective had attended the fast water mountain survival course and the module which covered rescues from vehicles, but he could remember the basics. Ropes were vital, but he had to be able to quickly detach himself should he become snagged. Sam tied the other coil of rope to the next lamp post, and shouted to the lad on the tree. But despite the shouts from the parapet the roiling muddy water drowned out all human noise. With many welcoming pats on the back and shouts of encouragement, the detective clambered over the parapet and lowered himself carefully down the dozen feet towards the stoved-in roof of the car. The vehicle had already lost almost all of its normal shape, the side panels and the roof battered from being repeatedly smashed against the pier of the bridge. The lad on the tree on the other side of the car looked across to him, and Gillard gestured up to the rope that Sam was trying to throw to him. The young man followed Gillard's gaze, and when she tossed the coils to him, he caught them. Gripping the rope firmly in one hand, the other on a branch of the tree, the lad gingerly made his way back up the tree towards the parapet of the bridge and to safety.

The woman in the car, who looked to be in her thirties, had one arm and her head out of the shattered driver-side window, a buckled space no more than eighteen inches wide and perhaps a foot high. She looked desperate. In her other arm was a crying toddler. Gillard squeezed himself down between the pier and the car, knowing that this was a dangerous manoeuvre. But it was equally clear to him that the roof on the other side was now so squashed down, there was no hope of her getting out on that side. He rested with his heels on a narrow ledge, no more than three inches wide, just above the water level. The movement of the vehicle banged him repeatedly against the stone of the bridge, making him thankful that he was wearing a helmet. The force of the water was incredible. What he needed to do was clear, yet seemed impossible. It meant challenging not only the oncoming force of the river, but the momentum of the vehicle itself. He was already drenched and very cold, his fingers rapidly numbing inside his neoprene gloves. He knew this was going to test him to the limits.

Finally close enough to the woman to be able to converse, he yelled that he was going to push the vehicle away with his legs and hopefully she could pass the child out to him. She nodded.

He looked up, his back to the bridge, sitting on the ledge, and braced his legs either side of the window. He picked a moment when the car was being drawn back by the current, and locked his legs in place. 'Give her to me now,' he shouted. The woman fed the child out through the window, into Gillard's arms. He used a loop of rope under the crying little girl's arms, and tightened the slip knot around her chest just as the next turn of the current pressed the vehicle back against the base of the bridge. He looked up to the parapet and saw helmets and the beige uniform of the fire service. Strong arms pulled the little girl up and onto the parapet above him. The water inside the car was now chin high on the woman, and she was beginning to scream in panic. He knew that there was a good chance the car would now turn over because there would be more air in the tyres than any other part of it. If it did that her chances of survival were slim.

He tried again and again to press the car back away from the bridge, but it was no good. As he looked up at the river which was now illuminated by more powerful lights from the bridge, he could see at least two caravans floating down towards him. Another figure descended from the parapet, a beefy firefighter on a harness with a hefty cordless cutter in his hands. After sharing bellowed greetings, he balanced on one branch of the tree, setting to work with the reciprocating saw. First he cut the edges of the windscreen and then the metal post between windscreen and side window. It allowed Gillard to peel back the roof and rip open a bigger gap. The woman began to wriggle out, sobbing with relief. Somehow, she was bundled up to a rescue harness, and then lifted to the parapet. Gillard followed soon afterwards, hauled up on his rope, into Sam's waiting arms.

'Well done, Craig,' she said. 'That was fantastic. I knew you could do it.'

'I didn't, but I had to try,' he replied.

The woman and her child had been put in a people carrier out of the rain, shrouded in various coats and plied with biscuits. A woman who said she was a nurse was tending to the child on the back seat. Gillard crouched down to talk to the mother through the window.

'Thank you so much, I'll never forget what you did for me and for Keeley,' she said. 'Did you get the other woman?'

'Which other woman?' Gillard asked.

'There was another car just round the other side of the pier. It was a little yellow one, I think, just rolling over and over and over in the water. There's definitely someone inside. I saw a glimpse of blonde hair when the cars were side-by-side.'

Gillard blew an exhausted sigh. 'Just a minute,' he said. 'I'll let the emergency services know.'

By now the fire service were in full possession of Loxcombe Bridge. Dozens of helmeted officers were guiding onlookers away from the threatened structure and using chainsaws to cut the tree which had separated the bridge crowd into two communities. Fire appliances had managed to work their way to the forecourt of the Jolly Boatman, where they trained arc lamps on the river. By the pub a fire service inflatable was being manhandled off its trailer by a crew of four. Gillard buttonholed the big firefighter who had helped him, and explained the situation. A call was put through to the fire chief on the other side of the bridge, and a thumbs up was given from the rescue boat.

The big officer relayed a message back. 'The manageress of the Jolly Boatman says she's got free dinner and a room for the night for you and your wife, for putting your lives on the line. She's offered the front dining room which is still dry for the woman and her daughter, assuming they don't have to go to hospital.'

–

As the crowds gradually seeped from the bridge, one man sat in his black four-wheel drive watching Gillard, once again at the centre of attention under the arc lights. What on earth was that damned detective doing here? Oh, and Sam too. That was a surprise. The man clenched his fists on the wheel. Always in the way. Wherever he was, whatever he wanted to do, Gillard always seemed to be in the way. Never mind, he could adapt the tactics. He'd proved that. He'd had to think quickly tonight after the power failed, but the solution he had come up with was ingenious. And it seemed to have worked perfectly. With luck it would give him many days' grace to clear up, without anyone suspecting. Overall, things were going to plan. To keep Gillard busy, working long hours looking for the missing girl, was a perfect feint to draw the detective away from the spectacular main event. The driver smiled to himself as he contemplated the next step in his campaign to destroy the man who had usurped him. What Gillard was involved in now was nothing compared to what would happen next. Nothing. He reversed the car aggressively out of the forecourt of the Jolly Boatman, forced a gap in the crowd of bystanders, then drove away, back into Surrey.

—

Wrapped in blankets in front of a roaring log fire in the lounge of the Jolly Boatman, Gillard and Sam sipped mugs of cocoa and nibbled the plate of chocolate biscuits they had been provided with.

'So what happened to the yellow car?' Sam asked.

'The fire service said it got pulled right under the bridge. It'll be downstream somewhere. They are telling me that more than forty vehicles have been washed away into the river. And there are still two caravans trapped under Loxcombe Bridge. The whole Lacey Dutton campsite has been flooded.'

'So if there really was a woman in it, she'll have drowned.'

'Probably.' He looked out of the window. 'It looks like it has stopped raining now.'

'Thank God.' She picked up another biscuit. 'It's funny how things turn out. I was a bit dubious about the mountain biking given the weather forecast. But all that gear of yours earned its keep this evening.'

'I always keep it ready in a big rucksack, in the car. You never know.'

She stared in wonder at her husband. 'Craig, you're ready for anything. You make me feel so safe.'

It was a sentiment she soon wished she had never voiced.

-

The Gillards' final journey home was hardly without incident, with heavy rain and gusty winds making driving conditions treacherous. Only five miles from Chipstead, they joined an unmoving tailback. Sam stuck her head out of the passenger-side window into the downpour to see what the problem was, and spotted an elderly motorist vainly trying to shift a heavy sycamore bough that had blocked the road. No one seemed to be helping him, so she and Gillard ran up to help. The detective shouldered the weight of the branch, which allowed Sam and the old man to pivot the bough so it no longer fully blocked the carriageway.

Once back in the car, the radio news was full of reports of flash floods right across Hampshire, Surrey and the Home Counties caused by an unprecedented intensity of rainfall, and made worse by a two-hour power cut. An elderly lady had drowned in her own basement attempting to rescue a family heirloom from the rising floodwaters. Two children who had been seen playing near the River Wey in the afternoon were missing. In all more than two dozen motorists had been rescued from their cars, including six wedding party guests whose vehicle had stalled under a flooded bridge in the New Forest. Their own involvement at the Lacey Dutton crossing was mentioned in passing.

Gillard could tell from monitoring the Surrey Police radio traffic, something he could do from his own smartphone, that emergency resources were stretched to breaking point.

'Thankfully, only one person seems to have died,' Sam said.

'I think we will have to wait until the morning to be sure of that,' Gillard replied. 'There were an awful lot of cars bobbing down the river. I wouldn't be surprised if they discover someone stuck under a bridge somewhere who didn't make it.'

He was right.

–

It was firefighter Geoff Holt who made the discovery, just before three a.m. His powerful torch illuminated a small yellow car bobbing upside down in what had been Lacey Dutton's riverside park, and was now a backwater of the river. Further progress downstream was blocked at the hamlet of Gorlaston by a slim and rather beautiful hundred-year-old stone bridge, now used only by pedestrians, and against which a dam of floating branches was lodged. The vehicle was entangled between the most leftward span and the lower limbs of a willow. This tree was one of a dozen which had originally marked the riverbank, but was now well within the vastly enlarged waterway.

Holt was in a fire service inflatable with two other fire service officers and a paramedic. During gaps in the rain they were taking the chance to inspect the many vehicles which had tumbled down the river. It was a risky plan, because the centre of the river was still a torrent with vicious 'stoppers', waves caused by buried obstacles that were quite capable of swamping their boat. But if anyone was still trapped in those vehicles, they couldn't afford to wait until first light. Exposure would kill in an hour. Boatswain Chris Marshall steered the boat expertly, watching out for the many underwater obstacles that a newly submerged shoreline could offer. They collided with only one, which turned out to be a cast-iron bench on what used to be the riverbank, just a foot or so below the waterline. Steering around it, Marshall powered the outboard until they could reach the car.

The hopes of finding anyone living were not high. When a vehicle has taken in so much water that it floats upside down, there is no place inside that offers enough air for survival. The tyres are the only buoyancy. Holt called out and rapped on the side of the vehicle, hoping for an answer. He didn't expect one, and he didn't get one. All the windows were underwater, just the bottom six inches of corroded door sills visible in the light beam. But there was good news. The driver-side door, on the far side, was open, and had bent in half against itself where it had scraped against the bridge. That gave some hope that anyone inside had escaped. With the inflatable next to the car, Holt tried to rotate the vehicle so that he could reach the open side. After a few minutes cutting of branches, he succeeded.

As the vehicle bobbed around, a great fan of fair hair floated up in the water. He reached down and felt a clothed female body beneath. He tugged gently, but she was clearly snagged. He felt for the seatbelt but it was snug in its holder. He wriggled in further, the freezing water coursing up his sleeve and down his neck as he forced the waterproof torch into the narrow cavity between the waters and the driver's footwell. Yes, a leg was caught deep in the water, tangled in the steering wheel, now at the base of this watery cell. The icy, bone-chilling unknotting of the limb allowed him to float her free. A young woman, no more than a girl.

She was as cold as stone.

Chapter Seven

Monday

Alison Rigby had demanded a seven a.m. incident room meeting on the Beatrice Ulbricht case on Monday, making no allowance for the after-effects of the flooding. She had somehow put Surrey CID on to continental time, always to be prepared for an early call from Germany. There was no doubt where her priorities lay.

Detective Chief Inspector Craig Gillard was in, on time, at 6.45 a.m. The CID block was virtually deserted. The overnight on-call detective inspector, John Perry, had just come in, dripping water everywhere. He was dressed for a Welsh bank holiday: heavy duty anorak, waterproof trousers and wellies. He sighed heavily as he dropped a head torch, laptop bag and various other bits and pieces on the nearest desk. With his hangdog expression, and prematurely greying hair, the forty-two-year-old looked more like the exhausted school physics teacher he once had been than a detective. To Gillard, and many of his more junior colleagues, Perry exuded that submissive resentment of the unsporty schoolkid, always forced to be in goal.

'Welcome to water world,' Gillard said. 'Found those kids yet?'

He nodded, which shook a few extra drips onto the desk and carpet tiles. 'They're fine. Turned out to be with a neighbour. But we've another death, a rather sad tale. A lady of ninety-three had a heart attack in her car while waiting at some defective roadworks lights. It was stuck on red for an hour and a quarter in the pissing rain, but even though others overtook her and went past, she wouldn't move. That makes three weather-related deaths.'

'Three?'

'Oh yeah, the fire service pulled out some teenage girl from a car stuck under Gorlaston Bridge in the early hours. Must've drowned hours before. Like to catch whichever bastard was the driver, leaving her there to die. They pulled her out by boat, and called me over to take a look. Poor kid.'

'Do we know who she is?'

'Not yet. Doesn't match any of the recent missing person reports, at least none locally.'

'Who is the on-call pathologist?'

'Delahaye. Poor bugger is run ragged. I think the coroner's office will call for reinforcements from London, but either way they'll not get to these bodies for a few days.'

Dr David Delahaye was Gillard's favourite forensic pathologist: a mind like a razor and a keen eye for details. With gangly limbs and with a balding dome of a head, he absolutely looked the part.

'My role in this is to dig up the dirty on the vehicle,' Perry said, shrugging off his anorak and dumping it on the back of a chair. 'Once I've got a coffee.'

Gillard looked around and saw that, in the absence of most of the required staff, the incident room meeting was not going to happen on time. 'I'm already logged into the DVLA. Pass me the registration number, if you go get us both a brew. Mine's extra milky, no sugar.'

Perry agreed, passed across his notes, and after thanking Gillard strode off to the refectory, shaking drops of water everywhere.

Gillard copied in the number and waited. The record came up quite quickly. The car was very old. A 1982 Austin Allegro, in canary yellow. SORN, since 2012. Statutory off road notification. That meant the car was not taxed for road use, had no MOT to prove it was roadworthy, and would therefore not have been insured. He wasn't surprised. Gillard's own father had driven an Allegro and had cursed it almost daily. Supposedly cheap and economical, they weren't much cop even from new. Those Allegros in good condition these days would presumably be worth a bit, but keeping them running would be the problem.

The last registered keeper was a Kevin O'Connell of Lacey Dutton Caravan Park. The detective quickly switched to the local database of criminal records, and typed in O'Connell's details. Bingo! He had form. Drink-driving, failure to stop at an accident, driving while disqualified. No jail time, but several sizeable fines. His last disqualification had not yet ended. Reading between the lines, Gillard reckoned he knew why this driver might have disappeared from the scene of an accident. He'd done it before, after all.

All they needed to do now was to find out who the girl was. He looked down Perry's very neatly written but rain-smeared notes, and saw an order number he recognised as being one from the largest independent forensic lab in the country. Good. He'd already sent in a DNA sample.

By the time Perry came back with the two coffees, Gillard reckoned he had a decent hunch about what had happened. The detective inspector was impressed. 'He must have just used the Allegro locally, he'd have been caught in a heartbeat if he ever went past an ANPR camera.'

'There's another thought I've had,' Gillard said. 'Put a chestnut wig, a mauve fedora, a coat and a scarf on this girl. Do you think she could have been on the train?'

Perry shrugged. 'Now she is surplus to requirements, is that what you're thinking?'

'Maybe,' Gillard said. 'If true it would put us in an even darker place, I fear.'

DI Perry's wife Melanie sat in the office above her wellness shop, going through the finances. Wholebods was doing quite well. Woking was prosperous and with just two part-time employees, a short lease and a business rates exemption, costs weren't too bad. The full body Shiatsu massages and the ear candling were doing really well. She had remortgaged their home once for the business two years ago, but now she had done so again, on the quiet. She moved the money, another sixty grand, into her personal account and set up the secret payment. John would kill her if he found out what she was doing, but he wouldn't find out. She had always looked after the finances. In fact it made her laugh that such a clueless man had ever considered becoming a detective.

Having a secret life gave her such a buzz. It pepped up the otherwise dull suburban existence she had at home. But what she had done recently, well, that was so much more fun precisely because of the risk she was taking. A colossal gamble.

She looked at her watch. Shit! She had to be home in half an hour to help Vanessa make a cake for a friend's birthday. At seventeen, her daughter was reasonably adept as a baker, but this had to be gluten-free. Vanessa had asked her mother to pick up fresh cherries, soya milk and polenta to replace normal flour, but she had forgotten. She picked up her bag and rushed out of the door.

–

Gillard caught up with DI Perry at ten. The detective inspector slumped at Gillard's desk with a sausage sandwich drowned in mustard.

'Are you still here?' Gillard asked.

'In body but not in mind,' Perry said. 'I'm going home now. Five extra hours on top of the nightshift is enough for anyone.' The man looked exhausted. 'Uniforms picked up Kevin O'Connell this morning, bailing out caravans at his mum's campsite. Admits the car is his, but swears absolutely blind it's been a non-runner since before he bought it. Claims it was stored on waste ground behind one of the static caravans, close to the river.'

'So he reckons it was just lifted up by the tide and floated down with this girl in it?'

Perry managed a laugh. 'Yeah. He says he has no idea who the girl is, or what she would be doing in the car. They've got the Allegro at Newsome Motors in Lacey

Dutton. I need someone to take a look. I'm formally SIO on the river death from tomorrow.'

Gillard looked at his watch. 'Rigby has rearranged the incident room meeting for midday, so I've got an hour. Leave it to me. I could do with a breath of fresh air.'

–

Within half an hour Perry was almost home, which was just as well because he didn't think he'd ever been so tired. The white VW Polo purred along happily enough to the outskirts of Woking, until he saw the developer's flagpoles which marked the Shepherds' Rest estate. A vast development of nearly 3,000 'exclusive executive' homes, of which just over two thirds had been completed. He drove along Southdown Way, past the sales office and show homes, and cul-de-sacs of five-bedroom detached homes with sizeable gardens, which had been the first phase built. He then turned left into Ryeland Drive, a meandering street of semi-detached three-bedroom boxes, all garage and no house. He and Mel had looked at one of these, but she thought them soulless, with a front garden no bigger than a tablecloth, and soon to be overlooked at the back by three-storey townhouses when the next plots were built. In the end they had bought a home in yet another bucolically-themed street. It was a big stretch financially, yet more piled on the family debt. As a policeman he had not been keen to live on a street named Romney Crook. But Mel had put her foot down. The houses were a tad more expensive and a little more secluded, and the teardrop-shaped wildlife garden around which the crook-shaped road ran boasted the only mature oak tree that the developers had seen fit to leave unfelled. For Mel, and even more for his daughter, this had been a clinching advantage.

It hadn't escaped his notice that his wife had seemed happier in the eighteen months they had been in their new home. They had been through a pretty bad patch before, and divorce had been mentioned. He really wanted to make Mel happy, but it wasn't easy. She was what you would call high maintenance, a bit out of his league. Not just in looks, though that was important, but in aspirations and expectations. She had come from a well-off background, and having earned an MBA expected to progress well beyond his level. That's why he was so reticent to tackle her about the mounting debts, even the never-never financing for the Audi soft-top, her pride and joy. He was simply delighted that her new wellness business seemed to be taking off.

There was very little crime in their new estate. He'd always kept an eye on the local community policing website. A few incidents of criminal damage, one of domestic violence, and then, just the other week, a high-profile incident. Five minutes' walk away, among the townhouses of Wensleydale Walk, a burglary and carjacking had occurred. Professional thieves stealing a high-value vehicle, presumably for export.

Apart from that, there was nothing reported. But as far as crime was concerned he had been looking in the wrong place. He knew now he should have been looking inside his own household. Trying to deal with it meant that Perry had his own dirty little secret, one that would quite possibly bring him down.

Chapter Eight

The bridge at Lacey Dutton looked forlorn in the watery spring sunlight. Though the water levels had dropped considerably, and the riverside path had re-emerged, each arch was still choked with uprooted trees and boughs, with car tyres, caravan panels, polystyrene containers and a thick sludge of mud and plastic. Every waterside tree sported a stork's nest of debris well above the reach of a stretching man, a clear high-water mark that would no doubt one day be engraved into the cast-iron flood record bolted to the centre of the bridge.

Newsome's Garage was on a side street opposite the Jolly Boatman, and had been spared the worst of the rising waters. It was a tiny place, petrol pumps removed a decade ago, two years after the BMW franchise was lost. Now it was just for repairs, and had only two employees. The Allegro, now right way up, had been pushed onto a lift in one of the repair bays.

Any idea Gillard had that the car may have been driven anywhere in recent years was instantly dispelled. The sills were rotted, there was only one hub cap, and there was mildew on the windows. Gillard, wearing overalls and latex gloves, was greeted by Brian Newsome, proprietor, a vigorous-looking seventy-year-old with greased back grey hair in a teddy boy DA, and the stub of a cigarette burning between fingers and thumb which he dropped on the ground and stamped out.

Newsome already had firm opinions about the car. 'There's no such thing as a good Allegro. But this one, well. Non-runner, guaranteed, a hundred not very careful owners. Illegal tyres, severe long-term corrosion, electrics well-fucked.'

'Show me.'

Newsome hit the button which raised the vehicle lift, hoisting the two-door saloon to shoulder height. It looked tiny compared to most modern vehicles. He pointed out the broken oil seals underneath, the worn bearings, the extensive rust like a Martian landscape.

'My guess?' Newsome said, though he hadn't been asked for it. 'It's been sitting in a puddle for a decade.'

Gillard nodded, unwilling to share any details.

'You won't get no forensics nor dabs off of this,' Newsome said with finality, folding his arms as if daring his expertise to be contradicted. 'I watched *The Bill*.'

'Things have moved on since the eighties,' Gillard said. 'Can you bring it down, please?'

Once the vehicle was down, Gillard opened the door. The interior stank of weed and stale water. Various insects of the crawling and sliding variety seemed to have made their homes underneath the seats and in the fabric roof lining. The hardest thing to gauge was how much of that had occurred since the waters carried it away, and how much before. It was conceivable that someone would willingly sleep in an old car if it was dry, or more likely may have sheltered in it from the rain. But it was hard to imagine that this car had been dry for a very long time.

So what had this young woman been doing in it?

He noticed something else. There was a great mess of vegetation entangled around the clutch and brake pedals, and a skein of something else. He reached down and untangled what seemed to be human hair, on which leaves, grass and muck had been caught. He took a small plastic evidence bag from his pocket, and gingerly dropped the tangle of fibres in.

Stepping back from the car and going outside, Gillard held the bag up into the watery sunlight. He'd been right. This hair wasn't blonde, like the girl found in the car.

It was dark.

–

Lacey Dutton Caravan Park was a sprawling piece of floodplain, about five acres on the outside bend of the River Wey, three quarters of a mile upstream from Lacey Dutton bridge. From previous visits he recalled it was a sprawling site, a dozen or so static caravans on the higher land, with a couple of dozen pitches nearer the river for camper vans and touring caravans. Now, with the flood-waters mainly receded, the entire site looked like a film set for a re-enactment of the Battle of the Somme. Two chocolatey-coated caravans were stuck in some willow trees, one vertical, one on its side, seemingly grappling each other like overweight mud wrestlers. Empty gas cylinders were strewn around the site like muddy corpses. The site office was the only element unmarked by the fight against the waters. A static caravan surrounded by a neat trellis fence and an Astroturf lawn, with gaily painted concrete gnomes and toadstools standing sentinel over a slimy moat. Approach was only possible across slippery planks recently laid for the purpose. Gillard parked on the road and donned his wellingtons. He met Mrs Deirdre O'Connell, Kevin's mother, as she emerged from the site office with a bunch of mops grasped in one hand and a vape in the other. They greeted each other casually.

'Insured?' Gillard asked, his inclined head indicating the entire sweep of disaster.

The woman gave him a weary look over her steel-framed spectacles which told him the answer. Gillard had known Deirdre on and off for many years. She was a tough cookie, having run the campsite on her own for several years after the death of her husband, with little or no active help from her tearaway kids. The business was only marginally profitable, he guessed, with the long-term prospect of a sale of the land for housing dangling like a jewel in the distance.

For the next few minutes he indulged her tour of the carnage and devastation that the river had brought on her life and livelihood. He gently guided her towards the subject of the yellow Allegro, as they squelched together through ankle-deep puddles, criss-crossing foot-deep muddy tyre tracks until they finally reached a leylandii hedge with a broken gate.

'This is Kevin's patch,' she said as they splashed through. The ancient mildewed caravan that was Kevin's home had survived the inundation because of its berm of sandbags, but his garden, as Deirdre called it, which ran for twenty yards towards the river's edge, looked like it had been swatted by some giant hand. The smooth mud was sprinkled with plastic bottles, lumps of polystyrene, and broken branches from the willows further upstream.

'That was where the Allegro was for the last however many years,' she said, pointing to the middle of the quagmire. 'He lost his Vauxhall Nova too, that's the one that worked.'

'Just to be clear, you say Kevin was with you throughout the flood?'

'Yes. He was backwards and forwards with ropes and sandbags. He did a great job considering he normally doesn't shift from sitting on his arse watching TV.'

'And there was no young teenage girl staying with you, or with Kevin?'

'No. But I might recognise her if you have a photo.'

'Not with me.' Gillard did indeed have an image on his tablet, but as it was of the face of a corpse, he didn't feel he could share it. That would eventually be Perry's decision as SIO for this case.

'Is there any other access here, apart from past the site office?' Gillard asked.

'Yes, the riverside path, which is actually a drive for two of the bungalows, went right past here.' There was no sign of it. 'I think a big chunk of the bank has disappeared,' she said. 'We owned it and we want it back.' She barked a brief sarcastic laugh. They made their way carefully down towards the river's edge.

Gillard opened up his Ordnance Survey map. 'So there was vehicular access?' he asked.

'Not after four o'clock on Sunday, I wouldn't have thought. Mike and Betty in the first bungalow said the waters were up to their front step. By midnight they were halfway up her new kitchen units.'

'Did you see any vehicles or any strangers on the site in the run-up to the floods?'

She shook her head. 'We had four bookings over the weekend. One was a regular from the statics, but everybody else from the lower pastures we brought up into the office once the river came over. Three cars got washed away, but we managed to save the Dutch camper van.'

'So what are you going to do?'

She blew out a huge vape cloud and watched it dissolve in the now bright blue sky. 'We'll carry on camping,' she said, and smiled at him, a survivor's mask that covered the pain. 'You've got to keep going, haven't you?'

–

Kevin O'Connell arrived pretty promptly at Epsom Police Station to give a statement. DI Claire Mulholland met him at the reception desk and escorted him into an interview room. O'Connell was a rough-looking slab of a man, in his early twenties and over six feet tall. He had a shaven, lumpy head and one of those bushy dark beards that looked like it had been bought from a joke shop and glued on. His stained trousers sagged, and as he sat at the interview table they revealed a wedge of hairy bottom, and stretched across it the word Friday on the purple waistband of his day-of-the-week underpants. Claire had bought her own teenage son a seven-pack of the same cheap brand, to remind him to change them every day. And like with O'Connell, the waistband day was always wrong. She reflected that unchanged underwear were worse than stopped clocks, only right once a week.

'That body was nothing to do with me,' he blurted out before the interview had even started.

Claire sat on the other side of the table and reassured him that he wasn't being accused of anything at the moment. 'We know the car wasn't a runner. We just want to know how the girl came to be inside it.'

O'Connell had brought in all his documents, which supported his mother's contention that the car had been bought two years ago for cash as a non-runner. 'Originally the bodywork wasn't too bad as it had been stored in a shed, and I'm pretty good mechanically,' O'Connell said. 'I thought that if I could get it running, and get in some of the spares, I'd be able to sell it for a fair bit. The old Austin Allegro is a classic car.'

Claire inclined her head dubiously. 'So where was the vehicle kept?'

'Under a carport behind my caravan.' He described the location, within ten yards of the river, easily accessible from the riverside path, and because all the rubbish containers were kept there, screened from the rest of the caravan park by a row of leylandii. 'There used to be a wire fence at the edge of our land, but it kept getting trodden down. So when the river flooded right up, there was nothing much to stop the car being floated off.' He paused. 'So have you got a photograph of her, then? The woman what was found inside?'

Claire knew they would get to this point, but couldn't show him either the historical photograph or the picture of the body. 'It's not the kind of image we can share at this stage.'

He shrugged and looked disappointed. 'Was she sleeping in there? In the car?'

'We don't know. It might be somewhere that you would shelter just to get out of the rain, if it was unlocked.'

'Yeah, not all the locks worked, so you could always get in. It was dry inside, all the seats were in good condition.'

Claire hoped that the girl had got in the car herself, but she had wanted to revisit Gillard's theory that she might already have been dead, taken out of one vehicle and dumped into the Allegro. 'Your mum said it is possible to get a vehicle down the riverside path, right?'

'Yeah, easy. The path is only an extension of the gravel drive that goes to a couple of other riverside houses. That's how the Allegro got in there in the first place. I towed it in. Still, it would have been a bit more challenging during the rain and the floods. Not impossible, but you would have needed a four-wheel-drive, a good one, and a bit of confidence, I'd say. You'd have to know what you're doing.'

Claire nodded. She believed O'Connell. On the balance of probabilities, this seemed like an unfortunate accident. She hoped the post-mortem would confirm it.

-

The delayed incident room meeting turned out to be frustrating. Gillard had called in dozens of CCTV recordings from the Earlsfield area. Public safety cameras at traffic lights and Pelican crossings, bank security footage and ATM cameras, internal video from off-licences and betting shops, anything that might give even a glimpse of a woman in a mauve hat and rainbow-coloured scarf. DCs Carrie 'Rainy' Macintosh and Carl Hoskins had worked all weekend coordinating the surveillance team, and had got a chain of four cameras which tracked the Beatrice impostor under the railway bridge heading north along Garratt Lane for a quarter of a mile until she turned right into Algarve Road, a tree-lined residential street. That is where she disappeared from view for good.

There were far fewer resources where the fake Beatrice's journey began. There were no CCTV cameras on the roads approaching Clandon station. The first glimpse of her approaching in the rain on the Tuesday afternoon was in the station car park. Gillard described to the assembled detectives how he and Claire Mulholland had driven all round the village of Westmeare, the last place that the real Beatrice Ulbricht was seen. They had visited plenty of quiet lanes and sunken rural drives where a body might easily be abandoned, while uniformed officers had leafleted and knocked on doors around the village. There were no obvious fresh leads.

'What about the London angle?' Hoskins asked.

Claire, who had been coordinating with the Metropolitan Police, answered that. 'None of Beatrice's fellow musicians are in the frame on this. We don't believe that the answer to this crime will be found within her musical community.'

'What about Adrian Singer?' Rainy asked. 'He's a wee bit creepy.'

Gillard shook his head. 'He may be the best suspect we've got, but he came out clean, forensically. There was no trace of Beatrice's DNA upstairs in his home, only on one dining chair and one seat cushion from the sofa, which matches his story that she came round for dinner and then left. His car showed some of her DNA on the passenger seat, but nothing in the rear seats or boot.'

'So do we really believe that she was just randomly snatched from a bus stop?' Rainy asked. 'It doesn't quite fit with all this elaborate cover-up and the impostor. That speaks of weeks of planning, surely, yet it happened within two days of her disappearance.'

Gillard nodded. 'That's an excellent point. I think the word to discard here is "randomly". It just doesn't fit. There has to be a reason.'

–

At two p.m. DCI Gillard Skyped Dr David Delahaye at Redhill Hospital, before he performed the post-mortem. The forensic pathology consultant appeared to be sitting in a small windowless office. Leaning forward into the fisheye lens his square spectacles and balding dome made him look like he belonged in a flying saucer. The right-hand side of the computer screen was dedicated to the photographs that they were sharing.

'This is the dead girl,' Delahaye said, as a close-up image of her face flashed up. Alabaster skin, bluish lips, eyes closed, dark blonde hair. But the overwhelming impression was of innocence; pure, fresh, and preserved for ever. The pathologist flicked through a series of images taken on arrival at the mortuary. They were mostly of her face. The last few were full body. Her clothing was intact, a woollen cardigan over what looked to be a white blouse, a pleated skirt, fawn tights and no shoes.

'No make-up,' Gillard said.

'Unpierced ears, no nail varnish,' Delahaye added. 'She may be even younger than she appears. She is the typical height of a thirteen-year-old. Forensically speaking, what we are missing, if she drowned recently, is foam. It would be normal to find froth in the mouth, and upper airways. I will perhaps be in a better position to assess this once I've opened her up. Froth in the smaller airways, oedema, even overinflation would give us a better guide.' He looked up at the detective. 'However, as you may know, determination of drowning is one of the trickiest areas in all pathology. Immersion in water can kill in many ways, not just by filling the lungs with water. Hypothermia, stress, hypertension and cardiac arrest can all kill, particularly someone who may be trapped in a partially submerged vehicle.'

'Not a nice way to go,' Gillard said.

'There aren't too many of those,' the pathologist said, peering over his spectacles. 'Well, I tend not to see them anyway. This' – he tapped the screen with a ballpoint pen – 'would not be one of them.'

'How long had she been in the water?'

Delahaye offered a weary look. 'You know full well we can't be precise about it, but unofficially I think we can bracket it. The corpse's core temperature was similar to that of the water she was recovered from, so she must have been dead in it at least a couple of hours. But from these photographs, and a brief external inspection, I would hazard a guess that it was less than twelve hours. There are few observable signs of the deterioration that one would expect.'

'One other thing,' Gillard said. 'I found some longish dark hairs entangled in the same vehicle, which are clearly not from this victim. I've asked the lab to copy you in on the DNA results.'

'Thank you. We could do without any more victims.' He paused and then asked: 'Any luck with finding Beatrice Ulbricht?'

'None, really. We've reached a hiatus. We know there was an impostor on the train, a woman who went to enormous trouble to draw our attention away from the

Westmeare area of Surrey. We guess she had an accomplice too, although we're still hazy about how that would work.'

'I met Beatrice, two years ago,' Delahaye said.

'You did?'

'Yes. She hadn't yet set up the Lysander Quartet, but was one of those jobbing semi-professional soloists that village music societies rely on. She came down to play for us in Kent, and we put her up in the spare room. She is, and I refuse to use the past tense, an absolutely delightful woman. Funny, self-confident, charming, full of *joie de vivre*. And I have to say that the Bach solo violin sonata that she played, for all the fact that it was not quite technically perfect, was so beautifully cadenced emotionally that most of us were in tears.' He blinked a few times. 'If she is not found alive, I'm going to ask somebody else to do the post-mortem. I don't think I could bear to do it.'

-

'I'm so sorry to hear this, Ellen.' Sam Gillard was on the phone to her friend, having seen a rather forlorn Facebook post after many days of no contact.

'I don't understand it. I did everything he wanted me to do,' Ellen sobbed. 'I knew he was always travelling, and I accepted that. I knew he could only come over one or maybe two nights a week, and I accepted that. I started going to the gym as he suggested, and dieting. I dropped two dress sizes. Even the sex stuff...'

'What did he make you do?' Sam asked, her interest piqued.

'I don't want to say. It didn't feel right, but I was so... so, relieved that anybody wanted me after all this time.'

Sam realised she'd never even seen a picture of Gabriel. When Ellen had come over for dinner she said that he hated having his picture taken because of a scar. It wasn't even a bad scar, Ellen had said.

'You're better off without him,' Sam said.

'But I don't want to *be* without him.' The tears began again.

With other friends Sam had also seen this kind of process at the death of a relationship. How longing and pain dominated at the start, and that learning to hate, even for a while, made you feel better. Hatred was the blister that protected the wound, useful for a while, but damaging if retained permanently.

'I gave him money too,' Ellen said. 'It was just a loan.'

'How much?'

'It's not about the amount, it's the breach of trust.'

'I agree, but are we talking a hundred pounds, or more?'

'It was the money left to me by my grandmother, for a deposit on a house. More than £14,000. It's all I have.'

'Oh Ellen.' Poor, poor woman, taken for a ride by an utter bastard. Sam waited for her friend's sobs to subside. 'Ellen, you can't let him get away with this. Give me his full name, address, phone number, place of work. I'll report it for you—'

'No, I'm sure he'll let me have it back. It's just awful to have to ask.'

'Ellen, trust me. Gabriel is never going to give you your cash back. If we act quickly, you might have a chance. But if you wait, well, there's a good chance he will get away with it.'

'I love him, Sam. How could he do this to me?'

'Get real, Ellen! This is what some men do.'

'Sam, please don't be horrible to me.' Ellen said in a meek voice.

'I'm sorry.' Sam realised that she was already nurturing a sizeable abscess of loathing for Gabriel, a man she had never met. As she rolled her mouth around her anger, feeling the texture and sensitivity that had once been very familiar to her, it flared into impatience with Ellen.

Her friend might not be ready to go ballistic, but she was. She would mention it to Craig.

—

Arriving home at a reasonable time, Gillard interrupted Sam showing their home to potential purchasers. It was a pretty standard three-bedroom semi-detached, but had attracted no firm offers in the months that it had been on the market. The market was soggy, the estate agent said, but there were other factors that Craig preferred to blame. His aunt Trish lived opposite in a bungalow she had bought shortly after the infamous Devon hit-and-run court case in which she was involved. She wanted to be close to her only nephew, but Gillard found her devious and manipulative, a baleful influence. She had been caught leaving messages on the windscreens of potential purchasers' cars warning them about undisclosed damp problems in the property. She was doing everything possible to stop them leaving.

The prospective buyers, a Nigerian dentist and his Indian-born wife, seemed quite interested, especially now that Sam had persuaded her husband to knock ten grand off the price. After they had left, Gillard embraced his wife and suggested they go out for a meal at the local trattoria.

Sam, who had picked up a couple of ready meals on her way home, quickly agreed. 'I never say no to an offer like that, Craig. I never know when the next chance will be.'

She was about to head upstairs to change out of her jumper and jeans when her husband scooped her up and kissed her on the nose. 'You look lovely as you are.'

'You're wearing a suit and tie, and I'm in trainers,' she said.

'The head waiter will just assume you're my niece. Besides, if we head off right now, we can walk – it only takes twenty minutes, so we'll still be in time for the early bird offer and we can share a bottle of wine.'

'No early incident room meeting tomorrow, then?' Sam asked.

'Not so far, but things can always change.'

Sam settled for the minimum refresh of eyeliner and lipstick, and as they walked down their drive and out of the cul-de-sac, he grasped her hand. To her, it was a good sign. When Craig was relaxed he was much more fun to be with. She liked him to be hers, not a possession of Surrey Police. She could admire his professionalism and his investigative brain, but at the end of the day she loved him for the more caring side of his personality.

After their meal of seafood fettuccine and grilled halibut, followed by chocolate sponge, Sam took her husband's hand across the table and asked what he was thinking.

'I've been thinking about you. It was something that Karl-Otto Ulbricht said, about how much he regrets not having made the time in his life to answer the emails and texts that his daughter sent him. It's the busy life, of course, and we all suffer it. God knows, I'm as bad an offender as he is, leaving everything for you to fix, from the broken window in the garage right through to showing round potential buyers for the house. But I can pay you attention, and I will.'

Sam leaned across the table, took her husband's face between her hands and kissed him forcefully. 'I love you, Craig. You're a good man.'

He smiled.

'Very few men are as nice as you, Craig. Remember my friend Ellen?'

He did. He had a very clear picture of her standing in his kitchen. 'How is she?'

Sam's face fell. 'That new guy has dumped her.'

'Oh dear.' He began to examine the coffee and liqueur menu.

'Craig, don't dismiss it like that. She's in love. And this bastard has swindled her out of her life savings.' Sam summarised the details.

She had his attention now. 'Has she reported it?'

Sam sighed. 'I don't think she is emotionally ready. She just wants him back.' Sam reached across and grasped his hands. 'Don't roll your eyes, she's very needy at the moment.'

They talked through the possibilities, agreeing that nothing could be done until a complaint had been made. He changed the subject to something less gloomy while they finished the wine, a fresh pinot grigio, and rounded the evening off with a fiery shot of grappa. The walk home was a delight; they cut across a darkened park away from the main road, and had a slightly drunken kiss and cuddle by the swings, just as if they were teenagers. For a dare they clambered over the wooden palings which marked the park's northern boundary, earning themselves a tut of disgust from a late-night female dog walker. Gillard carried his giggling wife over his shoulder the last 200 yards into the cul-de-sac, and with mock shushing and whispers tiptoed past his aunt's bungalow. Still holding Sam, this time like a battering ram, he ran across the street towards their front door, and pretended to bash it in with her head, yelling: 'Armed police!'

After numerous attempts to insert the key one-handed, Gillard opened the door, and toppled with Sam onto the doormat. Both laughing uncontrollably, they wriggled around, until he could kick the door closed behind them. The laughter suddenly ceased, the couple staring into each other's eyes, the kissing became passionate, and he said: 'Look, the Surrey bodice ripper strikes again!' He attempted to tear off her pullover, but Sam became entangled in the sleeves. She made short work of his suit and tie, and when they made love, passionately, it was on a pile of flyers offering pizza and curry delivered to your door.

Tuesday

Sitting with his head in his hands at his desk, DCI Craig Gillard contemplated the impasse he was at. What on earth had happened to Beatrice Ulbricht? All of the usual electronic and technical tools available to CID – CCTV, mobile phone cell site analysis, and finally ANPR – had so far either drawn a blank or simply created contradictory ideas. They couldn't find a single vehicle that had been both in Earlsfield *and* within the vicinity of Clandon station on that Tuesday afternoon, not even the van of the man who had seen Beatrice at the bus stop.

The breathless arrival of Detective Inspector John Perry broke into his reverie. 'Craig, you are not going to believe this.' He was waving his smartphone around excitedly.

'Try me.'

'The girl under the bridge has a DNA match on the national database, with a missing person called Jane Morris.' Perry turned back to the phone, as if reading it properly for the first time. 'It's a cold case last reinvestigated by the Met in 2006.'

'Let's have a look,' Gillard said. Perry passed him the phone, and he scrolled down the text. 'This can't be right, John. The girl in the river could only just have been born in 2006. Did she disappear as a baby?' Gillard scrolled down to the date of the original investigation. 'No, Jane Morris disappeared in 1982, aged fifteen. Is that just a familial DNA test?'

'No, I didn't ask for familial, just an ordinary match.'

Gillard suggested they download the full PDF onto a large screen so they could read it in detail. The results were astonishing.

'So it's not a familial test,' Gillard said. 'But it's impossible. They're saying that the woman in the Allegro *is* Jane Morris. But it can't be. Jane Morris would be fifty-two. The girl we saw was thirteen maybe, seventeen tops.'

'So what do I do now?'

'Get them to retest. It's possibly some cross-contamination. Thank God it's the kind of mistake we can spot immediately.'

The detective chief inspector looked up at the arrival of DC Hoskins, grim faced, with a polythene evidence bag which appeared to be full of mud. 'Another packed lunch, Carl?' Perry said, and chuckled at his own joke.

Hoskins ignored him, and said, 'This was found in a tree a mile downriver.'

'What is it?' Gillard asked.

'I'm told it's a scarf,' he responded. 'I'm off down to forensics, do you want to come?'

Chapter Nine

News of the find spread like wildfire. Five minutes later half a dozen detectives gathered round a large plastic sheet on the desk in forensics as technician Petra Amin used tongs to extract the item from the plastic bag. Filthy, stinking water sloshed out with it, and as the forensic technician stretched out the drenched woollen item to its full five feet, it was clear that it had once been multi-coloured. Muddied versions of red, orange, green, blue, indigo and violet wool, hand knitted by a loving mother for her talented daughter.

'Do we know who found this?' Gillard asked Hoskins.

'Geoff Holt and Chris Marshall from the fire service.'

'I'm impressed. They had enough on their plates with the floods, but still had time to read the missing persons round-robin.'

Hoskins nodded. 'I've emailed the senior officer there to ask them to keep a lookout for the hat and the violin.'

The door burst open to reveal Chief Constable Alison Rigby. She immediately made the room seem very crowded. 'I heard the news,' she said unnecessarily. 'The Environment Agency says the waters are now safe for police divers, and that's where I want all of the effort to go in trying to find Beatrice.'

DI Perry, standing at the back of the group, piped up. 'Ma'am, I put a request in this morning, but there is no confirmation of when we'll have them. As you can imagine with six people still missing in the county and a huge number of sunken vehicles across the Wey, Cranleigh Waters and the Mole, we're probably only going to get one team to begin with, as we're already competing with Sussex, Hampshire and Berkshire for resources.'

Rigby smiled. 'Fear not, John. The moment I heard the news about the scarf, I did a little calling around. As of five minutes ago I've been offered four teams coming in on an RAF flight from Scotland. The Home Secretary has agreed to pay the bill. Of course they should be useful not only for the Beatrice Ulbricht case but for the wider search for those missing in floods.'

'Friends in high places, ma'am?' Gillard asked.

'The very pinnacle, Craig.' She winked, and walked out.

–

Back at the incident room Gillard pulled out Ordnance Survey maps of Surrey, and using the largest available table spread them out. He called over DI Claire Mulholland, and they laid over some clear acetate so they could begin with marker pens noting the various events. They concentrated on the River Wey upstream from Lacey Dutton towards Hampshire. It was a good fifteen miles southwest of Westmeare and at least ten south of Godalming. Clandon was even further away.

'We've not got much here,' Gillard said. 'There are ANPR cameras on the A281 and A283, and there is a road safety camera on Loxcombe Bridge at the traffic lights. I think the best we can do for now is to try to see if anyone who has been in the vicinity of Westmeare on Sunday night has also been in and around Lacey Dutton in the last few days.'

'Whoever is clever enough to have constructed that girl on the train costume drama would certainly be smart enough not to get caught using the same vehicle in those two locations,' Claire said.

'I agree. But what else do we have?' Gillard asked. 'The DNA tests on the railway seat cushion came back with half a dozen different traces, one animal, almost certainly dog.'

'Why dog?'

'British Transport Police warned me to expect that on any DNA test of a train seat. It's from what passengers have walked in before they put their feet on the seat opposite.'

'Icky.'

'Yes. Anyway, none of the human traces are on the national database. We don't even seem to have a trace for Beatrice on it, even though the impostor was sitting there wearing her coat.'

Down the far end of the incident room, they could hear chuckling. Rainy Macintosh and Carl Hoskins were watching something that amused them. Gillard wandered over, feeling that he could do with a little light relief.

'You got to see this, sir.' Hoskins beckoned Gillard over to his computer terminal. Macintosh discreetly slipped away, returning to do some work.

'What is it?'

'CCTV from last Monday's Woking carjacking. I'm calling it the tale of the flying slipper.'

'I'm due in a meeting in two minutes,' Gillard said. He wasn't looking forward to it. The German minister and his wife were already waiting in Rigby's office.

'You'll only need half that, sir.'

Hoskins sat his boss in the chair, and restarted the footage again on quarter speed slo-mo.

It was domestic CCTV footage taken from above the front door of a house looking out across its short drive and onto a residential street. A dark Mitsubishi Warrior, an off-road monster pick-up with high suspension and a snorkel, reversed into the picture from the right-hand side close to the camera and swung in a fast clockwise arc down the drive towards the street. For the first one or two seconds nothing whatever could be seen of the occupant. However, a motion-sensor light further off to the left was triggered, and for a few seconds the car was bathed in dazzling light.

'Camera's mounted too high,' Gillard said.

'If it was a bit lower we could see his face,' Hoskins said, pausing the replay.

'Doubt it. Too much condensation on the screen.' As it was, there was only the sleeve of a dark car coat, with a single narrow hi-vis stripe on it visible through the side window.

'He's wearing gloves,' Hoskins said. 'You can see a hand on the steering wheel. But watch this.' He hit play again.

As the vehicle swung backwards and right off the drive and onto the road, a bathrobed figure sprinted into view from immediately underneath the camera. The man, who looked to be in his late thirties and athletically built, showed quite a turn of speed for someone in slippers, intercepting the car just as it ceased to move backwards.

He grabbed the passenger-side door handle, leaned back and tugged, but when it accelerated forward, the change of direction seemed to catch him off-balance. He was jerked off his feet and fell sideways, still holding on to the door. His dressing gown flapped open, hairy chest and parts south briefly visible as he rolled on the road.

'Ouch, that's going to hurt,' Gillard said.

'Yep, dragged up the road on his bare bollocks. Now watch the slipper,' Hoskins said.

The black item flew off the victim's foot as he was knocked sideways, shooting straight up and out of view before landing on the left of the picture, enough to again trigger the motion sensor as the vehicle sped out of picture to the left. It was in that final sharply illuminated frame or two that there was just a glimpse into the speeding vehicle.

'He's wearing a balaclava,' Gillard said. 'But there's a few pixels of face. He's white. See if you can get it enhanced.'

Hoskins nodded. 'Consider it done, boss. We've got only one ANPR hit on the vehicle, on the approach to the M4. Take a look to see if we've got any roadside cameras nearby.'

'Good work,' Gillard said checking his watch. 'How is the victim?'

'He got gravel rash on his bits, sprained ankle and some wrist tendon strain,' Hoskins said. 'But that was a week ago. He'll live. I'm going to see him today.'

The detective chief inspector suddenly lost interest in the comedy. An email from the lab had pinged into his inbox.

'Shit,' he said.

Hoskins looked up at him.

'The DNA test showed the dark hair I found in the Allegro belongs to Beatrice Ulbricht.'

Hoskins stretched his face in sympathy.

'Shit! Her mum and dad are upstairs,' Gillard said. He'd really hoped, against the odds, that the disappearance of this talented young woman would end happily, but that now seemed even less likely. What on earth was her hair doing in some ancient car that had been washed off a caravan site? It just didn't make sense.

He tapped on Alison Rigby's door, hearing the genteel clink of coffee cups within and a background hubbub of conversation. Called in, he was immediately tracked by the expectant faces of Karl-Otto and Lisbeth Ulbricht. The chief constable explained to him that she had already briefed them on the current state of the investigation. 'I was wondering if there was anything new since the start of the day?'

Gillard felt extremely awkward with the one nugget of depressing news that he had just heard. He was surprised that Rigby seemed to have taken upon herself the role of family liaison officer when they had more junior staff trained to do it. He hadn't himself really begun to assess what the discovery of Beatrice's hair could mean, and it didn't seem fair to anxious parents to just toss it out there.

'Nothing significant to add,' he said. He then trotted out the bureaucratic statistics of man-hours, CCTV hours, ANPR cameras checked and so forth, purely to justify his apparent lack of a conclusion. He was not proud of this evasiveness, but he felt dropped into an awkward situation.

Herr Ulbricht was staring at him intently. You do not get to be a senior minister in any country without a good bullshit radar, and Karl-Otto looked to have struck the motherlode.

'Detective chief inspector, surely by now you must have found out who this girl is who impersonated our daughter? The footage has been all over the television in both our countries. Does no one recognise her?'

'Yes, we have had literally hundreds of suggestions for who this person is. We have a team of ten who do nothing else but follow up on the helpline. But simply stating a physical resemblance doesn't help us too much, unless we know a little about the location and movements of each person. You have to bear in mind that she was probably wearing a wig,' Gillard said.

'That wide hat didn't help,' Lisbeth Ulbricht added, showing some signs of empathy with the embattled detective.

Gillard nodded and looked at her. 'The brim of the hat kept her face hidden from the cameras almost all the time. She was intending to deceive. It is not like a normal case where some dim criminal is caught casually on CCTV. This young woman, and whoever is assisting her, are extremely forensically aware.'

'We just need to know she is alive,' the father said, and banged the table with the flat of his hand.

'The surest sign of that would be if you had received a ransom demand,' Gillard said.

Ulbricht shook his head. 'There has been nothing. Of course, there are many sick people out there who send horrible messages on social media related to my political positions, but then there have been some very heart-warming messages of support too. I'm fortunate I have staff who just filter through the good stuff to me.'

A blue flash from Rigby's eyes indicated the meeting was over, so Gillard made his excuses.

—

Downstairs in the gents' toilet, Gillard was standing next to DI John Perry at the urinals. 'We need to have a chat as soon as you're done,' Gillard said.

'Absolutely. I've got something you just have to see.'

Gillard peered over into the adjacent receptacle and gave a mock wide-eyed stare. 'Nothing special there!'

When his laughter subsided, Perry said: 'I've got some photographs of Jane Morris from 1982. You will not believe them, I promise you.'

'Filthy pictures?'

'Anything but.' After washing hands and sharing the noisy blow dryer they emerged into the corridor, where Rainy Macintosh eyed them up and down. 'Having a wee meeting, boys?'

'You'll go down for a long stretch one day,' Gillard said, laughing.

Perry led him to his desk, and dragged over a chair to let Gillard sit side-by-side at the screen on his PC.

'This is the mystery girl, recovered from our yellow Allegro submarine. Photographs taken by CSI.'

Gillard nodded. He'd seen those pictures before from the Skype meeting with Dr Delahaye: the innocent teenager in her cardigan and fawn tights.

Perry clicked to the next image, which came up side-by-side. 'And this is Jane Morris, the picture circulated at the time of her disappearance.'

Gillard's jaw hung open. He looked from one to the other. They were identical, apart from the 1980s hairstyle on the old picture. Even the clothing looked identical. Same cardigan and tights.

'It's not possible, is it?' Perry said.

'When we talked earlier I had thought identical twins...'

'They wouldn't be identical *now*, would they?' Perry said. 'Jane Morris' twin would be fifty-two now. The DNA test was rechecked, and it comes back that this *is* the very same woman who went missing in 1982 at the age of fifteen. They look the same, and forensics say they are the same.'

Gillard shook his head. 'It's weird that the car was made in the same year Jane Morris disappeared. You might imagine she's been sitting dead in the passenger seat since 1982, except that she's way better preserved than the car.'

Perry scratched his head. 'Anyway, that's my mystery.'

Gillard blew a sigh. 'There's another complication. If that yellow Allegro is a time machine, it seems Beatrice Ulbricht has been in it too. I recovered some hairs entangled around the brake and clutch pedals which turned out to be hers. I suppose they had got caught when the vehicle was inverted during the flood, and her head was being jostled into the footwell.'

'How on earth did Jane Morris and Beatrice Ulbricht end up in the same car?' Perry asked.

Gillard stroked his chin. 'If your body is also the impostor on the train, then it's possible Beatrice's hair was on the coat she used. I think it's quite a neat idea.'

'But that doesn't square with her being Jane Morris. Someone magicked out of the past to commit a crime in the present. It's not possible.'

'Claire Mulholland is convinced the perpetrator is a woman,' Gillard said. 'Maybe two women.'

'Okay, I'm all for female empowerment,' said Perry. 'But whether she's right or wrong we've still got the same problem.'

Gillard tapped his fingers on the desk. 'There's only one answer. It *is* Jane Morris, the DNA and the resemblance can't both be wrong. But we have to explain how the corpse is so well preserved after nearly four decades.'

'Freezer?'

'No. I worked on the Franklin case in Esher back in 2009, where the wife had kept the dead husband in her freezer in the garage for eighteen months. Once forensics thawed him out he looked in a far worse state that Jane Morris does. There's a reason why you're supposed to eat frozen food within three months.'

'So what can it be, then?'

'Embalming. That's my guess.'

Perry sighed. 'So our perpetrator isn't only forensically aware, good with mobile phones and electronics, but also knows how to preserve a corpse.'

'Maybe time to check out funeral directors,' Gillard said.

–

Boatswain Chris Marshall steered his Zodiac inflatable expertly along the edge of a mass of tangled tree boughs and branches that seemed to embrace the full width of the river. He was about a mile downstream from Lacey Dutton, and had that morning been involved in the recovery of seven cars, vehicles that had originally been jammed against the arches of various bridges, but as the water level had dropped had the space to float through to the next obstruction. A few had even made it over the weir. Fortunately, none of them had contained a body. What he was working at now was potentially more troublesome, with too many underwater obstructions to allow the inflatable to make any progress. Divers from Police Scotland had been working all morning, picking through this great Sargasso mat of detritus, much of which had accumulated against a fallen riverbank sycamore. The huge tree, well over 200 years old, had acted like a giant net, hooking in everything that would float: fence panels, broken caravan sidings, polystyrene, and enough pub garden furniture to host a wedding reception. For those underwater, it was dangerous and awkward work, always the risk of a tree rotating and trapping a diver. The water beneath was still thick with silt and visibility was non-existent.

Marshall saw that one of the divers had raised his hand. He seemed to have made his way almost to the middle of this tangled mass. He was pointing at something and beckoning, but Marshall couldn't bring the Zodiac any closer to get a better view. The frogman moved, clambering partially onto a submerged bough. His weight rotated the entire floating tree. As his side dipped, on the far side of the trunk another branch lifted, dripping from the river.

Hooked over it a second arm could now be seen. This one was not sheathed in a wetsuit, but bare, pale and slender. It lifted in a balletic arc, a graceful female hand giving the briefest flick of acknowledgment, before it slipped between the twigs and slid back into the water.

Chris Marshall knew whom he was searching for. In his remembrance of this moment years afterwards he would sometimes wonder whether he had imagined the hand grasping a violinist's bow, or whether what he had seen was simply a long twig, caught between her lifeless fingers.

–

PC Lynne Fairbanks and DC Carl Hoskins stood outside the front door of 16 Wensleydale Walk, Woking and surveyed the drive from which Kyle Halliday had attempted to save his two-year-old Mitsubishi Warrior from being stolen. It was late afternoon, just over a week after the incident. They pressed the doorbell, and the victim himself eventually opened it. He was leaning on a metal crutch, wearing jeans and a loose checked shirt. His left wrist was still bandaged, his right ankle too.

'Ah, better late than never,' he said affably, as he hobbled backwards to let them in. In the flesh he was quite a hunk, Lynne thought. Dark wavy hair, penetrating hazel eyes and an easy smile.

'We're sorry about that,' Hoskins said.

They followed him into the house. His movements were limited; he couldn't put any weight on his ankle, and the obvious pain showed through the smile. 'I'm surprised that nobody's been round to check for fingerprints on the door handles and stuff,' Halliday said. 'I mean, it's more than a week.'

Hoskins gave an expansive shrug. 'CSI is a bit stretched at the moment, as you might have heard with the kidnapping and all. There's no point doing it now of course, as we'll only get the dabs of you and your missus.'

Halliday sighed, then caught Lynne's eye. 'Well at least there was one advantage of you lot being asleep at the wheel. I wouldn't have wanted the CCTV I sent you being shown on *Crimewatch*. I would have been highly embarrassed,' he said. 'I'll think twice next time about being Mr Have-a-Go. I'm still in agony.'

Hoskins laughed. 'Nobody wants their meat and two veg flashed around on the teatime news.' He didn't mention that almost everybody in CID had enjoyed a good laugh at it, particularly some of the female officers who seemed quite impressed with what was on view, considering the number of times they had crowded round a screen to watch it on slow motion. 'Besides, as I said before, your car is probably already in a container on its way to Albania or somewhere like that.'

'I'll miss it,' he said. 'I did loads of work on it, spent thousands. All wasted.'

Lynne already had Halliday down as a petrolhead, having seen the brand new Mercedes saloon and one-year-old Range Rover crowded onto the small drive. 'You'll be covered on insurance, I imagine,' she said, offering him her business card. She had seen the video, and copied it onto her personal phone to show her friends. 'Let me know if you need more details from us.' Their hands touched briefly, his finger stroking the interior of her palm.

'Thank you. I've already got my claim in,' he said with a smile. 'Of course they give you the run-around, bloody insurers.'

'You need better CCTV, mate,' Hoskins said. 'And a proper burglar alarm. It's not uncommon for professional thieves to break in for keys for top end cars. If you had a second camera you might even have caught the approach on foot of the thief. There would at least be an idea what he looked like.'

Halliday shrugged. 'I already gave you a description. White bloke by the face, prop-forward sized, with a ski mask or something. I told you about that car coat, with the stripe.'

'Yeah, you have,' Hoskins said. 'But you can tell a lot from CCTV. The way they walk, stuff like that.'

Halliday nodded, and then asked: 'So how are you doing finding this German woman?'

Lynne was about to issue the usual disclaimer about not discussing current cases when Hoskins said. 'Well, between you and me, we've been given the right run-around. Not made much progress.'

Halliday shrugged, thanked them, and hobbled his way to show them out. Once the door had closed, Lynne said: 'I didn't think you were supposed to tell them anything.'

Hoskins' eyes slid sideways to the young woman. 'Just a bit of banter. Does no harm. He seems like a nice bloke. Clearly fancies himself.'

Lynne was aware that Hoskins had left a conversational gap for her opinion about Halliday. He was never interested in her opinion on the case, so she wasn't going to share on this. 'Don't you hate these new estates?' she asked, casting her eyes across the road. 'Hardly a blade of grass, and most of the trees are stumps.'

'Yeah, DI Perry lives just down the road. Dunno why he'd shell out for one of these. All balsa wood frames, tiny rooms, built on the hurry-up.' Hoskins sniggered, and inclined his head back towards the door behind them. 'Do you think his knob is still raw?' he whispered.

'What a charming thought,' Lynne muttered, rolling her eyes, and strode back to the car. She had decided long ago that Hoskins was a sexist pig, with little piggy wandering eyes. The less time she spent with this repulsive man, the better.

'Wait for me,' said Hoskins, staring at his phone. 'Got to get back right now. They've found another body.'

'Is it Beatrice?'

He nodded.

'Oh no,' Lynne said. 'That's so sad. The poor girl.'

'It's the way of the world, love. If the world wasn't like that, we'd be out of a job.'

Chapter Ten

Hoskins got back after Gillard had already begun the presentation to a packed room. 'As everybody will be aware, this is just the outcome that we feared,' he said. Many of the officers were visibly upset, and not just the women. Working on crime quickly erodes and numbs human emotion, replacing it with a weary cynicism, oiled by the kind of dark humour that gets you from day to day. But every so often, the humanity of a potential victim reaches across the boundaries, rekindling feelings and the unlikeliest kinds of hope. It is always manifest with child abductions, the quintessence of innocence facing an unknown evil, and often with the elderly, when attacked in their own homes. Over the last week or so Gillard had seen so many of his colleagues almost visibly willing Beatrice to be safe and alive, volunteering extra hours to make it so. The discovery of her body now seemed the cruellest of fates.

'The body was lodged under a tree a mile downstream from Lacey Dutton, which is why it had not been spotted. It was freed by divers an hour ago.' He posted up some enlarged images of the corpse, still wearing a bra but no other underwear. Considering the substantial amount of time she may have spent in the water, the features were still surprisingly recognisable.

It was clearly Beatrice.

'Poor kid,' Hoskins muttered.

'At the chief constable's request, these two investigations are now being unified, as Operation Hawkeye,' Gillard said. 'I will remain senior investigating officer, DI Perry will be in charge of any further flood recovery developments, working with DI Mulholland. Other reporting lines will remain unchanged.' He turned to a whiteboard on which the new developments had been scribbled up.

'News management is vital. Christine McCafferty and her team will confine themselves to the bare bones, which is that the search has been scaled down following the discovery of a body which is believed to be that of the missing German music student. That is embargoed until six o'clock tonight, so no mention of it to any of your sources until the family has been informed. We will then be asking for information about anyone who saw her in the vicinity of Lacey Dutton in the last week.'

Gillard handed over to Claire Mulholland, who detailed the public response to the TV reports showing footage of the woman on the train. 'It's been a nightmare to be honest,' she said. 'Almost all of the respondents have simply guessed about a physical resemblance to someone they vaguely know. Local police forces all over the country have then been trying to establish the current and previous whereabouts of those identified people. It's a slow task.'

There then followed reports from other team leaders, including Rob Townsend on computers, as well as the CCTV and ANPR searches which had been broadened.

Macintosh had a hand up. 'Yes, Rainy?'

'Are we not going public about the wee blonde girl in the yellow Allegro?'

'At this stage, no. Once we have the results of the autopsy, and can get our heads around the bizarre results of the DNA test, we might be able to make further progress.' He pointed at the whiteboard. 'First, what we all have to get our heads around is this: two women, one a twenty-five-year-old German music student missing for five days, and the other a fifteen-year-old missing thirty-seven years, seemingly turn up in the same vehicle, in the same flood, at the same time. From the state of the car we know they didn't drive there – the flood simply lifted the vehicle off the caravan site where it had stood unused for several years and carried it away towards the Lacey Dutton bridge.'

Rob Townsend had his own suggestion. 'Maybe the same person killed them both, and stuffed them into that car.'

Gillard nodded. 'It's the obvious answer. The trouble is, assuming the second body genuinely is that of Jane Morris, that indicates the first of the crimes was committed as long ago as 1982.'

'Some murdering pensioner, then?' came a voice from the back.

'But however old he is, he has a young female confederate who is happy to help in misdirection.'

That quietened the room completely.

'What's next?' Perry asked.

'We're going to hope that Beatrice's body has retained some forensic clues to where she's been for the last week. Dr Nina Summers will be doing the autopsy.' He looked at his watch. It was just after five. 'My next job is to go to the hotel in Guildford where Beatrice's parents are staying and break the news.'

—

A soft knock at the hotel bedroom door was quickly answered by Ulbricht, a balloon of brandy already in his hand. He offered Gillard a drink the moment he arrived, and showed him into the room. The detective was accompanied by Family Liaison Officer Gabby Underwood, a woman trained to deal with the emotional fallout they knew was coming. The top floor suite where the Ulbricht family was staying had been turned into a shrine to their daughter. A dozen framed photographs sat on the grand piano, and on a coffee table sat a laptop with her YouTube channel playing on a loop.

Mrs Ulbricht was already seated, and had just begun to rise when Gillard suggested they should all sit down. 'I'm afraid we have finally got some news for you.' He said nothing more for a moment, just watched as the patrician visage of Karl-Otto Ulbricht reddened, crumpled and distended, like time-lapse photography of a dying leaf. His shoulders narrowed, shook and an undulating wheeze squeezed out somewhere from his lungs.

'A body has been found which we believe to be her,' Gillard said. 'I'm very sorry.'

'My Beatrice, oh my Beatrice,' he whispered, grasping from the piano a large portrait of his daughter. He embraced it tightly, arms folded around, eyes squeezed shut. Gillard heard a crack, the portrait glass. A glinting shard clinked to the floor by his feet. Lisbeth Ulbricht sat still and pale, her eyes brimming and then overflowing, tears tracking down her handsome face. She had already known. Only her husband had hung on to hope, which had just shattered in his arms.

Wednesday

Rainy Macintosh was doing her usual morning check through the weirdos and loonies who had sent messages to the various helplines. One member of her team had forwarded one email and marked it urgent.

You'll not get me Craig, but I'll get you. IC

She recalled that someone signing themselves IC had sent a previous personalised message which she had forwarded to Gillard. Looking back at the reply, she saw that the detective had acknowledged and filed it, but said he was unaware of a personal connection. She walked across to his desk, which was unoccupied, and was told that he wouldn't be in until midday.

'Dental appointment,' Carl Hoskins said.

'I've got this,' she said, showing him the printout. 'It's from a Samsung phone. Seeing as it's a threat, I could try and trace it.'

'It's up to you,' Hoskins said, clearly indicating that he wouldn't have bothered. 'We get lots of that type of shit.'

'I'll go and see Rob.'

She found the young research intelligence officer bent over his desk with a huge stack of electronic data requests to look at. She added hers to the pile, but reminded him that it included a threat to Gillard. 'We'd never forgive ourselves if something happened,' she said. Getting only a grunt by way of reply, she wandered away muttering sarcastically to herself. 'Aye, thank you Rainy, I'll be sure to look into it. Yer wee fucking dobber.'

–

Wednesday morning, bright and clear, and the chance to breathe. Craig Gillard stood up on the pedals as the slope got too demanding even for the lowest gear. Getting out on his road bike was precious time. Since the Beatrice Ulbricht case had begun, there had been barely an hour for him to get the exercise that he felt he needed. This wasn't just about the body, but letting the mind breathe, unpacking stress and complexities and really getting a chance to think. He wasn't one of those cyclists who ploughs on along major roads, doggedly breathing in noxious traffic fumes. He always preferred minor lanes, cross-country routes going nowhere, even if that meant he couldn't keep up the speeds that the smoothest tarmac offered.

Years ago, he'd been able to get out regularly on Sunday with a group of other off-duty officers, but now pressure of work meant you could never be sure anyone was available. More often than not he just slotted in a quick solo ride when he could. Today was one of those stolen moments. A dental appointment at 10.15 allowed him a free two hours beforehand.

He was just a few miles north of Redhill, heading up on the North Downs on a tiny, steep road between Bletchingley and Caterham. The wonder of this lane was that it took you over the M25, and its belching perma-jams, on the kind of winding and barely used route that many drivers would be surprised to find still existed so close to the capital.

It was on the very steepest part of the hill, a slope of nearly 17 per cent, that he could hear the approach of a vehicle behind him. There would be no room or visibility to pass for a couple of hundred yards. Not every motorist had the patience to accept being slowed to seven or eight miles an hour behind a cyclist on a steep hill. The engine note alone, high revs and a big engine, communicated the mindset of the following driver. He had learned to read that many years ago.

But the impact from behind took him completely by surprise.

A flash of bull bars in his peripheral vision, then he tumbled over the handlebars to the ground, the vehicle ran right over him, a dark growling monster swallowing him and spitting him out the other end. He glimpsed blue sky above with little puffy white clouds, then pivoted to look uphill. His face and neck were in agony, and there was blood and a screaming fizz in one ear, but he had no time to deal with that. The four-wheel-drive fifty yards further up was now reversing back towards him, transmission whining. Survival clicked in. He rolled to the side of the road, into a thick patch of nettles, and tumbled down a damp bank into a culvert. But not before he had taken a mental photograph of the back of the pick-up truck: Mitsubishi Warrior, olive green, double cab, and a Reading registration number beginning RG, from 2016.

Brakes and the slam of a car door heralded that the attack was not over. Gillard scrambled to his feet, now woozily aware of blood pouring down his left cheek. He was standing in a small ditch which ran alongside the edge of the lane. Behind him was a steep upward slope, thickly wooded and carpeted with freshly green bracken. His assailant was now revealed. A big, broad man in a dark car coat with a ski mask. He had a two-foot-long adjustable spanner in his hand, and was scanning the roadside vegetation for someone to hit.

The detective knew he would be found quickly, so began to scramble up the bank behind, his cycling shoes too smoothly soled to get much purchase, so it was hand over hand grasping and pulling his way through saplings of hawthorn, rowan and spiky blackthorn. The pursuer roared at him, in almost choking anger: 'I'm going to fucking kill you.' Gillard had no doubt that was his intention, and hauled himself up the steep slope. A quick look behind showed the pursuer, shod in yellow Caterpillar boots, had set off after him, but had to stow his weapon to get a grip on the foliage, and was cursing to himself on every clumsy, scrambling footstep up the disintegrating bank. Over fifty years old he might be, and panting with the exertion, but with years of climbing experience, Gillard was clearly more nimble than his heftily built and seemingly younger attacker. Now, twenty feet above the road, and hearing the heavy breathing well below, the detective risked a look behind.

The man had a fist-sized stone, and was weighing up his aim. The shot when it came was all power and no accuracy, embedding itself with a thunk! into the ground to his right. With a few seconds of respite while the assailant looked for more projectiles, Gillard reached behind him for the phone that he kept in a small pocket on the back of his cycling tunic. A photograph or two, and some video, might be invaluable.

It was gone.

All he felt was his bare back through the torn textile, and a weeping fag-packet-sized graze that was, from nothing, now agony to the touch. The pursuer was now following a shallower lateral route through the bushes that in a minute or so would bring him across from the left-hand side. Gillard, now with shallower woodland above him, would need to move to keep ahead of his assailant. But had an idea. He unbuckled his new digital watch from his left wrist, wrapped it in his torn cycling glove, and tossed it underhand down the slope into the bed of the vehicle. The dull clang of its impact drew the attention of his pursuer, who scanned the slope and road looking for the source of the noise.

The detective, now feeling a little more confident, settled for a little diversion. He held his right hand to his ear, as if it contained a phone, and loudly said, 'Yes, police please, and an ambulance.' He read out his mobile phone number, as would be required for a real emergency call, and then continued. 'Yes, hit-and-run, Mitsubishi Warrior, olive green...'

Before he'd even finished the sentence, the attacker had begun to flee back to his vehicle, with a final parting shout of 'fucking cyclists'. Gillard continued the charade call as he watched the Warrior roar off and up the hill. Only after two or three minutes of silence, when he was sure that he was safe, did he check himself over. He was lucky. His arms, pulled in to protect himself, had not been crushed by the big fat front tyres. The Warrior's high suspension had enough clearance not to grind him to pieces. As he was later to discover it was his own bike that caused the worst injuries. Partially embedded in the bull bars of the four-wheel-drive, it was dragged over his shoulders and face, a sharp pedal slicing up his cheek and ear.

Five minutes after the attack, agonising bruises making themselves felt all over his body, Gillard stood on the tarmac and surveyed the crushed and twisted wreck that was his expensive racing bike. Plastic fragments on the road depicted the destruction of his mobile, his wraparound sunglasses, and various other bits and pieces. He'd need to hitch a lift, get someone with a mobile who could genuinely call emergency services. This was a quiet road, but someone would surely be along in a few minutes. In fact it only took one. The squeal of brakes, something coming downhill, just one invisible bend above him. He looked up, ready to flag the car down.

One second later, he realised he'd made a huge mistake.

Green Warrior!

The vehicle thundering down to him was doing at least forty. The driver had given Gillard just enough time to get down from his haven in the woods to make him a target all over again. With just thirty yards before impact, the cop instinctively threw himself to the inside of the curve, the other side from where he had been knocked off, making himself much harder for the assailant to target. The Warrior went the other way on the outer curve, brakes squealing as it slid to a halt another fifty yards down the road.

Now the detective really was stuck. The bank on this side was impossibly steep, and he might not be able to get across to the other side in time. A renewed climb would be agony. Every part of him was screaming in pain.

Help arrived immediately. Another vehicle could be heard descending the road, much more cautiously and slowly. Gillard tried to run uphill, as best he could, towards it. A white Nissan Micra, *Eric's School of Motoring* emblazoned on its side, did a perfect emergency stop. There was a young woman behind the wheel and a tall man next to her. Gillard staggered up to the passenger-side window, which slid down to reveal a thin-faced, grey-haired fellow of sixty or so.

'I'm an off-duty police officer,' Gillard gasped, holding up an expired Surrey Police ID card that he always kept in a thigh pocket of his cycling trousers. 'I've just been a victim of a hit-and-run and I need you to dial 999.'

'You mean that vehicle ahead?' the instructor said, pointing at the Warrior, which was now driving away.

'Eric, shouldn't we chase him?' the young woman asked her instructor, her eyes lit with excitement.

Gillard sensed the dual controls being firmly depressed on the instructor side. 'No, Briony. Not on your third lesson. I think hot pursuit comes some weeks after reversing around a corner.' He shared a thin smile with the detective.

–

It was later that afternoon when Sam came to pick up her husband from Redhill A&E, with a big bag loaded with everything he'd asked for. He had a blanket around his shoulders, and was wearing only the shreds of his favourite red and green cycling trousers. They had patched him up but he still looked quite a mess, even worse than she'd expected, given how together he seemed when he had rung her. He got up gingerly as she approached but he held up a warning hand when she tried to embrace him. He flipped up the blanket to show her his back, where there was an enormous dressing. 'That's what my iPhone did to me as it broke up,' he said. 'And this was a bicycle pedal.' He pointed to the five inches of fresh stitches on the top of his cheek and across his ear.

'I love you,' she said. 'And I've been so worried.'

'I'm fine really.' They hugged carefully and he said, 'I'm sorry to say your Christmas present to me is gone for good.'

'Broken? Is that why you need the paperwork? You should look after yourself before writing your insurance claim.' She opened the bag and handed him the papers. She had also brought him a complete set of casual clothing, and thought getting dressed properly should be his first priority.

Gillard was reading the watch instructions. 'It's got a fitness tracker on it with GPS. I managed to chuck it in the open back of the Warrior, so once we get the details and unique ID to Rob Townsend, he can get on to the manufacturer and track the truck.'

'Wow, that watch was a better gift than I realised,' she said. 'So was this just casual road rage, do you think?'

Gillard shook his head and then winced slightly at the pain it caused. 'He wanted me to think it was random, by cursing cyclists in general. But when the driver is wearing a ski mask on what is not a very cold day, you know that it was planned in advance.'

Sam was horrified. 'But how would he know where you would go?'

Gillard shrugged. 'I don't know. I've had plenty of time to think about all the people who might hate me, going back years. Some of them, like Charles Allerdyce, Paddy Kincaid and Ronnie Evans, are still inside, though that doesn't mean they don't have mates who would do such a thing. There's lots of others: Rodney Wells, Sam Akos, a few of the Croydon gangsters from when I was in the drug squad. And of course we mustn't forget your old mate, Gary.'

Sam shuddered at the mention of her old boyfriend Gary Harrison. 'I think you frightened him off for good. I'd be more worried about Paddy, seeing as he's ex-police. But who's your favourite candidate?'

'Ronnie has got to be my favourite. Today is the tenth anniversary of putting him away. He'll be eligible for parole in a year. And it has to be said he's a totally psychopathic bastard who would arrange something like this.' He looked at the bag. 'Did you bring my spare phone?'

She nodded and passed it to him. As her husband started tapping out numbers she realised that even now, an hour or two after a near-death experience, sitting half dressed in A&E, he wasn't able to stop working. Even as he waited to see the neurologist to get the all clear, he was thinking ahead. She listened as he first spoke to Rob Townsend about fitness trackers, and after that asked to be passed on to Carl Hoskins.

'Hi Carl. No, fine really, just a few bruises.' He winked at Sam. 'You know that car theft from Woking. Yeah, that's right, the flying slipper. What was the plate on that olive green Mitsubishi Warrior?' He waited while Hoskins checked. 'Yeah, that's the one. And it was driven by a bloke in a balaclava and a navy car coat with high-vis stripes on the sleeves.' He laughed at some joke Hoskins had told him. 'Yeah, well that same guy has just had a go at me.'

Chapter Eleven

The moment that DC Rainy Macintosh heard Gillard had been a road rage incident victim, she messaged Rob Townsend to see if any of the details of the threat message signed by IC had been traced. It took a while for the research intelligence officer to reply that the phone in question was a pay-as-you-go, and had been used only a few times.

She walked over to his desk. 'Rob, I think cell site analysis on this would be useful. If someone is making threats, however vague, against the senior investigating officer, and someone has just tried to kill him with a car...'

'Okay, okay,' he said, not really looking up. 'I'm really snowed under, I'll get to it as soon as I can.'

Rainy felt exactly the same kind of disappointment she had got when working as a junior doctor. Not quite the exacting hours, perhaps, but a feeling of being under-appreciated, her judgement questioned because she was junior, and because she was a woman, a woman of size. It was that curious version of physics, where a woman was progressively less visible to the male gaze the larger she was. The police were, if anything, even more misogynistic than the medical profession, something that had come as an unwelcome shock to her.

She leaned forward and whispered in Townsend's ear. 'Laddie, when I was on A&E at 4.30 a.m. at the dog end of a sixteen-hour shift, I sewed up the torn scrotum of a young man who looked just like you.'

She had his attention now, a kind of crazed horror scribbled all over his face.

'He had slipped trying to climb a razor wire fence during a burglary. Went right through his jeans and sliced into the scrotal sac. Imagine that, eh? Needed nine very careful self-dissolving stitches.' She mimed the action, slowly, her hand just above Townsend's crotch.

'Anaesthetic?' croaked Townsend, his eyes bulging.

'Aye, but only a local.' She held up one hand between their proximate faces, as if grasping something tiny between finger and thumb. 'A wee sharp needle. I just want you to remember what I'm capable of. A bit of respect might be handy. Okay?' She tweaked his ear.

Townsend's head moved like one of those dogs from the parcel shelves of 1990s cars. 'Okay, Rainy. I'm really sorry. I'll get it started now. Should only take a couple of hours.'

–

It was early afternoon when Gillard hobbled in to the Mount Browne incident room for the meeting that he had called. He had a bandaged ear, a dressing on his cheek, and hobbled like a man of ninety. He got plenty of sympathy from the female members of the team, and plenty of jokes from the men.

'Blind dentist you were seeing?' Hoskins asked.

'You'll be blacklisted as a no-show for your appointment,' Rainy Macintosh warned.

After he had given them a brief account of the morning's hit and run, he turned the meeting over to DI Claire Mulholland, so he could sit down. It seemed that it was his back, and the wound caused by the disintegrating mobile phone, that was causing the most pain.

In his absence, Hoskins had combed the police national computer and the DVLA to see what exactly they could learn about the Mitsubishi Warrior. Of course all the information pertained to the owner, Mr Kyle Halliday, not to the thief who'd stolen it. Hoskins rang Halliday, who said it did not have a fitted satnav. In fact the detective constable fully expected to find the vehicle burned out somewhere, having outlived its usefulness, but so far there were no reports.

'The first thing I want to concentrate on are the messages from IC,' Claire said. 'As you know some of them referred to DCI Gillard by name. It could simply be a hoax, but then it could be significant, particularly in light of the attempt on his life. Using cell site analysis we've traced the location where the first message was sent from, and as close as we can establish it is the bus stop from which Beatrice disappeared. The second message was sent from an even more significant location. Just north of the village of Bletchingley, almost the same spot at which our SIO was attacked, and just a few minutes later.'

A gasp went around the room.

'So I think the entire inquiry is morphing.' She turned to a whiteboard on which the various salient points had been listed. 'We're now linking the murders of the two women whose bodies were found in the River Wey to the attempted murder of our own SIO, and the theft of a Mitsubishi Warrior on Monday of last week.'

Rainy put up her hand. 'Ma'am, do we know yet who the second woman is?'

'Not for certain. I was hoping DI Perry would be able to tell us.' She looked around and could see he wasn't there.

Hoskins spoke up. 'He's on the phone to Dr Delahaye. He told me he'd be here in a couple of minutes.'

The detective constable's prediction was spot on. The incident room door burst open, and DI Perry stood in the doorway looking amazed.

'So have you an answer to our little conundrum?' Gillard asked.

'Yes. Delahaye has all the test results now, and believes it almost certainly is Jane Morris. Her body has until recently been deep frozen, at a temperature low enough to preclude any deterioration.'

'What, since 1982!' Rainy exclaimed. 'Like a thirty-seven-year-old fish finger?'

Perry nodded, walked up and took a seat. 'Cause of death seems to be strangulation.'

'Well, perhaps that's him then, the one sending messages,' Rainy said, her face suddenly lighting up. 'Maybe IC aren't initials, but the word icy, as in frozen water.'

'That's certainly plausible,' Gillard said.

'One thing we can be certain about,' Claire said, 'is that whoever was strangling a woman to death in 1982 would have been, let's say, a minimum age of sixteen back then. They would be fifty-four now. How old would you say your assailant was, Craig?'

'I didn't see his face, but from the speed he moved at I would be surprised if he could be in his fifties. More like mid-thirties to early forties. But that's only a guess. It could possibly be the same man. From his build it was definitely not Adrian Singer.'

'And definitely not the bird in the hat on the train,' Hoskins said. Gillard saw him looking around expectantly for the eye-rolling from female colleagues. They did not disappoint. Hoskins grinned, another successful feminist bait trip concluded.

The DCI popped out another couple of painkillers for his throbbing ear, and washed them down with lukewarm coffee. 'I'm getting more optimistic about this. We've got three separate crimes to map, a male and a female suspect, and two dead bodies recovered. That's a lot more to work on than we had a week ago.'

'On the other hand,' Rainy said, 'our wee killer seems quite active. There may be other bodies out there that we don't know about.'

Gillard and Claire shared a glance of agreement. 'We hope you're wrong, Rainy,' Gillard said.

'We also need to think about your security,' Claire told him. 'How can this man have known where you were cycling? You started from home, didn't you?'

He nodded. 'I've been thinking about that, and haven't come up with any satisfactory answers. However, I do believe we can make a lot more progress on the vehicle. The manufacturers have promised a trace on my fitness tracker by this afternoon.'

–

PC Lynne Fairbanks rang the doorbell of 16 Wensleydale Walk. She heard the gradual clattering of a metal crutch as Kyle Halliday came to answer. He'd obviously got her text, as he was wearing a dazzling white shirt and well-fitting jeans, and had the same big broad smile she had noticed before.

'You got my message, Mr Halliday,' she said, with faux formality.

'Call me Kyle,' he said, inviting her in. 'Coffee?'

'Let me help,' she said. They moved around the kitchen together, an awkward *pas de deux of* kettles and mugs, and jars of instant. The proximity was quite unsettling, in a good way. She noticed he was looking at her in the same way he had on her first visit, his knowing hazel eyes roaming around her face. Suddenly they were in each other's arms, kissing fiercely, his hands on the back of her head. He plucked off her clip-on tie and threw it aside.

'You've got a nerve,' she said. 'And I've got a boyfriend.'

'And I've got a wife.' Halliday checked his watch. 'Back at five. We've got two hours.' His large hands skated down the front of her tunic, undoing buttons.

Lynne blinked. She couldn't quite believe that she was going to do this, but she knew there was a reason why she had left her stab vest with its built-in bodycam in the car.

'I wanted you the first time I saw you,' she whispered.

'And I wanted you.' He put the crutch aside and effortlessly lifted her onto the kitchen counter. He then slid one arm up her skirt.

'I'm not wearing any.' She grinned. 'Saves time.'

—

Two hours later Research Intelligence Officer Rob Townsend and DCI Gillard sat hunched together around a screen in the surveillance suite at Mount Browne's forensic unit. They were looking at a Google map of the position of the Teikin Athlo-Watch, Gillard's fitness tracker that he had tossed into the back of the Warrior. A flashing red dot showed it was currently at an industrial site on the edge of Gosport in Hampshire. It hadn't moved in eighteen hours.

'What is that place?' Gillard asked.

'It's an aggregate yard, full of big quarry lorries. I've rung them up and nobody at the site has seen the green Warrior. There's a patrol car on its way to double-check.'

'Okay, good work. Let's go back and look at the trace from start to finish.'

Townsend rewound the data feed. It had taken more than twenty-four hours to get the Korean manufacturer's legal consent to download the Teikin's GPS trace from the head office in Seoul. That delay was frustrating because, unlike cell site analysis for mobile phones, the GPS trace was very nearly real-time. The first few minutes of the route were from Gillard's home to the point of the hit-and-run. Soon after, with the watch now in the assailant's vehicle, the dot started moving at speed down the winding road, over the M25 heading south. The trace joined the A25 south of Bletchingley and started heading west, through Redhill and towards Guildford. That matched the ANPR route that Townsend had tracked the day before, based on Gillard's accurate recall of the number plate, relayed as he was on his way to hospital. ANPR was great, but the coverage was patchy, and the Warrior had disappeared from the A25 at some point between Redhill and Guildford. The GPS at least would show them exactly where.

Townsend fast-forwarded the trace until it seemed to be travelling at several hundred miles an hour, heading on minor roads towards Woking. Then it hesitated at the junction of the A3 before heading off rapidly on that major road to the south-west. Townsend speeded up the trace again, but Gillard asked him to stop. 'Rob can you go back to the turn-off on the A3?'

The young officer did so. Gillard asked him to zoom in on the map, until it started to be populated with road names and other details. The minor road crossing the A3 was called Rose Lane, heading from West Horsley to Ripley. 'Just what I thought,' Gillard said. 'The minor road goes over the A3 here. But the trace shows him turning off onto it.'

'Yes, it's a bridge.' Townsend tried to drag the little Google man icon across to the bridge which would link to a Google Street View photograph. He wanted to see whether it was possible to get onto the A3 here. But the icon kept bouncing back, indicating that this particular lane had not been traversed by the Google mapping cars. He was however able to get a Street View image of the bridge from the A3. It showed that there was no slip road or track of any kind.

'I don't get it,' Townsend said, staring sullenly at the screen.

'I do,' Gillard said. 'Our suspect probably heard the watch rattling in the back, stopped to take a look, guessed what it was and thought he'd fool us. Leaning over the bridge, he was probably able to drop it into the back of some quarry lorry or similar.'

'He's very forensically aware, isn't he?' Townsend asked.

'Did you do the ANPR searches for the Warrior over the preceding days?' Gillard asked.

'Yes, as you suspected, it was the vehicle stolen from the address in Woking. There have only been a few ANPR camera hits, in the rough area bordered by Woking to the north, Guildford to the west, and the M25 to the east. One was from a mobile patrol vehicle.'

The detective rubbed his chin. 'That's all a little surprising, isn't it?'

'Why?' the young officer replied.

'Look, if you have just picked and stolen a newish, high-value and quite distinctive four-wheel-drive from some poor sod in Woking, the last thing you would be doing is driving it round the same area he lives, right?'

'I suppose so.'

'If you were a professional thief, you'd change the plates for a start, and sell it to someone on the Scottish Borders, in West Wales, or even get it shipped abroad to Albania where they never ask questions.'

Townsend nodded again.

'If he continues to drive it round just in this small area, we can catch him,' Gillard said.

'Maybe he's not so smart.'

'Don't count on it. Everything he's done so far has been clever. Very clever.'

Chapter Twelve

Thursday

DI Perry had made an appointment to see Dr Nina Summers at the mortuary in Redhill, and Gillard wanted to come too. The Home Office forensic pathologist was one of the most senior and experienced in the country, and had agreed to undertake the post-mortem of Beatrice Ulbricht at Dr Delahaye's request. Dr Summers was there to greet them.

'I've now had a chance to examine Beatrice Ulbricht,' she said, leading them in to the examination room, where a half open body bag was already on an examination table. Perry looked nervous; he had admitted that this was the first time he'd ever been inside a room where bodies were dissected. Dr Summers was a tiny dark-haired woman with a Mediterranean look, dark eyes and olive skin. But there was nothing in her accent to hint that she had ever lived anywhere but the south-east of England.

The forensic pathologist unzipped the body bag to reveal the naked girl in her entirety. Perry gagged audibly next to Gillard. Beatrice was an alabaster statue, a Halloween Snow White; perfect in every detail but for the crudely stitched Y-shaped incision in her thorax where her viscera had been removed, and the less obvious cut around her crown. That was where the top of the skull had been removed by an electric saw and had now been popped back, the scalp held on with a few stitches. Gillard and Dr Summers exchanged a quick glance as Perry turned away to compose himself. The detective chief inspector could see from the dead woman's body that she had sustained cuts and bruising around her face, throat, forearms and feet.

Dr Summers continued: 'The trickiest element in this case is to establish to what extent, one, did her immersion in water cause the injuries we see and, two, erase evidence of previous injury. Typical external injuries for a submerged body, which normally floats face down, include lateral abrasions to the forehead, nose, chin, the backs of the hands and the shins. There are patently very few such injuries. The corpse was trapped underneath a floating tree, but not for much of the time she was in the water.'

'She may well have been in the Allegro with Jane Morris,' Perry said.

Summers nodded. 'In my estimation she was in the water for roughly twenty-four hours. Skin maceration was moderate, and she had not sloughed off significant keratin from hands or feet. Moreover, there's no water in the stomach and nothing suggesting inhalation, which may well indicate she was already dead before immersion.'

'So we can rule out accidental death?' Perry asked.

'Probably,' Dr Summers said. 'The cause of death seems to be strangulation prior to immersion, which I note chimes with Dr Delahaye's conclusion for Jane Morris' cause of death. In this case, self-evident bruising in the strap muscles and a fractured hyoid bone are indicative. There are also a few petechiae still evident in the face.'

'What's petechiae?' Perry asked.

'Broken blood vessels. In strangulation or drowning, they can often be seen in the eye.'

'Oh, you mean bloodshot?'

'Yes.' She turned back to Gillard. 'There is strong evidence of blunt force trauma throughout, including fingernail marks externally on the throat which I think you will have noticed.'

Gillard nodded. 'I think she may have put up a fight.'

'Yes, I am gratified that despite her immersion there are fibres and skin and a little blood still retained under the middle fingernail of her left hand. DNA as you know decomposes fairly rapidly in water, but we might be lucky. I sent them off for analysis this morning. Here is something interesting, too.' She brought over a small torch from another table, and shone it on the body. It revealed a fine mist of glittery particles on her hair and right temple under the ultraviolet light.

'What's that?' Perry asked.

'It's a dye from some security product,' Summers said. 'Probably pepper spray.'

Gillard nodded. 'Beatrice's friends said she had a pepper spray. Most of them have a permanent dye, but some of the better ones have a UV marker. They're generally illegal in the UK, but it's further evidence that she fought like crazy to save herself, and even had the time to use the spray. With luck the perpetrator will be similarly marked.'

'Was she sexually assaulted?' Perry asked.

'I was going to come to that,' Summers said. 'There are scratches to the vulva, and traces of bleach internally, which indicates to me she may have been washed post-mortem, even before the immersion in the river.'

Gillard blew a sigh. 'That tells us the perpetrator is not only a sexual predator but a calm one. He has somewhere to work on the body before deciding how to dispose of it. It just reinforces the notion that this is a man who is comfortable with the dead. A first-time murderer often panics, and just wants to get rid of the corpse as soon as possible. We already know that this man is in a different league. Forensically highly aware too.'

'Ex-police?' asked Perry.

'It's certainly possible,' Gillard said.

'There is one final thing,' Summers said. 'A particular question about the time of death has been puzzling me. I understand that the victim went missing on Sunday. However the decomposition profile of the corpse is rather strange. The internal organs and digestive tract would normally decompose first, but they are in almost perfect condition. No discolouration of the abdomen at all. That of itself would indicate that she was alive until shortly before immersion.'

'So the abductor kept her alive?' Perry asked.

'That's possible,' Summers said. 'But I favour a different answer, given what we already know about Jane Morris. I think she too was frozen, for a couple of days at least.'

Perry's eyes widened. 'One frozen for almost forty years and one for a couple of days.'

Gillard nodded. 'If our murderer has those kind of facilities, there could be many more victims. He has solved the biggest problem that most killers face: how to dispose of the body.'

Gillard sat in the hospital car park for half an hour, waiting for Perry to finish being sick in the toilet. He passed the time by listening to the Lysander Quartet CD. When you take apart a person to their constituent components, as Dr Summers had done, where does all that music, all that creativity, all that emotion end up? The bone, the gristle, Beatrice's beautifully moulded flesh, were merely an extraordinary piece of scaffolding for the woman's achievement, a rocket launcher for her destiny. The violin. To be able to communicate such extraordinary emotion through the judicious scraping of horsehair over wire. It was a wonder of the world. One now lost.

He looked up to see the detective inspector lurching towards him across the car park, wan face above a dark grey raincoat, hunched against the chill wind. He still didn't look too chipper. Gillard quickly ejected the CD, and slid it carefully into its cardboard sleeve.

'Feeling better?' he asked him, as the DI slid into the passenger seat.

Perry nodded. 'Yes, thank you. I've seen the odd body before. You know, the old man who died in a toilet, the drug overdose in a doorway. But there's something about seeing a young woman like…' He ran out of words, his left hand rotating as if it could conjure a eulogy from thin air.

'She's got to me too,' Gillard said, as he drove off. He knew that this was where, had they both been women, a bonding conversation of mutual emotional revelation might begin. But they were blokes, and it couldn't be done that way. First of all there was silence, for a few uncomfortable minutes.

'Did you see the England match the other night?' Perry asked.

'Yeah, total rubbish. He was *never* offside.'

Back on safer ground, they laughed.

–

Perry nipped home mid-shift to pick up a couple of data-sticks that he had forgotten. He was surprised to see a black Range Rover parked on the road outside, blocking in his wife's baby-blue Audi soft-top. Just as he was putting his key in the front door, it opened and Mel was there in a bathrobe, looking a little flustered and sweaty, her hair damp at the forehead. 'I wasn't expecting you back,' she said. 'I was just about to take a shower.'

'I forget a couple of datasticks. Isn't this your day to work full-time?' He squeezed past her, and headed to the kitchen.

'Normally, but Kate wanted to swap with me. So I just came in half an hour ago. I've been at the gym.'

'Who's car is that at the front? It's blocking you in.'

She hesitated, and pursed her lips. 'I don't know. Look, John, do you have a few minutes? We need to talk about Vanessa.'

He turned to her. 'God, what is it now?'

'Come on through.' She led him to the sun lounge at the rear of the house. It wasn't very sunny, and the room was cool. 'We need to do something about her drug taking. You said you would talk to—'

Perry sighed. Last weekend their seventeen-year-old daughter Vanessa had been among a dozen youngsters caught in possession of drugs at a rowdy party raided by police, in the centre of town. The number of ecstasy and amphetamine tablets she had on her seemed indicative of a custodial sentence, even as a first offence.

'I've had a word, against my better judgement. Her file has been "lost". She won't be part of the case going up to the CPS.'

'That's brilliant, thank you so much.'

'It's not brilliant, it's corrupt. I could go to prison if they find out.'

'But they won't find out, will they, darling?'

Darling? Not a word she used often.

She reached out for him and kissed him with unusual passion, her hands holding his face, her tongue probing inside his mouth. It had not been *there* for a very long time. As her bathrobe came undone, the tips of her breasts brushing against him, he started to feel aroused but, more than anything, surprised. After a minute, he gently pulled away and looked quizzically at her face. 'Mel, that's really nice, but I don't have time. I've got to get back.'

She gave him a look, not of disappointment, but something else. As if they had just had an argument which he had lost and she had trumped it with: I told you so.

'What's up, Mel? Has something else happened?'

'I found some more drugs, in her room.'

'What kind?' He started to move towards the stairs, to start examining this domestic crime scene.

She held him back. 'I don't know exactly, I flushed them all down the loo.'

'What? Why did you do that, Mel? How are we ever going to—'

She seemed distracted, glancing over his shoulder towards the door into the house.

'Is she here?' he asked, turning to look too.

'No, John. She's not. She is never here at a Thursday lunchtime, she's got that part-time waitressing job, remember?' Mel said, looking back at her husband. 'I've not seen her since Monday, but she texted me a few times.'

Now released, he went upstairs to the spare room which he used as his home office. In doing so he passed Vanessa's room, 'Keep Out' in large stick-on letters on the door. He took a deep breath, turned the handle and peered inside. Many crime scenes were tidier. The bed, a double mattress on the carpet, was unmade and there were clothes all over the floor. The place reeked of sex. Clearly, despite Mel's certainties, Vanessa *had* sneaked back with her boyfriend. Perry went inside, and opened the window. As he looked out, he saw that the black Range Rover had gone. He wished now he had made a note of the registration number.

'Mel, I think she's been back recently,' he called down.

'Really?' she shouted back up to him.

'For God's sake, didn't you notice the whiff when you were up here? It's like a bloody bordello.' He pulled back the duvet on her bed. A used condom, scrunched up tissues and a tell-tale patch on the dark blue sheet, not yet dry. Christ almighty! The girl is seventeen.

'Mel, it's disgusting.'

'I've not been up there today. I can't face it every day.'

'I can see why,' he replied. Then, looking at his daughter's pillow, he saw something on it. Something that changed everything.

–

Later that afternoon, Gillard and Perry sat in one of the meeting rooms going through everything that was known about Jane Morris. They started with the news-paper coverage, finishing with one piece on the one-year anniversary of her disappearance.

It was a chilly October evening when fifteen-year-old Jane Morris left the sweetshop where her friend Sarah worked, to walk the half mile back to her home in Balham, South London. The shy, mousy-haired schoolgirl was well known to many of the stallholders in the Hildreth Street market that adjoined Balham High Road. Her uncle Harold was one of them and described how he saw the girl talking to a young dreadlocked man with a Bob Marley T-shirt. It was the last time she was seen. Detectives initially arrested and charged a local man, Dudley Jives, who matched the description, but he was acquitted when it became clear that there was no forensic evidence against him, and his initial confession had been provided under duress. Since then police have had little luck tracing the man, despite extensive door-to-door enquiries in the area. It is now a year since Jane disappeared, and her parents Frank and Eileen fear that she may never be found.

They leafed through several box files full of paper evidence, including the confession of Dudley Jives, which displayed a dead, passive police-speak. It was hardly in the man's own words. The deeper into the documents Gillard reached, the more he was convinced that the initial investigation was botched. The assumption of a black perpetrator was never questioned; detectives had never apparently stepped back to doubt the witness statement of the uncle.

Perry, meanwhile, was leafing through the 2005 cold case review. With more modern forensic techniques and DNA analysis, there had been hopes for a breakthrough. But without a body, it was much harder to make progress. Before the review had been published, Jane's mother Eileen Morris had died. Her husband Frank, a bookmaker with a shop on Balham High Road, had died of a heart attack in 1997, and the key witness, Harold Garrison, the girl's uncle, passed away in 2002. Harold's wife Linda had succumbed to breast cancer in 1998. There were no other brothers or sisters in the family, and the only child was Jane.

'There's no one left to interview,' Perry said. 'I don't see how we can get back into the case.'

'What about Jane's childhood friend Sarah, the one who worked in the sweetshop?'

'Checked that. She emigrated to Australia in 2003, died of skin cancer in 2015.'

Gillard turned to the younger man. 'Lateral thinking, John. What I'd like you to do is start at the other end. We know that Jane Morris has been kept deep frozen for nearly forty years. If you do that in a normal household freezer, at about minus twenty centigrade, then you get deterioration over the years. But as we know, Jane Morris' body was in pristine condition. So, the question we have to ask ourselves is: who supplies the kind of freezers that can keep a body that long without deterioration? Who are their customers? When did they first supply such a freezer? What's the longevity of these type of freezers? Who services them?'

Perry nodded. 'That's a better route into the case.'

'Take a couple of days to research that, and I think you should also take a closer look around Balham market to see if anyone remembers our key witness, Uncle Harry.'

–

'Do you think I'm stupid?' Perry yelled at his wife, as they stood on opposite sides of the kitchen table. 'Doing it right *here* under my nose.' It was six p.m. and he been stewing about this all afternoon. 'I found your hairs on her pillow.' Vanessa had long, naturally blonde hair. The teenager didn't have dark roots. Mel did.

'A fat lot you care,' she retorted. 'You're never here. No wonder your daughter runs wild, taking drugs, smashed out of her head at parties. This is like a single-parent family.'

'Our daughter,' he shouted. 'Ours. Don't you wash your hands of her.'

'Oh, yes, hark at the loving dad,' Mel said, folding her arms. 'At least I care for her.'

'I have always cared for her.' He jabbed a finger at his own chest.

'Really? At least *I* was there for her birth!'

'That's kind of obligatory,' Perry smirked, a point won. The only reason he hadn't been present was that the car had broken down, but Mel had taken umbrage, as if he had done it deliberately. Mel's counter-attack had taken him by surprise. She seemed to be even angrier than he was. 'I cook her meals, I clear up after her, I talk to her about her problems, which is more than you ever do,' she shouted.

Unsure how he had so quickly been forced back on the defensive, Perry returned to the main line of attack, stabbing his finger for emphasis. 'Who is he, then, this lover of yours?'

'I'm not telling you. Actually, he could be anybody, John. I'm so starved of affection, I made a pass at the Ocado lad, but he ran away back to his delivery van.'

Perry flexed his fists, bewildered at what was happening to him. 'You used our daughter's bedroom, so that if you got caught I'd blame *her*. That is pretty low.'

'I always change the sheets, like a good caring mum. Well, I would have done if you'd given me a few minutes.'

Was she really blaming him for coming home? 'I can't believe I'm hearing this,' he yelled. 'How long has this been going on?'

She turned round to him, her lips twisted in anticipation. 'A long time. Before we moved here.'

'What!'

'Yes. I got us to move here so it would be easier and more convenient for me to see him.' She folded her arms and watched him. *So how do you like that, then?*

Perry was speechless. He hadn't even wanted to leave their previous home, a tidy two-bedroom 1930s terrace, which they could easily afford. They had moved in here eighteen months ago. Now here he was in hock up to the neck for a flimsy new build. And it was all to facilitate *her* ongoing affair. 'I want to know exactly how long this has been going on, Mel.' He seized her by the arms, gripping her tightly enough so that it would hurt. 'I want to know how long!'

She smiled. 'A good eight inches, since you ask. And quite thick with it.'

An involuntary snarl tore across Perry's face, his arm raised itself, fist clenched. When it comes to inflicting pain, a spiteful woman is a match for any man. Less power maybe, but unerring accuracy.

Some cooler and detached part of him now recognised what was going on. She was goading him to hit her, something he had never done to any woman. Or man, come to think of it. Her closed-eyed expression was one of a saint, waiting to be validated by crucifixion. That was what she wanted, he could see it now. If he nailed her with a punch, the exit strategy would kick in. Of course. He was being stupid. He'd only just discovered her infidelity, but *her* plan for a divorce, mentioned first a couple of years ago, was obviously simmering nicely. And thinking about it, it was a pretty solid plan. She'd get the house, but he'd have to continue to pay for most of it. Of course if he hit her and she pressed charges, he'd lose his job too. In fact, he was trussed up like a turkey. The deliberately lost evidence file, at her insistence, meant she had the whip hand over him in every way. An anonymous call to Crime Stoppers would do the trick. If he touched her, he was lost.

He grabbed his coat and his car keys, and headed for the door.

'And John? Just so you know. He made me come more times this morning than you have managed in our entire marriage,' she yelled after him. 'I was screaming the bloody house down!'

–

Perry jumped into the car, and screeched off to drive around the estate. If she wanted a war, she'd get one. Just not one of her choosing. He had resources that he could use against this man, whoever he was. He was looking for a black Range Rover, but it was just his luck that he couldn't find one anywhere. A grey one, yes. A black Freelander, yes. But not the exact vehicle. Fifteen minutes later, Perry parked by the developer's site office. He now realised that in his fury he had, for the second time, forgotten to pick up the datasticks and would have to go crawling back for them.

Idiot.

He turned off the engine, and, resting his hands on the top of the wheel, placed his chin upon them. He stared out across the bleak treeless entrance, the banners crackling in the wind, a tundra of new build misery laid out before him. He thought it through. Mel's lover, whoever he was, had been hiding up there in Vanessa's room as he arrived. Mel manoeuvred him into the sun lounge to discuss their daughter, so that the bastard could slip out of the front door. Of course, that's why she had kissed him so passionately, her hands holding his face. Over his ears! So he didn't hear the door. What was most unforgivable was that he hadn't a bloody clue. Here he was, a detective inspector charged with trying to find the culprits on a couple of murders, and he couldn't even see that his wife was having an affair under his very nose.

The truth remained that he loved Mel. And he had trusted her.

More fool him.

All that stuff about Vanessa and drugs in her room, Mel might just have made it up. John Perry took a very deep breath, and realised quite why it is that they say that love is blind. He began to recognise in himself something he had been taught about in the training courses on domestic violence. Why is it that women rarely press charges against abusive husbands? It's because their self-esteem is at rock-bottom and they believe they deserve everything that happens to them. He had found it hard to believe at the time.

Not now.

John Perry certainly felt worthless: five foot seven, not particularly fit, and obviously, really obviously, not very smart. Big debts. Newly corrupt, too. And to top it all, the banner headline news, that not one of his three previous girlfriends, all those decades ago, had ever seen fit to tell him. That he was rubbish in bed. How on earth could he expect to run part of a complex murder inquiry for Surrey Police, when his own life was such a mess?

For the first time in his life he considered killing himself.

Chapter Thirteen

Claire Mulholland's warnings about Gillard being targeted had hit home. The detective chief inspector rarely had any worries about his own safety, but his thoughts always turned to Sam. They had been trying to sell their home for many months now, partly to get away from his annoying aunt, but also to move away from the Chipstead area closer to Guildford, where most of his work was now based. It wouldn't be the first time someone connected with a case had discovered where he and Sam lived. He made a mental note to suggest to Sam that they drop the price again, to generate more interest in their home. He was sure she would agree.

Missing her, he tried to ring her extension in the police control room, but it went to voicemail. She was almost always on the line, and wouldn't be finished for another couple of hours. The way his ear and cheek were throbbing he quite felt like going home early, perhaps to make her a surprise meal. It was a rarity for him to be home before her, but something she always loved. He had just about made up his mind to ask DI Perry to cover for him in the ongoing search for the Mitsubishi Warrior that evening, when he was summoned by email to the office of Alison Rigby.

He groaned inwardly, and made his way out of the CID building into Mount Browne's historic redbrick building. Rigby was dressed informally, and peering at her screen through reading glasses. 'Come in, Craig. How are your injuries?' she asked, peering at the dressing on his ear.

'It's not too bad. I'll live.'

'I'm not going public on the details of this assault against you. Although it almost certainly was a targeted attack, I'd prefer not to confirm that one of our officers was a victim. But I strongly suggest you recheck all of your personal security assumptions. You tangled with an Albanian crime gang a year or so ago, and it might be possible that this is associated with them. They would certainly have the resources.'

'Possibly. However, that would not fit with our assumptions about the Beatrice Ulbricht abduction, and the falsified rail journey.'

The chief constable shrugged. 'The investigation is well resourced already. But if you feel you need more, do let me know. We can tack it on the end of the Ulbricht budget that the Home Office has allowed me. Speaking of which.' She looked up at him from her desk, a brief flash of the infamous blue stare. 'We seem to be making progress in most aspects of this sprawling case, except on the murder of Beatrice. Herr Ulbricht rings me most days. It's a call I have to take.'

'I think you know we are doing our very best, ma'am,' Gillard responded.

'Perhaps you could write me a summary report.'

'Yes ma'am.'

'No hurry, Craig. Any time this evening will be fine.'

He groaned inwardly. That was the end of Gillard's plan to give Sam a pleasant surprise.

–

It was almost ten when he got home that evening. The report hadn't been hard to write, but it lacked a conclusion, which made it feel unfinished and unsatisfactory. As Gillard reversed the car up the drive, he saw that Sam's little black Renault was gone from its normal position in front of the garage, next to his RAV4. The usual lights in the house were on, in the hall and kitchen, plus one of the bedrooms upstairs. He let himself in and called her name. No reply. The burglar alarm had not been set. There was no note on the kitchen table, and no evidence of any meal except the unwashed breakfast plates.

Gillard checked his phone. He had sent Sam a text when he was almost finished with the report, to say when he would be home. That was just before nine, and there had been no reply from her, which was unusual. He rang her mobile, which was turned off. He left a message. This was all very strange. He went upstairs, and checked the lit bedroom. The bed was made, there was no evidence of a hurried change of clothing, which is what he would have expected if she had come in and then gone out again to see a friend.

A ragged edge of anxiety crowded his consciousness, but he refused to let it dominate. This was a problem of logic. Had Sam returned home at all? The kitchen and hall lights were on a timer, so would go on automatically at seven p.m. However the bedroom light was not, and he was pretty sure it would not have been left on when Sam left in the morning, because it would already have been light. That would tend to indicate she had come home. But why would she not leave a note or email or text him to let him know?

He checked the landline answer phone, which indicated no new messages, then logged on to the Internet upstairs in his office. He used Sam's laptop and went straight to Facebook, which took him to her account. There was plenty of recent activity, particularly from Ellen, but no indication on direct messages of any hurriedly arranged girls' night out. Sam's parents lived in the Lake District, a major expedition, so she wouldn't have gone to see them on a whim.

Baffled, and increasingly alarmed, the detective went back into the kitchen and looked around for evidence from first principles, as if it was somebody else's home. Instantly he noticed the kitchen table was not quite in its normal position. Discoloured square marks on the linoleum, evidence of its usual alignment, were visible. One of the three chairs was not tucked under the usual edge of the pine table. He crouched down and peered under the table, and spotted something glinting in the shadows. An earring. A small dangly butterfly that he recognised as one of his wife's favourites.

Anxiety clicked up to fear. He hurried back up to the office, found his emergency backup briefcase, and extracted a tiny evidence bag, latex gloves and tweezers. He held the earring carefully to the light, but could see no sign of blood. That at least was a minor relief. There was no good reason for this little piece of costume jewellery to have found its way under the table.

There was one final and possibly large resource that he could use. He was reluctant to go across the road to ask his aunt Trish if she had seen anything. Sam had often complained that the woman spied on her, particularly when she was at home alone. But right now, that could be an asset. The detective looked out of the front window towards Trish's bungalow.

Her car was gone too. That was highly unusual, because she always claimed she didn't enjoy driving the big Ford Ranger that she had acquired from her sheep farmer sister. Trish had groceries delivered, and was more likely to walk to local shops than take the car. Gillard walked across the road and rang Trish's doorbell. Only one light was on, the hall light that seemed to be on twenty-four hours a day. There was no reply. Gillard tried his own next-door neighbours on both sides. Only one was in and hadn't seen anything.

Enough was enough. Gillard took out his own mobile and alerted the control room to Sam's absence. He asked them to get the duty detective inspector to put a request for a trace on Sam's mobile and flag up her car registration as a matter of urgency. He might look an idiot if she showed up, but he was prepared to take that chance.

Then he went back inside his cold, empty home, sat at the kitchen table and stared at the earring. How could he have been so complacent? So foolish as not to imagine that whoever it was who could find out where he was cycling on a particular day, probably already knew where he lived.

He held his head in his hands. For all his steely professional resolve, he was now just plain old Craig Gillard. For the first time in many years he had no idea what to do next.

It was nearly eleven when DI Claire Mulholland pulled up outside Gillard's home, having driven at breakneck speed from her home in Staines. They had earlier had a long conversation on the phone. Claire had an enduring affection for her boss, who had acted as mentor and an inspiration during her early years on the force. She only once before witnessed him this distressed, and that was a few years previously when he had discovered a blood-soaked crime scene at the home of his long-ago former girlfriend Liz Knight. But if Sam had been abducted, this would be of a different order.

A police patrol car was parked on the front drive, and when Gillard answered the door to Claire's ring, she was immediately part of an urgent conversation in the hallway. Two large and grim-faced uniformed officers turned to look at her, and the Surrey Police lanyard dangling around her neck, but she only had eyes for Gillard, who was as white as a sheet.

'Have you found her?' she asked, fearing the worst.

Gillard shook his head. 'There was a 999 call at around half past eight, from Trish, saying that a man had driven away in Sam's car.'

One of the uniforms, a sergeant with a moustache, took up the story. 'Mrs Gibson rang in at 8.27 p.m., apparently from her vehicle, saying that she had decided to follow the stolen vehicle. She described seeing the man close the garage door, he was tall and of a muscular build, wearing a bulky car coat and a ski mask…'

'That's the same man!' Claire said. 'The one who tried to run you down.'

'I think he's got Sam,' Gillard said. 'She doesn't keep her car in the garage. So the only reason it would be seen driving out of there is if he had reversed it in to load...' His voice cracked. '...her into the back unseen.'

'Oh, Craig,' she rushed forward to embrace him, ignoring the presence of the two officers.

'CSI are on their way, ma'am. We've got an alert right across London and the Home Counties.'

Craig had already told her about discovering the earring. Since their phone conversation he said he had found a clump of Sam's hair trapped low in the hinge of the door into the garage. 'I've taken a peek, and there doesn't seem to be anything obvious, but I thought I'd await CSI rather than step inside.' He looked around at his home, as if seeing it for the first time. 'I'll need somewhere to stay...'

'Of course, Craig, you can stay with us.' She turned to the two uniforms. 'Is there any news on Craig's aunt, Mrs Gibson? Any ANPR hits? Any further phone messages from her?'

'Yes, one further phone message to say she was pursuing Mrs Gillard's car on the A217 heading towards Sutton,' the sergeant said. 'Unfortunately, the call handler asked her to confirm that she was using a hands-free phone, otherwise she would be committing an offence. At that point Mrs Gibson swore at her and then hung up. We've heard nothing since, but do have two ANPR hits which correspond to a northbound A217 camera.'

The uniformed constable was on the radio to the control room, the very place where Sam had been working until earlier that evening. Squawks and crackles filled the hallway, but the laconic message being relayed by the female call handler was clear enough. A vehicle had been found in a back road off the A217, a gravely injured female inside. Two patrol cars, the fire service and paramedics were on the scene. CSI was due to arrive shortly.

Gillard's eyes widened. 'Which vehicle? Is there a description?'

The constable on the radio asked for confirmation of vehicle make or registration number, but was told none was available yet. 'I'll get right on it,' she said.

The arrival of a white van and another patrol vehicle filled the hallway with the glare of headlamps. 'Come on Craig,' Claire said. 'CSI is here. You can't do anything but get in the way. I'm taking you back home to Staines.'

'Not until I've seen that crashed car.'

She could see the set of his jaw. 'Okay, Craig. We'll go there first.'

—

She wouldn't let him drive. Claire took Gillard's unmarked Vauxhall, allowing her to blue-light it the eight miles to the country lane where the vehicles had been found. During the journey Gillard worked his phone, chasing every little detail of the unfolding incident. The first confirmation came quite quickly that it was Trish's Ford Ranger that had been discovered, but it took arrival at the scene to take in the full horror of what had happened.

Such was the press of emergency service vehicles close to the little church of St Botolph's in Banstead that Claire parked 200 yards away, intending to walk. But the moment they stopped Gillard jumped out and hurried up towards the blue crime tape, and the big blue SUV, doors open, just by the lychgate of the churchyard. White Tyvek-suited figures lit by powerful floodlights were busy inside. Bloodstains could be seen on the seat. Claire found her boss by an ambulance, where the crew were in the process of confirming to him that it was an elderly lady who had been inside the car and was now in hospital.

'She's sustained severe head injuries,' one of the paramedics volunteered. 'I've just been on the phone to intensive care. She's in a coma, with a bleed on the brain. I'm sorry, but the registrar says the prognosis isn't good.'

Claire took Gillard's arm. He had no coat or jacket, no lanyard for ID, and was still dressed in his white shirt and dark work trousers, his tie askew. He looked ashen, as if in shock. But her attempts to restrain him were futile. He marched on towards his aunt's vehicle, recognising one of the CSI technicians, Kirsty Mockett, the girlfriend of Research Intelligence Officer Rob Townsend.

Claire listened in as Kirsty described what seemed to be a savage attack against Gillard's aunt. 'I don't think she stood a chance,' Kirsty said.

'Are there any eyewitnesses?' Gillard asked.

'Uniforms are doing door-to-door, but no houses look out just here,' Kirsty said.

Gillard looked around, eyes swivelling crazily, as if there would be evidence ripe for the plucking if only he could spot it. 'Look for tyre tracks for Sam's car. She had Michelin radials, front left replaced just three months ago. Look out for her other earring, a tiny butterfly. She lost the first one in the house.' He barked out another half-dozen pieces of forensic advice to the young CSI, who merely blinked.

'Come on, Craig,' Claire said, taking him gently by the arm. 'Don't try to do everybody's job. We need you calm, well slept and focused tomorrow, because there are certain things that only you can tell us. For tonight, there is nothing more you can do.'

He nodded, accepting the advice.

'I'm sorry about your aunt,' Claire said. 'I know you are no great fan of hers, to put it mildly, but she has put her life on the line to save Sam. That's redemption, isn't it?'

'Yes, she has done us all proud.' He blinked and seemed to be reassessing his least favourite relative. Eventually he emerged from his reverie, and steepled his hands either side of his nose. 'I can't sleep, Claire, not knowing where Sam is. There has got to be something I should be doing, because every minute counts. I just don't know what.'

Friday

Gillard awoke with the dawn chorus in an unfamiliar bedroom. It was 5.17. a.m. A loudly ticking clock metronomed his anxiety, as if counting down the time available to find Sam. The alarm he had set last night was not due for another hour, but he flicked on the light anyway. Claire had shunted out her eldest son to his girlfriend's place, to make room for him. The posters on the walls were hardly reassuring, dead-eyed skeletal zombies wielding knives above the name of the latest computer game in which they featured.

He grabbed at his phone, a lifeline to hope. He'd been copied in on every development. Trish had undergone an emergency operation to relieve the pressure in her brain, but was still in a coma. Elsewhere there wasn't much to learn. Sam's black Renault hadn't triggered a single ANPR camera since ten p.m. It had just disappeared, much like the Mitsubishi Warrior. He wasn't hugely surprised. Surrey had an enormous network of tiny back lanes, many of them ancient, even within the great encircling loop of the M25. Those who could read a map could easily navigate a way anywhere within the county without having to use motorways or dual carriageways. He flicked back through all the emails and official notifications going back to the moment that Sam's car was first reported missing. Then he went through his voicemail, which included many messages of support and encouragement both from his colleagues, and those who worked with Sam in the control room.

He found it too upsetting to listen to them all, and decided to use his energy in a more practical fashion. He shrugged on the borrowed bathrobe, and padded off to the bathroom. The heating hadn't kicked in yet, and the water was cold, but he welcomed the invigorating chill as he splashed his face. Claire had manhandled him out of his home so fast he had neither a change of clothes, nor any toiletries. She had left for him a new toothbrush, and a deodorant. That was all he needed. He couldn't quite face a cold-water shave, and dressed hurriedly into last night's clothes.

Trying not to wake anyone, he padded carefully down the stairs, but on his way into the kitchen ran into Dexter, Claire's boisterous and waist-high Irish wolfhound. The dog eyed him suspiciously, presumably half remembering the smell from previous encounters years ago, but unsure why someone who was almost a stranger should be sneaking about his mistress's home in the twilight. A low growl confirmed the animal's concerns. The detective's whispered hello and attempt to stroke his head engendered only a raucous bark. A half minute stand-off ended with a sleepy shout from upstairs from Claire, telling Dexter to behave. The wolfhound would have none of it, so Gillard abandoned his plans to leave a thank you note in the kitchen, simply scooping up his keys and racing for the door.

The first blush of dawn was searing a slatey horizon as Gillard fired up the Vauxhall and roared off to Mount Browne. The traffic would be light, and with luck he could be there in just over half an hour. He realised that with Claire's car at his home, she would be a bit stuck about getting to work. Husband Baz would hopefully be able to give her a lift. For now, he had consideration for just one person: Sam. Where on earth was she, and who had taken her?

Running through the radio for something to distract him, Gillard stumbled across Radio 3. He wasn't quite in the mood, but nevertheless heard a snatch of some rather enticing violin piece. It made him think of poor Beatrice Ulbricht. A disappearance, dwindling hopes, and a dead body at the end of it.

His eyes pricked with tears as he considered the same fate for his own dear wife. He was approaching the slip road for the M25. Angrily, he flailed for a different channel, and found something with heavy metal. 'Highway to Hell' by AC/DC. As the bass drum beat kicked in, he squeezed the accelerator the last half inch, hit the blue lights and blasted down into the fast lane.

He would save her if it took every atom of his being.

Mount Browne seemed almost deserted when he burst in. No ID, no jacket, no shave. He was lucky that the receptionist was an old buddy, Tony Williams, who had heard the story. He tossed Gillard a spare pass card, and told him that he'd fill in the paperwork himself. Like a man possessed, Gillard strode through the empty corridors and into the incident room. Michelle Tsu and Rainy Macintosh were both there, scouring every report of abandoned vehicles, car thefts and ANPR hits.

Gillard returned their greetings, and sat down at Carl Hoskins' crumb-flecked desk. There were two terminals side-by-side, and he wanted them both. He was going to search the police national computer for every person who could hate him enough to do this. It was often slow, so while one search was clunking through, he could try another.

Those same dozen or so names had been circulating in his head in the middle of the night, but now he wanted to close down the unlikeliest so he could concentrate on the possibles.

Charles Allerdyce: Lincoln, four years to run on his sentence.

Paddy Kincaid: Winson Green, another nine.

Ronnie Evans: out since 2016. Out? He hadn't expected that. Evans was a drug smuggler, and very nasty. He'd done some early time for car theft too, which helped tick a box. The only trouble was, he was a lanky individual; there was no way he matched the description of the man in the car coat, now verified by three witnesses: himself, Trish and the bloke who had tried to stop him stealing his Mitsubishi Warrior. No, it couldn't be Ronnie. At least not just Ronnie. Maybe there were two Ronnies? He smiled at his own joke, the first smile in many hours.

Sam Akos. Well, he was out, but he was black, a huge Ghanaian. Wearing white face under his ski mask would be an interesting disguise. It seemed wrong. Gillard looked through Akos' record. He was six four. Car coat man was perhaps six one, max.

Skin tones and body shape seemed to rule out another half-dozen drug dealers, organised crime operatives and general lowlifes. Colin Ellis, a double murderer who was definitely out on licence, looked promising. He was the right build, and he was certainly physically capable. But he had spent the entire Internet revolution inside, was probably a bit too old, and wasn't the brightest spark in the first place. Gillard couldn't imagine Ellis working out how to send a delayed text message. Posting a letter was probably his limit, so long as someone wrote it for him.

That left Rodney Wells, who was an international fugitive last seen on the Costa del Crime. Wells was certainly smart, and elusive. But why would he come back to Britain? Then he considered those who didn't have a criminal record. There were a couple of travellers who had made threats against Gillard's 'children' a few years ago after he had arrested them for stealing quad bikes. The two men were unaware that the detective was childless when they claimed to know where his kids went to school.

All in all, it just didn't seem a very promising crop of possibilities. So perhaps it was someone he didn't know.

–

Detective Inspector John Perry had needed something to keep his mind off the state of his marriage. So he tracked down the man in charge of the original Jane Morris case. Retired Detective Superintendent Wilfred Mottram lived pretty close to the scene of the abduction in South London, just half a mile south in one of the big double-fronted Victorian houses on Bedford Hill, near Tooting Bec Common. The man who answered the door was a Ronnie Kray lookalike, in his late sixties, a sizeable slab of a bloke, with tinted glasses and a big pockmarked face. Mottram led Perry down a hallway past stacks of cardboard boxes through to the conservatory at the back of the house. There were more boxes here, with Samsung and lesser-known electronic brands emblazoned over them.

Seeing Perry's gaze, Mottram volunteered: 'It's my post-retirement business. I buy in mobiles in bulk, and sell them on eBay and other online marketplaces.' They chatted about the rise of the delivery economy, until the detective inspector decided they'd had enough small talk to lubricate the more serious questions.

'So as I said on the phone, I've come to ask you about the Jane Morris case.'

Mottram remembered the case very well. Over tea and jaffa cakes he relayed to the younger man the difficulties that they'd had.

'The governor wanted a quick result. We must've interviewed five hundred West Indians looking for the guy with the T-shirt. That created a lot of resentment in the local community, which even then had quite a high ethnic population.'

'What about Harold Garrison, the uncle?'

'I interviewed him a few times. He was gutted, as befits a fishmonger. Very fond of Jane he was. Frank and Eileen only had the one child, and to lose her like this. Well.' He shook his head.

'Was it just a stall he ran at the market?'

'No, a proper shop. Shellfish, mainly. The old days of jellied eels, cockles, whelks. The old London food. Of course these days, it's all ciabatta, gnocchi and fucking avocado. The Hildreth Street market has been gentrified to death. Most of the old stallholders and shopkeepers have long gone. Even the halal butchers. The only one I recognise these days is the West Indian hairdresser's which has been there decades.'

'Did you ever visit his fish shop? Did it have a big deep-freeze?'

'Don't remember. I suppose he must've had one, in his line of business. He closed the shop a year or two after her death, and moved away.'

'Still in the fish business, was he?'

'No idea. I was moved on to other cases by then.'

Perry had been keeping his trump card for the end of the interview. 'I can tell you now, that we found Jane's body floating in a river in Surrey just a few days ago.'

'You're kidding me.' His jaw hung open, revealing tiny white flecks of saliva at the corners of his mouth.

'I've got some photographs,' Perry said, getting his iPad out.

'Go on then,' Mottram said, switching his specs to a half-moon pair. 'I don't imagine I'd recognise her after all this time.'

'I think you will,' Perry said. He flashed up the image that had been taken in the mortuary, while she was still wearing the skirt and cardigan she had worn on the day she disappeared.

'Nah, that must be an old photo,' Mottram said. 'It's exactly the same apart from her hair.'

'That photograph was taken four days ago. The post-mortem showed she has spent the last thirty-seven years frozen solid.'

Mottram blinked, and removed his spectacles to wipe his eyes. 'Oh Jesus, it's like time has stood still.'

Perry looked at this big powerful man, and then a few thoughts dropped like coins into his mind: Mottram is the right age to have killed Jane Morris, and even today could still have overpowered Beatrice Ulbricht too. Maybe a bit too unfit to have chased Gillard up a hillside, but the combination of police experience and electronics expertise might give him the forensic nous that their killer had shown. The hairs on the back of the detective's neck stood up. He didn't like Mottram, and he didn't trust him.

–

Friday afternoon saw DI Perry sitting in the cavernous and poorly lit basement of Tooting Police Station in South London. He was looking up the original interview notes from 1982 with Jane Morris' uncle Harold Garrison, and much else besides. There was a huge archive of historic police records kept down there, culled from the various local police stations which over the years had gradually closed. Much of it had been put on microfiche, the favourite archiving system of the immediately pre-computer era, but one that had now been superseded. The librarian had shown Perry how to manoeuvre the lens over the dark blue sheets of microfiche on the light box's glass plate to get the correct part underneath the magnifying glass, which then projected it onto the large screen, which was very much like a computer monitor. After a few minutes he got the hang of it, and was able to whizz from one sheet of evidence to another. The construction of a misdirected investigation was quite easy to uncover from this perspective.

Garrison, a forty-two-year-old fishmonger, claimed to have seen Jane Morris on the evening of Friday, 17 October 1982. He waved to her as she passed the shop, then noticed her talking to the young man with dread-locks. His statement included the line, 'I kept an eye on her as I'm not overly fond of them sort, you know.'

His was the only witness statement to mention the dreadlocked man, but Mottram and his team took it at face value. That assumption informed the rest of the investigation, all the interviews with young West Indian men, and the community uproar. Perry had to cross-reference the original file notes for photographs, because few of these had been recorded on the microfiche. The case had attracted an enormous amount of interest, but the thing that particularly piqued his curiosity was a picture taken by a photographer at the *South London Press* on the first anniversary of Jane Morris' disappearance. It showed Garrison and his wife, Linda, with a pram. The accompanying article was all about how much they missed their niece, but now had some fresh joy in their life. Perry stared at the picture. Linda Garrison was clearly in her forties, like her husband. He'd have to check her exact age. The article said they had been trying for a baby for years, and had finally been lucky to be blessed with little Graeme. If it had been a girl they would have called her Jane. None of the photographs of the bereaved family at the time of Jane's disappearance showed anyone who was obviously pregnant.

If there was a child in the pram, could it really be theirs?

He had a growing suspicion, and decided to check it from the present-day evidence. He logged on to the police national computer upstairs, and keyed in his personal ID. He then downloaded the full PDF of Dr Delahaye's post-mortem of Jane Morris, after she had been found in the flood. There was a lot of medical terminology he didn't understand, and he laboriously looked each term up. One sentence intrigued him. 'Beta HCG test positive, but uncertainty of effective freezing on human chorionic gonadotropin may cast doubt on nulliparous state.'

The word nulliparous turned out to mean never having had a pregnancy or birth. Perry picked up the phone and after numerous attempts managed to get hold of the forensic scientist. Delahaye briskly explained the terminology.

'Forensically speaking the most reliable way to determine whether a woman has ever been pregnant is to detect in her bloodstream a particular chemical which is released by the placenta after implantation. It does not in itself indicate whether the foetus was brought to term. However there can be other reasons for the presence of an elevated level of chorionic gonadotropin, and as my report made clear the uncertainties of what happens to this chemical after the body has been frozen make it quite unreliable to deduce pregnancy from this measure alone.'

Perry was scribbling down notes as fast as he could go. 'So on balance, doctor, would you say she had been pregnant?'

'At the time of death obviously not. There was no trace of foetal tissue, and the uterus was of a normal weight. But the more vexing question is had she ever been pregnant, and on the balance of probability, assuming no false signal from the beta HCG, I would say yes. That of course is a provisional conclusion.'

Perry thanked him and hung up. Speaking to a real scientist was refreshing. The man's mind was clearly as sharp as a scalpel. The detective knew he needed more evidence, and turned to an experienced-looking desk sergeant to help him. 'In 1982, where might a young girl have dropped off an unwanted baby in this neck of the woods?'

The sergeant, a thick necked and grizzled officer narrowed his eyes and said. 'You'd be best off looking for press coverage. Abandoned babies were news. Try to go via the NHS, and you'll get tangled up in privacy and data protection issues.' He logged Perry into the database of the local newspapers from that time. Nothing came up about abandoned newborns a year either side of the date of the crime.

The detective inspector leaned back in his seat with his hands behind his head and his face creased in concentration. What other possible lines of analysis could he undertake? If the Garrisons had adopted a child born to their niece, there should be school records. Again he asked for the help of the sergeant. Fortunately, they were looking in the days before 'choice' became the key word in education, so generally speaking most kids went to the nearest infant and junior schools. The two of them put in calls to all the relevant school offices, but considering it was after five o'clock, they knew they would get no answers before the following Monday.

One idea kept circulating in Perry's head. That the fishmonger had first impregnated his own niece, and had adopted the resulting baby. Someone in Jane's family would have known she was pregnant, surely. He conceded it was going to be very hard to prove now, but clearly if he was right, any family cover-up would be a huge issue for the police to have missed. The next thing was to try to find records for the child.

Perry picked up his coat and emerged into the grey drizzly car park, the drone of traffic all around. He contemplated a long and tedious drive through the rush-hour traffic until he got to Woking, and his own not-very-welcoming home. Work, the best part of the week, was now over. It was Friday night, and all he had to look forward to was the prospect of emotional hand-to-hand combat with his estranged wife, a woman who had the verbal equivalent of a black belt in karate. He dreaded it. If there was anywhere else he could have gone, he would have. He wasn't due on shift, but he'd go back in to the office first thing tomorrow anyway.

—

It was Friday afternoon before Gillard was allowed to return home and collect some clothing. CSI chief Yaz Quoroshi was just leaving, the last of the crime scene vans just reversing out of his drive as Gillard drove into the cul-de-sac. They greeted each other through open vehicle windows. 'What have you discovered?' Gillard asked.

'The good news is that there is no blood. There was clearly a struggle. The hair you spotted in the hinge of the door matches Sam's. My guess is she was being carried, probably unconscious, for her head to be that low.' Quoroshi must have seen Gillard's jaw clench, because he added. 'Craig, we have no reason at this stage to think she is dead.'

'Anything in the garage?'

'No. The door was neatly closed after he departed. Your aunt's emergency call seems to dovetail with that.'

'Rigby won't let me stay here, so I've just got to nip in and get toiletries and clothing.'

'She's quite right. If the abductor knows where you live, it's crazy to stay. If he's trying to get you, there will probably be another message. That's why I think she is still alive.'

Gillard nodded. 'Thanks, Yaz. I'll be staying with Claire for now.'

As the crime scene van pulled away, the detective looked at his house, no longer cinched in by blue crime scene tape, and with an unsmiling female PC on guard. Gillard didn't know her, and in his unshaven and lanyard-less state, with a creased shirt and borrowed jacket, he struggled to convince her of who he was. In the end, he briefly put on the blue lights of the unmarked Vauxhall, then dug out some paperwork from the glove compartment. She still forced him to sign in on the clipboard on his telephone table. She thawed a little when he re-emerged from upstairs, showered, shaved and suited.

'Just doing my job, sir,' she said.

'I know.' He invited her in for a cup of tea and a bowl of soup, which overrode her initial refusals. He didn't want to admit it, but he couldn't bear to be alone in the kitchen from which his wife had been snatched.

Gillard was almost back in Guildford when he got a call on the hands-free. It was Detective Chief Superintendent Brian 'Radar' Dobbs. 'I'm sorry to tell you this Craig, but Rigby has asked me to take over as senior investigating officer.'

'What?'

'I think it's obvious that your mind will be drawn to the one aspect of the case that is of a personal concern.' Dobbs was a grey and dour individual whose huge ears had earned him his nickname. He'd been on long-term sick leave with depression on and off for a couple of years, and everyone had expected him to retire. His return a couple of months ago had surprised everyone.

'Yeah, the fact that my wife has been kidnapped, what a surprise!'

'There's no need to take that tone,' Dobbs said. 'The chief constable will undoubtedly give you her reasons directly. In the meantime you should take some time off and try to relax…'

Furious, Gillard cut the call, floored the accelerator and swore inventively for a couple of minutes. How on earth did anyone expect him to relax while Sam was being held by some maniac? Wouldn't it be better to focus that nervous energy on cracking the case? He was quite prepared to work a hundred hours a day until she was found. There were things he knew that nobody else knew, there was information he could find that no one else could find. How dare they!

Most of the civilian day staff were just leaving as Gillard's Vauxhall bullied its way into the car park, blues on, and slewed to a halt untidily in the bay reserved for a riot van. If ever there was going to be a one-man riot, it was now. The moment he burst into reception, the duty officer's phone rang. His eyes flicked up to Gillard. He mouthed one word and gestured at the handset – 'Rigby' – and pointed him towards her office in the next building.

Two minutes later, Gillard was standing in front of the seated chief constable, having thrown every possible reason at her for having him continue to run Operation Hawkeye. Rigby steepled her long fingers, her nails short and glossy, and gave him the full benefit of the icy blue stare of death. 'Craig, the sheer intemperate nature of your appeal to me makes it obvious that you're in no emotional state to run a large, complex investigation. If you would calm down for just a moment, that would be perfectly obvious to you.'

She shuffled some papers on her desk, and then looked up at him. 'I've passed the search for your wife to the National Crime Agency's anti-kidnap and extortion unit. The AKEU have people who know exactly what they are doing. An officer will be here before midnight, and the rest in the morning. Now, I know you have unique information, and they will undoubtedly call on that. But I don't want you here, getting under everyone's feet.'

'But ma'am, you won't let me stay at home, because of the so-called threats to me. Where the hell am I supposed to go?'

Rigby sucked her cheek. 'I advise you to moderate your tone, Craig. This is in your interests. We are doing absolutely everything we can to find Sam. I understand you have the keys to your late aunt's house. Perhaps you could stay there? I understand she has cats that need feeding.'

Gillard could think of nothing worse. He had compartmentalised the prospect of his aunt's death, someone he knew he would never miss even though he was grateful to her for pluckily following Sam's abductor. But to be in her house, looking after her damn animals, would be like returning to the nightmare of his childhood that he thought he had escaped.

'I can't do that, ma'am.'

'As you wish. But I don't want you here. I've just authorised the suspension of your passwords for the PNC and the other databases. Give me your security pass and work phone.' She even clicked her fingers at him.

Sullenly, he dropped them on her desk. He was waiting for her to ask for the keys to the unmarked Vauxhall, but as her phone rang she already seemed to be moving on to the next thing. 'This is a call from Germany, Craig. Perhaps you'll forgive me?' She picked up the handset and exchanged a warm greeting with Karl-Otto Ulbricht.

The interview was over. Gillard turned and made his way down the carpeted corridor, lined with the stern portraits of previous chief constables going back over a century. He had made his marriage vows to Sam almost three years previously. To love, honour and cherish. To protect may not have been explicit, but to Craig Gillard it was central. Few people are better placed than a policeman to protect a woman he loves. But Alison Rigby had just taken away the tools for him to do it.

–

He drove into the centre of Guildford, unsure what to do next. He had an overnight bag in the car, and was welcome to stay with Claire and Baz Mulholland, but he could hardly mooch around there all day getting under the feet of her numerous kids, and being a target for Dexter, the crazed wolfhound. It was nearly six p.m. and he was hungry, so he put the car in the car park and had a lonely meal for one in Pizza Express. It was only when he was halfway through eating that he realised he and Sam had once shared a meal there on one of their early dates before going to see a film. The thought rather ruined his appetite.

Like most of the other solo diners, he spent time working his personal phone. Presumably warned off by Radar Dobbs, no one in CID nor anyone in CSI would take his calls. His texts and emails went unanswered. Only DC Michelle Tsu sent a brief reply, saying: 'Sir, we're all feeling your agony. I just want you to know that we won't rest until we find her.'

Gillard creased his face, trying to suppress the emotion he felt. He became aware of a waitress standing at his shoulder. 'Was the pizza okay?' she asked. He nodded mutely, paid up and tipped extravagantly before staggering out. He stared around the streets, shop windows still lit up, even as staff began to lock doors. The streets were busy, the frenetic start of the weekend commute home. All right for those with a home. In the pedestrianised area everything seemed to be moving fast, except the homeless. They occupied most of the benches, grimy plastic bags and shopping trolleys containing pitiful possessions. He found a clean end of a bench at the other end of which perched an elderly lady in a headscarf and a raincoat whose colour could once have been described as coral, sucking on a can of cider. She didn't see him, she didn't even see the multitudes who strode past. Her rheumy unfocused eyes, canted skywards, seemed to await a message of salvation from on high.

For that, he envied her.

He tried Claire for the fourth time, and she picked up. 'Craig, where are you?'

'I'm sharing a bench with a lady of the road in the centre of Guildford.' He told her Rigby's advice about using Trish's bungalow. She immediately renewed her offer of the spare room in Staines, but he declined.

'I need to be close to the investigation. I'm going nuts.'

'Don't, Craig. Rigby is serious. If you cross her she'll destroy you.'

'How's the investigation divided up?' he asked.

'Dobbs as you know is SIO. He's appointed Perry to look after the Ulbricht and Morris killings, and I'm going to be working with the AKEU guy, Rajinder Otara, who arrives tonight, to find Sam. There's a total news blackout of course.'

'I'm relieved it's you, Claire.'

She chuckled. 'Mainly because you think I'll feed you up-to-date information.'

'And will you?'

'Within reason. I'm working on the basis that as Sam was abducted and driven away in her own car, the kidnapper must either have left a vehicle nearby or arrived on public transport. We've got the CCTV in from both Woodmansterne and Chipstead stations, as well as buses in the area.'

'It's not going to be much help when we don't know what he looks like.'

'True enough. I guess he wouldn't be dim enough to wear the car coat.'

'What did ANPR show?' Craig asked.

'There are no hits on the Mitsubishi Warrior, but then I'm not surprised. He'd be crazy to use such a distinctive vehicle again. But it's not been reported abandoned either.'

'That sounds good. I've got my own plans.'

'That sounds ominous.' Her voice was cautionary.

'Don't worry, Claire. I'm just picking up a loose end. You might recall that Sam had an ex-boyfriend called Gary Harrison. A nasty piece of work, serial liar, used to knock her about. He'd have a grudge against both Sam and me.'

'I don't recall he was on your list?'

'No, he wasn't. I actually overstepped the mark when I put the frighteners on him when I first met Sam.'

'I see,' said Claire.

'Five years ago he was married with two kids, and lived in the Addiscombe area of Croydon. I'm going to sneak back and get my notes from home, but if you would be kind enough to forward everything we have on him, and a proper address trace, I'd be very grateful.'

'I will if you promise me not to go freelance on this.'

'I promise, Claire. I won't put you in a difficult position.'

'Okay. I'm trusting you.' She hung up.

—

Wallington Close in Addiscombe was a typical piece of 1990s infill development. Forty units of social housing, squeezed onto the sold-off gardens of 1930s semis. More vehicles than space for them, a good half of them parked on municipal lawns, which made the otherwise tidy homes look run down. It was 8.30 p.m. when Gillard's Vauxhall cruised to the dead end of the street looking for number fifty-nine, the last known residence of Gary Harrison.

It was a few years ago now, when he had only just met Sam, that Gillard had taken illegal revenge on Sam's ex for breaking into her home and beating her up. He had sneaked into the back of Harrison's car and ambushed him when he drove off, almost suffocating him by sliding a plastic bag over his head, twisting the neck then punching him. It was necessary, but he wasn't proud of it. He'd never even told Sam the details. And here he was again, breaking the rules to look for his nemesis.

There wasn't a number fifty-nine.

The last home was forty-seven, a three-bedroom end of terrace without a garage, but with bin sheds and external meter cupboards beyond the paint flaked ranch-style fencing. A child's BMX-type bike leaned against the wall just outside the porch.

He walked up to the door and rang the bell. An Asian woman in traditional dress answered the door. She hadn't heard of Gary Harrison, nor of the family with two kids who had supposedly lived at number fifty-nine. The detective knocked at two other doors nearby, but gained no more information. The address was the one Harrison had used when he was employed as a chef in a college at Bromley seven years ago. Gillard had already checked with the employer, an educational trust which had since sold off the Bromley site to concentrate on others that it owned. Harrison's manager was no longer on the payroll. Thanks to Rainy Macintosh, Gillard already knew that no contributions had been made on Gary Harrison's national insurance record in five years. The home address that HMRC's national insurance unit in Long Benton had for him was the address of the college.

More dead ends.

It was clear that Gary Harrison had reinvented himself under another name, was almost certainly in another relationship, and quite probably some way away from this, his old stamping ground. There were pages and pages of Gary Harrisons on Facebook, on LinkedIn, in the National Archives, and presumably in phone books and electoral registers across the country. In all probability the man himself would not be found under this name in any of these places. With enough resources, and lots of time, it might eventually be possible to find him.

They just didn't have enough time.

And the abductor might not even be him.

It was at that point Gillard decided to abandon the search for Harrison and concentrate on more promising leads. If there were any.

-

Gillard was dreaming about one of their holidays, a five-day trip to the Arctic Circle to see the northern lights. He could almost feel the warmth of Sam's hand in his as they crunched through the thick snow, towards the soft shimmering searchlights that seemed to emanate from the pine forests ahead. Wakefulness slid like a knife between his ribs, the realisation of her absence. He was in his own bed, but lying on Sam's side, clasping one of her navy blue pullovers to himself as if it was a hot water bottle. The aroma of her enveloped him, a comforting miasma.

He had let himself in at midnight, having driven around the Chipstead area trying to spot any suspicious vehicles. It was of course a complete waste of time, as he didn't know what he was looking for. Gillard had parked the Vauxhall in an adjacent street and walked back, just in case someone was watching his home. Rigby didn't want him staying there, but she could hardly prevent him from doing so. The PC was no longer stationed at the door, seeing as he wasn't expected to be there. In theory, back home and on his own, he was at risk.

Well, bring it on. He was ready.

The largest carving knife in the house was on his bedside table, and he was wearing a tracksuit and socks. Not for him the fate of poor Kyle Halliday, skin ripped on the road while trying to save his car. If whoever had taken Sam wanted him too, he would go down fighting.

Now he heard again the noise that had woken him, which in his dream he had interpreted as the breaking of an icy Arctic crust. It was something at the back door. Leaping from the bed, knife in hand, he opened the bedroom's casement window which looked down over the back door.

Of course. Trish's bloody cats. Not fed for a day or so, and now trying to get into his home through the cat flap which he had glued up months ago. Napoleon, the green-eyed ginger tom and leader of this feral brood, cried up at him. No human can quite match the sense of entitlement of a cat.

He suspected he would get no sleep now.

–

Seven a.m. on a cool Saturday morning in April found DI John Perry sitting at his desk at Mount Browne, looking at all the DNA tests that had been ordered for both the Ulbricht and Morris murders. The vast majority of positive results were elimination samples, where a CSI technician or a police officer had left traces on evidence. DC Hoskins, for example, had managed to leave a DNA sample on Beatrice Ulbricht's multi-coloured scarf. Gillard had left his traces on the inside of the evidence envelope in which Beatrice's hair had been found. Perry himself had left a trace on the cardigan which had been found on Jane Morris' body. Unfortunately the tiny amount of blood trapped under the fingernail of the middle finger of Beatrice Ulbricht's left hand had been too degraded by contact with water to yield a reliable DNA sample.

What he really needed was to find the location where Beatrice had been strangled: a house, a bed, even a car seat. A genuine crime scene where there was a good chance of the attacker having left his DNA. They already knew that it could not be Adrian Singer's house. Neither his DNA nor hers had been found anywhere that did not match the story he had told. The gap in Beatrice's life between her disappearance late on Sunday and her failure to arrive at the concert on Tuesday night was like a yawning chasm in the evidence record. After mulling all this over for half an hour, Perry turned his attention to Jane Morris. For all the fact that this was a very cold case indeed, the line of inquiry seemed more straightforward. He went to the forensic lab and asked the male technician to fetch one of the six DNA samples taken from Morris by Dr Delahaye.

'What kind of test are you after?'

'Familial,' Perry replied. 'I want to find out if anyone whose DNA we have in any of these linked enquiries is related to her.'

'Okay. We'll be lucky to get that back by Monday,' the technician said.

Perry returned to his own desk, and once again flicked through the hundreds of microfiche documents he had photoed and copied onto his datasticks, hoping for some kind of inspiration. There was one very short witness statement from someone called Betty Garrison. It wasn't a name he had heard before, and the statement merely said that she hadn't seen her granddaughter Jane for five days before she disappeared. Ah! Betty was the missing girl's grandmother. The statement gave her date of birth as 9 December 1918. The chances were that she was no longer alive. Still, worth checking out.

–

A phone call cut into Gillard's slumber. He was shocked to see that it was a quarter to eleven on Saturday morning. He answered sleepily, propping himself up in bed. 'Hello Claire, any news?'

'We've picked up a text from Sam's phone to your work mobile.'

Gillard was instantly awake, and very glad that Claire had the good sense to monitor traffic over the phone he'd been forced to surrender. 'What did he say?'

'He said that she is "under the bridge".'

'I mean what *exactly* did he say?'

She read out the exact text.

Under the bridge/ That's where you'll find her/ cold, with the fishes/ drowned by your own hand. IC

'Shit.' The only bridges that he could think of were at Lacey Dutton, the Loxcombe and the Gorlaston, near which two bodies had already been recovered. Could she be alive if she was there? It could equally be a bridge near where they lived in the Banstead or Chipstead area, anywhere over a river where fish could be found.

'Craig, we're tracing Sam's phone as we speak. Maximum priority. I'd pre-arranged it with the service provider even though the phone has been off since she disappeared. We should get a cell site analysis within the hour.'

Gillard rubbed his face, trying to coax his brain to perform. 'We can do better, Claire. There's GPS on it—'

'The Google geolocation is encrypted though,' she said. 'We tried this before, it takes weeks and the involvement of lawyers—'

'No, listen. Sam has the Android Find My Phone app on her laptop, which CSI has. We don't have to break into the Google geolocation. The GPS data is copied into the app. Speak to Rob Townsend, he knows how to do it. We can extract the data remotely, unless the phone has been tampered with and some of the apps close down.' He picked his way through the various bits of paper on the bedside table until he found Sam's laptop password. He then read it out to Claire. 'CSI may already have got into the device, but if not, this will get you in.'

'Brilliant,' Claire said. 'Okay, I'll get onto that. What are you going to do?'

'What can I do? I'm going to drive over to Lacey Dutton and have a look around the two bridges, maybe get some ideas.'

Gillard hung up and rubbed his face. He'd been awake until at least five, tossing over in his mind all the various possibilities. That he'd had fallen asleep until mid–morning shocked him.

–

The detective was in the shower when the phone went fifteen minutes later. Heedless of the water over the bedroom carpet, he lurched out of the cubicle and grabbed his mobile. It was Claire.

'We've got a trace,' she said excitedly. 'You're not going to believe this, but Sam's phone was on Sandy Lane, just outside the University of Guildford Law Department, when that message was sent.'

'What?' Gillard knew the building. Just two minutes' walk from Mount Browne. Sandy Lane was the shared access road to Surrey Police headquarters. 'There's ANPR in the university car park!' he said excitedly.

'Hold on, Rob's right here telling me something,' she said. There was a bit of background noise and some raised voices. And then Claire's exclamation. Gillard was shocked. He had never heard her use the F word before. Certainly not twice in one sentence. There was a huge amount of background hubbub, raised voices. If he didn't know better, he'd say it was panic.

'Claire? Claire? What is it?'

She took a few seconds to answer. 'Craig, sorry, I've got to go. Whoever's got the phone is here, in the building.' It sounded like she dropped the phone on the desk. He could hear her still, but faintly, calling someone else. 'Rob? Rob? New message. No, now!'

The line went dead.

Gillard rang Claire's number, but the line was busy.

The last thing she had said that made any sense was: *here, in the building.* All sorts of scenarios were running in parallel in Gillard's overactive brain, but the most worrying was a US-style mass shooting. Why else would this man go to the very heart of Surrey Police? Maybe he was an ex-cop, or even a current officer. Only that would explain what was going on.

One thing was certain. Everything had changed. His place was not skulking around at home, even if that's what the chief constable demanded. It was to be with his colleagues. It was to be at the centre of the action, looking for his wife.

Chapter Fourteen

Gillard now regretted parking in the adjacent street last night. It took a minute's sprint to get to the Vauxhall, and get moving. He flipped on the blue lights and siren, and left rubber on the road as he tore off on the journey to Mount Browne. That should save him ten minutes on the usual forty to get there. As he drove, he tuned into the police radio monitor which allowed him to overhear the uniforms talking to each other. It was clear that a search was taking place at Surrey Police headquarters. Reading between the lines of the laconic and formulaic interchanges, it was clear that whoever the intruder was, he had not yet been spotted. There was no mention of gunfire.

His phone in the hands-free cradle, Gillard tried twice to get Claire and failed. He then tried Research Intelligence Officer Rob Townsend. There was no reply. Of course as this was his personal mobile, it would come up as an unidentified number in most of his colleagues' handsets. Right now no one would have time for dealing with strangers.

Foot to the floor, the Vauxhall was soon at the A23 junction with the M25. Traffic reports confirmed that London's orbital motorway was clear between junctions seven and ten, but it was always a risk. The blue lights cleared traffic more effortlessly here than on any A road. He was about halfway when Claire called him back.

'What in the hell is happening, Claire?'

'Sorry, Craig. We've got two dozen uniforms crawling all over the building. It's bloody mayhem.'

'Have you found him?'

'No. The GPS trace on Sam's phone shows it's here, somewhere in the CID building, and has been for half an hour. There were only a couple of guest passes granted today, officers from Essex, and they are now down in reception. The cell site analysis confirms what the Find My Phone app is telling us. The GPS resolution is about five metres, so whoever's got it should be visible.'

'Sorry, I'm not getting this,' Gillard said. 'You're saying the phone has walked itself into the building on its own?'

'Well, obviously not. But we've had another text message since it got in. "Catch me if you can". He's obviously taunting us.'

'We know these messages can be sent in advance, and this guy is capable of organising it,' Gillard said. 'But someone, possibly unwittingly, has brought the phone in.'

'Everyone is being escorted out of the building in rotation so they can isolate who it is. It's massively disruptive. All the incident rooms are going to have to be searched.'

'Don't you see, Claire? This is another subterfuge. This is our perpetrator telling us he can run rings around us. And while Surrey Police is busy examining its own orifice, he's probably doing something else, somewhere else.'

All he could think of was Sam. Hostage somewhere. Dead or alive. Under the bridge with the fishes.

–

Detective Constable Carl Hoskins lifted his legs and rotated in his chair. His jaundiced eyes took in the major incident room, the central hub of this ever-broadening murder inquiry. First into Beatrice Ulbricht, then Jane Morris, and now the abduction of Samantha Gillard.

'I don't get this,' he said to Rob Townsend, the only other person remaining. 'There's no one been in this room today that doesn't come in here every day. There's me, Perry, Mulholland, Michelle Tsu and you,' he said.

Townsend, arms folded behind his head, scowled at the screen. The GPS map of the movements of Sam's phone showed it in Sandy Lane at 9.34 a.m. and inside the building within half an hour. 'Yet it says it's definitely either here or in the corridor, or maybe upstairs in the storeroom, and it's not moving anymore. It can't be downstairs because apart from reception there's only that big meeting room, and it's been locked all day.'

'But what gets me is who brought the fucking thing in?' Hoskins said. 'Find the person, find the phone. I mean, any of us would notice the weight of a phone if someone slipped one into our pocket, wouldn't we?'

Townsend nodded. He'd already been through his own briefcase, and the drawers on his desk. Several of the drawers were locked, belonging to officers who weren't on shift, but by the same token no one could have put a phone in them.

One thing that they were all grateful for was that it was a Saturday. Alison Rigby wasn't in to witness the perpetrator making a fool of the entire force. If they weren't able to crack this quickly, the chief constable would inevitably hear about it and would begin banging heads together.

'It would really help,' Townsend said. 'If the phone finder app used the full GPS trace. If we had altitude, for example, we would instantly know which floor it was on.'

Perry and Claire Mulholland came back into the room, having been cleared of inadvertently carrying the phone. 'Any progress?' Perry asked.

'Nope,' Hoskins said, taking another spin around the room on his chair.

'What about a drone?' Perry asked. 'It could have been dropped on the roof.'

'Good thinking,' Hoskins said. 'I'll take the lift.'

–

The detective constable was not fond of heights, and the flat roof of this, the highest building on the Mount Browne campus, reminded him of that fact. Keeping away from the two-foot high parapet at the edge, Hoskins made his way past the ranks of solar panels, looking underneath to see if anything had been deposited. The one place you couldn't easily check was the top of the emergency exit onto the roof. There was an aluminium ladder screwed to the wall, but that was a bit too exposed for him. Besides, from the trace on the app, the phone should be roughly in the middle of the roof, not on one edge.

He was getting ready to go down, when he heard a car race into the car park. He looked across and spotted Gillard's Vauxhall. It didn't surprise him for a moment to see the detective chief inspector unable to stay away. By contrast old Radar Dobbs, despite being SIO, claimed to be working from home. Hoskins had had his run-ins with Gillard, and just a month ago had seen an attempt on the detective chief inspector's life result in the death of his colleague DC Colin Hodges. But he trusted Gillard's instincts like he trusted his own mother. The arrival of the best detective he had ever worked with gave him renewed confidence that they could crack the case.

–

At reception, Gillard confronted Ray Collins, a Mount Browne lifer with a gigantic beer belly and a fondness for sweets. Collins knew every officer in the building.

'I can't let you in, sir,' Collins said. 'I think you know why.'

'It's all right, Ray. But I understand there's a kerfuffle about my wife's phone being loose in the building.'

Collins sucked in his cheek. 'I've no idea what is going on, and I guess I'm not supposed to talk to you about it. But yeah, there's something happening.'

'Is there anyone here who isn't normally about?'

'We've been through that, sir. Two guests from Essex Police, but they never even stayed in this block.' He tapped a fat finger on the edge of the desk. 'They had a meeting in forensics.'

Gillard looked around. 'Get any post today?'

'A bit, mostly internal. Some stationery from a commercial delivery.' He indicated behind him a box that looked like printer paper, which had been shoved aside under a desk.

'Just the one? Seems a bit odd.'

'Who cares? The resource manager isn't in until Monday. He'll log it in and find out if it was what we expected.'

'May I?' Gillard asked.

Collins shrugged. 'Be my guest.' He bent over, and heaved the heavy box onto the counter where Gillard could see it. As he was doing so, Claire descended the stairs and greeted Gillard.

'What are you doing here, Craig?'

'Solving a mystery, hopefully.' He looked at the parcel, which was franked and had a typed sticky address label but no business dispatch information. He was just about to start tearing off the parcel tape, when he stopped himself. 'Hope it's not a bomb. I wouldn't put anything past this guy.' He gently picked the parcel up and walked out and down the steps into the car park.

Claire followed at a safe distance, and watched as the detective chief inspector put down the box, then brought out his own mobile phone. He punched out a number, put the phone to his ear, and then knelt down in the car park with his other ear to the box.

'It's in there,' he said. 'I've rung her number. It's on silent but I can hear the buzz.'

He walked away from the box. 'I think you'd better get the bomb disposal people to have a decko. I'm going to have a look at the bridges at Lacey Dutton.'

–

Sir Robin Loxcombe had in 1763 donated money to build a 'great stone bridge' over the River Wey at Lacey Dutton, to replace the narrow Gorlaston Bridge half a mile downstream. Gillard reckoned the local aristocrat would be turning in his grave to see the state of it now, less than a week after the flood. Reopened to traffic and controlled by temporary traffic lights, it was splinted in scaffolding. Contractors' vehicles were squeezed behind cones on the upstream side of the bridge, which had been damaged by the trees and cars that were ground against it.

The detective watched from the car park of the Jolly Boatman, before going inside to briefly greet the landlady who had been kind enough to provide him and Sam with blankets and food after the flood rescue. The detective looked at his iPad, on which the report of the fire and rescue service was displayed. It was absolutely clear that a full search had taken place at the time of the flood. But what if Sam's body had been dumped here in the last few days? He couldn't bear to hold that thought in his head, but he had to check it out.

He made his way along the bridge, walking the narrow pavement on the downstream side. He looked over the parapet, and saw that the river was getting down towards a more normal level. His earlier scouring of the Environment Agency website, and a conversation with the duty officer, had revealed that the depth of the river here was not normally sufficient to hide anything like a body for very long. The water was a thick brown mud, rather than the usual clear-running waters, and there was plenty of debris still in it. One new and quite substantial sandbank in the lee of the middle pier of the bridge held a child's pushchair, a broken table and a moped. Nearer him was a more general raft of timber: everything from bits of garden shed, right through to rustic planters and a kitchen chair, all woven together with a dense mass of torn willow branches.

Gillard made his way right over the far side of the bridge and crossed through the kissing gate into the pastures at the far side. Fortunately he had brought wellingtons, because the grassland leading down to the water on the downstream side was like a swamp. He splashed up to the water's edge, and looked under the first vaulting span. He tried to get closer, but the newly formed mudbank sucked him down almost to the top of his wellies within a few steps. He was still a good fifteen feet from the water. He shone his torch into the shadowy gloom. Endless amounts of plastic rubbish washed down from God knows where, the full David Attenborough eco-disaster. He supposed it would eventually be washed out to sea to choke some poor turtle.

The detective stared at the waters, the gentle herringbone ripples like melted chocolate. Any of this, from the sandbank to the waters themselves, could conceal the body of the woman he loved. Being here now seemed essential, an act of faith and loyalty to Sam, to look for her in the place she would most probably be found. Yet at the same time, the professional side of him knew it was a complete waste of time and effort, because unless he was to don a wetsuit and get right in there, there was no hope of spotting her.

> Under the bridge/ That's where you'll find her/ cold, with the fishes/ drowned by your own hand

That was the thing that really mystified him. Drowned by your own hand. It didn't make any sense. There was nothing he would ever do that would put Sam in danger. He just couldn't find the answer to the riddle. Even as he turned his back, he felt like he was abandoning her. Meanwhile, whoever it was who'd kidnapped her had the entire Surrey constabulary rushing around at their own bloody headquarters.

Returning to the pub, Gillard ordered a round of roast beef sandwiches with chips, and pulled up a bar stool next to the log burner, which had filled the public bar with a toasty heat. He checked his phone to see if his contact at the fire and rescue services had got back to him. Ideally he wanted a fresh search underneath not only the main Lacey Dutton bridge but at Gorlaston too, where the yellow Allegro had been trapped. He'd repeatedly viewed the YouTube footage of the inverted vehicle, bobbing away like a disconsolate toy duck.

The landlady, a solidly built woman with a helmet of dyed blonde hair and a shrewd expression, asked him about the investigation. He answered mechanically, giving away as little as possible.

Drying glasses and placing them on a rack above the bar she asked: 'The women who were in the car didn't have anything to do with each other, did they? That's what the papers say.'

'Sorry, I hope you don't mind, but I can't discuss operational matters.' He took a bite of his sandwich, which had been well seasoned with a fiery horseradish.

'Of course, they must have been connected by one thing,' she said, turning away to get more glasses from the dishwasher, and releasing a huge cloud of steam into the air. 'That is, whoever killed them, must have known them both.'

Gillard smiled and ordered a half pint of Kelham Island bitter. He recalled that the Sheffield-based brewery had itself been flooded in the past. She offered him a pint, on the house, but he demurred. He wasn't on duty, but a recognisable police officer can only be seen to down minimal levels of alcohol if he is to retain the respect of the public.

The landlady, doggedly pursuing her theme, said: 'Of course, he'd have to be quite an age to have killed one of them, wouldn't he? She's been missing for decades. Unless he was working with someone else.'

The detective looked at her. 'How's the repair work going?'

She clicked her teeth and sighed, clearly a practised expression. 'Hasn't started. Bloody insurers won't get a loss adjuster down here for a week. Got more important things to do supposedly. Luckily, the cellar didn't flood.' He let her trot out the various frustrating details of trying to put right what nature had done wrong, knowing that a sympathetic ear is in itself a small piece of catharsis.

After twenty minutes, thoroughly warmed by the heat and the food, he bade her farewell, and walked out to the car park. Just as he did so a text came through from Claire to say that the package in the car park had been detonated with a controlled explosion, and unfortunately Sam's phone had been destroyed in the process.

'Idiots!' he yelled at the phone. They weren't supposed to do that. They needed the SIM card to find out if the texts had been set in advance. That information was probably lost for good now. He got into the car and sat head in hands, wondering what he could do. Then his phone rang. It was the head of the anti-kidnap unit. He wanted to see Gillard ASAP and was on his way to meet him.

–

Gillard sat in the front passenger seat of an unmarked Ford Galaxy in the car park of the Jolly Boatman, watching the rain patter down on the windscreen. In the driver's seat was Detective Chief Superintendent Rajinder Otara, a veteran of anti-terrorism operations and an experienced hostage negotiator. Over the last forty minutes, Gillard had told the Sikh officer everything that he knew about the abduction and murder of Beatrice Ulbricht, his near-death experience with an olive green Mitsubishi Warrior, and the abduction of his wife.

Otara had listened carefully. 'We've already had a chance to re-examine the CCTV footage from the train and the platforms, the cell site analysis of the various mobile phones, as well as your fitness tracker. We've been impressed, actually, by the resourcefulness of many of your team, including you.'

'Thank you.'

'We're expecting the hostage taker to contact you or Surrey Police again, to try to twist the knife a little. To that end, the first thing we did last night was to put a full real-time monitoring system in place on your home and work phones and mobiles, as well as your email. We should get us an almost immediate trace on the location of any caller. It's not foolproof, of course. It's clear that you are up against at least one perpetrator who has advanced technical skills. And at least one, possibly the same one, who has a grudge against you.'

'I've put a few people away in my time.'

Otara stroked his neat beard. 'Yes, but I'm particularly intrigued by your wife's ex-boyfriend Gary Harrison. DI Claire Mulholland thinks he is possibly the best candidate, although it's unclear whether he would have the technical skills we have seen exhibited. We have two research specialists trying to trace him, going back through everything we know from him in his army days and when he was a chef.'

'If it is him, he might kill Sam,' Gillard said. 'It won't be about money, it's about getting even with me.' He described his own attempts to trace Harrison's whereabouts.

'I agree. Having seen the messages, this is clearly not a conventional kidnap case. That makes it difficult because there are no demands, no cash we can offer and precious little to negotiate about.'

'What is your strategy then?' Gillard said.

'Trace the car. Our perpetrator has been moving around a lot, transporting corpses and who knows what else. That is the weakest link, and unlike with phones it's more difficult for him to give us a false signal.'

Gillard nodded. It was a logical conclusion.

'So, as he seems to be pretty good at staying off main roads, we are ramping up a surveillance operation with twenty mobile ANPR cameras concealed in parked vehicles on various back roads between Woking and Lacey Dutton on the western edge, and right across to Croydon and Caterham in the east. We are putting together an analysis of all the cell site data we have accumulated, not only on Beatrice Ulbricht's phone, but on your wife's too, or what we've been able to recover from it. We are monitoring her social media accounts to see if anything pops up there.'

'That's all very well,' Gillard said. 'But I think our suspect has gone to ground. He's done all the driving, all the texting, and all the setting up he needs. He's watching to see if we can find him. And my gut feeling is that he has eyes and ears in the police.'

–

With Mount Browne like a disturbed ants' nest, and overrun with the bomb disposal people, NCA officers and miscellaneous spooks, DI John Perry took Rainy Macintosh to a small conference room, where they could shut out the mayhem and he could give his full attention to what she'd learned in the Jane Morris case.

'Boss, after yuz alerted me to the chance that Jane Morris had given birth, I checked through one of those ancestry websites. You might not know this but you can get school attendance records from it as well as births, marriages and deaths. Because of the unusually common name, it took me a while to work out which South London secondary school wee Janey had been to. Then I realised I was being stupid, because one of the photographs released at the time showed her in school uniform. What I discovered was that she had not attended at all in the six months prior to her death.'

'What is the significance—?'

'Och, sir, it's obvious. Schools didn't like to have pregnant schoolgirls swanning about. Advertises moral degradation, all that shite.'

'When I was a schoolteacher we had several pregnant girls,' Perry said.

'Aye, but that is since the 1996 Education Act, which made it compulsory for teenage mums to complete their education. Back in the 1980s, well, it was still a stain on a school as well as a family. The parents may well have kept her away.'

Frank and Eileen Morris. Perry wondered just what they might have known of their daughter's activities. If she looked pregnant, they might well have withdrawn her from school. And what did Uncle Harold the fishmonger really see the day she disappeared? As before, the answers could only come from evidence in the present day.

'Have any DNA samples come to light for our suspect?' Perry asked.

'Nope. Every sample we have has been accounted for by a witness or one of us.'

'That's a shame, I just had a little theory that I was going to test. But as I've got nothing to test it against, I'll have to leave it.'

'What's your theory?'

It seemed so outlandish that Perry was reluctant to tell her. 'I was just wondering if Jane Morris' baby grew up to be our killer.'

'You mean the wee twisted lad hung on to his frozen teenage mum as a kind of keepsake?'

'Yes.'

'But that means someone else killed and froze the poor wee hen.'

Perry laughed nervously. 'It would be just too bizarre, wouldn't it?'

She put her hands on her ample hips. 'So you're looking for someone a bit more normal to be responsible for two stranglings and an abduction?' Macintosh gave a dry laugh. 'You could be on to something, sir. It's just a shame the bomb squad blew up the package containing Sam Gillard's phone. You could expect a DNA or fingerprint lift off that screen when he was sending messages.'

'We didn't get one off Beatrice's phone.'

'Aye, that's because it was smeared in Coca-Cola. That stuff's super-acidic. One other thing, sir. I checked up the witness you asked me about, Betty Garrison. The dead girl's grandmother is still alive, at the grand age of a hundred and one, living in a care home in Carshalton.'

–

Perry set off for Carshalton with a sheaf of cuttings. It seemed like the perfect time to visit, and it had the great benefit of deferring having to go home. He found Mrs Garrison in her private room, sitting up in bed watching TV. She gave him a waspish look, and demanded: 'Who the hell are you?' She muted the TV with her remote.

She was a substantial old lady with wattles of blotchy skin hanging down from her chin, and swollen arthritic hands the size and texture of old gardening gloves. Only a few wisps of hair clung to her skull. The care worker who had escorted Perry in had reassured him that Mrs Garrison was still lucid and in control, but did have a bit of a temper. 'It's probably what has kept her alive all these years, even after her children have died,' the woman said.

Perry introduced himself and showed his detective ID card.

'Did I just park my Rolls-Royce in the wrong place?' She guffawed at her own joke.

'No, Mrs Garrison. It's about something—'

'Ah, yes. Still digging for my granddaughter after all these years, then?' she said softly, her face tightening.

Perry explained slowly and carefully about the recovery of Jane's body. 'We believe she has been kept frozen for nearly forty years.'

'I heard about it. I expect you think that my son Harold did it, don't you? Him having a fish freezer and all.'

'We are keeping an open mind.'

'Are you now?' she asked with a slight smile. 'That would be a first for the filth.'

Perry thought carefully about how to approach this prickly woman, his last remaining potential witness. If she didn't cooperate, he'd be stuck. 'Before I get to all that, Mrs Garrison, can I ask you about your grandson, Graeme?'

She began to cough violently, bringing up something liquid into a handkerchief that she apparently kept for the purpose by her bedside. 'I've not seen that one for a long time.'

'Since when?'

'He came crawling round asking for money more than ten years ago. He knew that we'd finally sold the Balham properties, that was my house and the shop in Hildreth Street, for a tidy sum, so I could come and live here. He just assumed there would be lots spare. Just like his bloody father.'

'That would be Harold.'

'Yes, my Harold, God rest his twisted soul.'

'Tell me about Graeme's childhood. I presume you enjoyed playing with him in the early years?'

She narrowed her eyes and pursed her lips. 'He was a difficult baby, always crying as I recall. By the time he was seven or eight, he was quite big and he used to bully the girls out in the street. Hair pulling, pinching, stuff like that. My Harold tried to thrash it out of him, but it was no good. What comes from bad always turns bad doesn't it?'

'Why do you say Graeme comes from bad?'

The old woman licked her lips, but said nothing.

Perry saw his opportunity: 'Graeme wasn't Linda's child, was he? He was Jane's.'

A shadow passed over her face, an ancient agony which distended her mouth. With a supreme effort she organised her features into the matriarchal antagonism that had presumably served her well for decades. 'Well, well, the good old British bobby gets there in the end. Even if it takes nearly half a century.' She felt for a fresh tissue, and dabbed the corner of her eyes.

'Care to tell me about it?' Perry said.

She sighed deeply, clicked off the TV, and then continued. 'Look. I've seen everyone I ever cared about die, you know. First was Linda, then Frank, my Harold and finally Eileen. She hung on until the end, hoping to find out what happened to her daughter before she died. But in my heart I always knew. It was a truth too terrible to tell.'

Perry waited while she composed herself. 'Jane told her mum, when she was about three months gone. Frank was enraged, concerned about his standing among the neighbours, many of whom were regulars at his betting shop, especially after Harold whispered to his brother in law that he'd seen her talking to West Indians. Eileen was religious, and wouldn't hear of letting the girl have an abortion. Jane wouldn't say who the father was, but I thought I knew.'

'What gave you the suspicion?'

'Linda and Harold had tried for a baby for years and got nowhere. Linda was just consumed with the desire to be a mother, and I think Harold had suggested years ago that they adopt. I had known that my Harold liked young girls, but I never guessed that he had taken advantage of his own niece, until Eileen whispered to me one day that her little Jane was pregnant.'

'How did they conceal it?'

'I think Harold threatened Jane to keep her mouth shut. And it would have destroyed the family, no mistake. Harold and Linda offered to bring up the child, and Linda dressed up for a pregnancy that she didn't have. It seemed like the best solution. Frank got a bent doctor to write a series of false sick notes for Jane saying she had glandular fever, and pulled her out of school. Harold and Linda moved across to a rented flat on the other side of the High Road, to be on the safe side, away from nosy neighbours and Jane's friends. The girl didn't leave the flat for months once she began to show. So in November 1981, on the settee in that poky flat in Wandsworth, I delivered my granddaughter's baby. It was a tiny little thing, just an angry red bundle of noise and fists. But it wasn't black, thank God.' Seeing Perry's expression, she hurriedly added: 'Not that I'm racial, mind. It just would have been harder to pass off as Harold and Linda's.'

'What about registering the birth, midwife visits and so on?'

'The same bent doctor sorted that out. He had some gambling debts that Frank let him off. By the time social services and the NHS heard about little Graeme, he was already a toddler.'

'But he would only have been six months old when Jane disappeared,' Perry said. 'I'm really surprised police didn't look more closely into the origin of that child when your granddaughter disappeared.'

'The Garrison family knows how to keep its gob shut. Besides, we had a story to tell that the police in those days liked to hear: gone off with a darkie.'

Perry recoiled at the epithet. 'Did you suspect that Harold had killed her?'

'Not at first. But I had noticed how she looked at him so accusing like. I think she wanted her baby back. And she used to cry a lot. We told the police how she'd been quite listless and down with the glandular and all that, and that was true. She was a living misery after we gave her baby away to Linda. I think everybody was worried that she was going to grass her uncle up.'

'When did you know it was him?'

'I think it was when he sold up the business, and bought some warehouse space somewhere to set up a fish wholesaler. I thought, "I bet poor Jane is in the freezer".'

'Weren't you ever tempted to tell the police?'

'And throw my family to the wolves? Not on your nellie. No, the nearest I got was when Harold died in 2002. Graeme came to see me, and said he would sort out the sale of all his fish stuff, which had lain unused in some warehouse somewhere since he got ill and closed down the wholesaler. Hello, I thought, what's going on here. That Graeme never offered to do anything for nothing. Even then he was a smarmy one, trying his charm to get round me.'

'Did you have an address for this wholesale business?'

'No. I'd lost interest. I think it was somewhere in Surrey. But as they always say, tell me no secrets and I'll tell you no lies.'

–

After he had finished the interview Perry picked up his notes and drove off towards his home in Woking. The datasticks now contained photographs of all the historic case records, witness statements, interview records and so on from 1982 that he had picked up from the archives in Tooting, and now this crucial evidence on tape from the grandmother. He emailed off a digital copy of the interview to DC Rainy Macintosh and DCS Rajinder Otara.

He wasn't going to go straight home, though. His sanity depended on not having to confront Mel again. Last night he had slept in the car in a country lane, and if necessary he would do it again tonight. He could keep the laptop charged from the USB port in the car, and could pretty much do what he needed to do.

Perry parked his unmarked VW Polo by the site office of the Shepherds' Rest estate and set the dash cam so it would capture all the vehicle movements through this, the only entrance to the estate. If a black Range Rover passed, he would spot it.

He rang Rainy Macintosh, who had been researching all the British suppliers and distributors of ultra-low temperature freezers. 'Hiya boss,' she said with her usual level of cheerful Glaswegian insubordination. 'Still at work on a Saturday evening?'

'Not exactly,' he replied. *Just planning revenge against my wife's lover, as one does.*

She told him that most of the freezers were used in medicine, mainly designed for small samples. They would generally be too small to hold a human body. They were also pretty expensive.

'I've been on to the four biggest suppliers, and they do keep customer lists because of a servicing requirement. Most of them are companies or universities or research institutes.'

'What about the exceptions?' Perry asked.

'Aye, if you go on eBay or Alibaba, there are all sorts of manufacturers you can deal with directly. If it's a Japanese tuna freezer, or walk-in freezer room, you can get one made to order. These are going to be much harder to trace so—'

'Sorry to interrupt. I'll call you back later.' Perry had spotted a black Range Rover entering the estate. He shut the laptop lid, tossed it onto the passenger seat and watched as the vehicle went past him. The driver was a bulky male wearing sunglasses. Once it had turned onto Southdown Way, Perry followed at a discreet distance. The target turned left into Ryeland Drive. His own home was on Romney Crook, the next turning on the right. He willed the vehicle to make the turning, but it did not. Instead it continued up the slight hill, and into Wensleydale Walk, parking outside number sixteen, in the same half on, half off the curb fashion that Perry had witnessed outside his own home. This must be him. The man who makes my wife howl with pleasure.

Bastard.

Perry didn't dare draw attention to himself by stopping, but drove past and into a cul-de-sac beyond. He turned the car around, stopped for a couple of minutes and then drove back at low speed. The driver was nowhere to be seen.

That was fine. Perry would come back later.

He drove home, and was relieved to see no sign of his wife's Audi. Ideally, he wanted to get his hands on her phone and examine the call records to really work out what had been happening, but Mel was a very canny woman and the device was never out of her sight. In fact it was a toss-up whether Mel or Vanessa spent more time glued to their phones.

Once into his home office, he picked up the phone, intending to ring Rainy back. Then he stopped. There was something he wanted to do first. Something about the Wensleydale Walk address was familiar. He logged on to the local crime database and discovered that, yes, this was the house from which the Mitsubishi Warrior had been stolen a couple of weeks ago. He looked up the details of the couple from the electoral register. Kyle Halliday and Angela Wright. There were no previous entries for him.

Perry looked back through his emails, and found one that had been sent all around by DC Hoskins, headlined 'The tale of the flying slipper', attached to which was the video from Halliday's CCTV. He had glimpsed it once at the office already, but now took a more detailed look. His adversary in love had certainly been courageous, rushing out to stop the thief. The comical partial disrobing, and the obviously painful fall, made Perry chuckle. Whichever German coined the word *schadenfreude*, delight in the misfortune of others, had clearly understood the innate cruelty of the human soul. The man was certainly muscular and well-developed. Trying to confront him physically, however tempting, might be stupid. There would be better ways.

After three viewings, Perry set aside project vengeance, and got on with the day job. But at last he had a smile on his face.

–

Twenty-four hours on from the start of Project Hawkeye, NCA resources had filled up the surveillance suite at Surrey Police headquarters. The mobile ANPR units were parked along key junctions on the patchwork of minor roads within the target area. They sent in a constant stream of data which was assessed in real-time by two specialist officers. So far, the Mitsubishi Warrior and Sam's black Renault had eluded them. On the row behind, a supervisor and assistant were overseeing another five plainclothes officers in the field, visiting places within Surrey where ultra-low-temperature freezers were known to be installed. Next to them were two officers tasked with monitoring the various phones.

The usual bane of electronic monitoring in policing is delay. But with the power and technology available to the National Crime Agency, that had been almost eliminated. There was one final thing that Otara wanted, and it could not be obtained without the signature of the Home Secretary. On a Saturday, and even with the help of the chief constable, making the case to the Home Secretary's duty officials had taken a few hours. But finally, permission had been granted. Reading the confirming email, Otara raised a fist above his head and yelled: 'We've got permission! GCHQ are sending us their top expert. First thing tomorrow.'

One of the officers monitoring the phones hissed for quiet. 'I've got something,' she said. She turned on the microphone, and they listened in mounting horror to a message just left for Gillard on his home landline.

Chapter Fifteen

Gillard was back at home by five. He had been encouraged by his meeting with DCS Raj Otara. The National Crime Agency had the resources to get to grips with the kidnap, but he still felt that he should be contributing. Otara had encouraged him to ring if he had any fresh ideas, but there were one or two things he wanted to do himself. He was aware that the person Sam had spoken to most in the last couple of weeks was Ellen, the old friend who had been a police cadet with her. She was the only person who'd been given their address in the last two weeks.

He had no idea what the surname was, and CSI had taken Sam's laptop, which would have given him access to her Facebook page. Using his own laptop, he tried to log into Sam's account, making a number of guesses at the password. After fifteen minutes he had got nowhere. At one level he was impressed that it wasn't easy to guess, but right now it was very frustrating. He recalled that Ellen worked as a receptionist at a vet's practice in Bedfordshire. Going through Sam's address book, he found a number for a vet, and rang it. As he did so, he heard the landline downstairs going, and then half a minute later the call-waiting flashed up on his mobile. It was DCS Otara from the NCA. Nobody had replied at the vet, which was probably closed for the evening, so Gillard hung up and took the waiting call.

'Craig, the kidnapper has just left a message on your landline. Listen to it, and call me back with your thoughts ASAP. We're getting a trace.' Otara cut the line.

Gillard ran downstairs to the telephone table in the hall and saw the new message light was flashing. With an unsteady finger, he pressed the button.

> 'Craig. You are being rather dim. It's gone five in the afternoon, and I'm here with Sam. I can't put her on the line, because she's gagged. In fact she is rather trussed up alto-gether. I've been enjoying her again, Craig, in a variety of ways, but I'm getting a little bored now. And you know what happens when I get bored. She only has twenty-four hours to live. That's five p.m. on Sunday afternoon. Tomorrow. Do you think you can find her in time? Frankly, I doubt it. But I do know you'll try.'

The hinted abuse made the detective's guts feel like they were trying to turn inside out. He forced down the rising bile, and tried to quarantine his emotions. Poor Sam. What she must be suffering. He didn't have time to indulge his rage, but it was there, a gathering shadow over everything.

Twenty-four hours!

The voice, that's what he must concentrate on. He didn't recognise it at all. It was hard to match it against his memory of the shouts of the man who tried to run him over. What he could hear now was a southern accent, almost jaunty, not London particularly, nor Essex. Could it be Gary Harrison? He had been her boyfriend, so enjoying her 'again' might reference that. Gillard had never heard him talk. The one perfect person to have answered that question was of course poor Sam herself. This was a really important piece of evidence. The NCA would have access to linguistic experts who could narrow down the origin of this accent to within a few square miles. But probably not within twenty-four hours.

Gillard played the message again, recording it on his mobile, then rang the incident room, getting straight through to Otara. The NCA expert was ecstatic about the trace they had got on the caller's mobile. 'Fantastic, we were hoping for a breakthrough like this. We've got a location, in the village of Westmeare.'

'Westmeare?' His first thought was Adrian Singer, who lived there, but had gradually been sidelined as a suspect. The voice Gillard had heard on the message was quite different from the more cultured tones of the music teacher.

'We've three cars on their way, the first is just three minutes away,' Otara said. 'Stay strong!'

He cut the line, leaving Gillard staring at the handset. He had never felt so impotent. He was just thinking about how to track down Ellen when the landline rang. He picked it up.

'Is that Craig Gillard?' The voice was female and vaguely familiar.

'Yes,' he said cautiously.

'It's Ellen Bramley, Sam's friend—'

'Ah, what a coincidence! I've been trying to track you down.'

'Craig, I'm so sorry I didn't call earlier. I heard from one of the other former cadets that something terrible's happened to Sam. That she's disappeared or something.'

Chief Constable Alison Rigby had made clear that not a whisper of the kidnapping was to leave Mount Browne, not even to family members or close friends. A round robin from her to all Surrey Police staff warned that even a single article in the press might jeopardise Sam's life. Gillard had only been given permission to let Sam's parents know after reassuring the higher-ups that they could keep a secret.

'Ellen, this is really, really important. I can't tell you what has happened to Sam, except that her life is in grave danger.'

The cry of sympathy, and a great rush of questions, brought Gillard's own emotions close to the surface. He fought hard to keep his own voice steady. 'Ellen, we don't have much time and I need you to help me, even if you think the information I'm requesting may be sensitive and not relevant. I need to ask you some questions about your ex-boyfriend.'

'Gabriel?'

'Yes. Do you have a surname and an address for him?'

'Gabriel Hallam.' She read out an address in Fleet, Hampshire. 'I don't think he's there much. Why are you asking about him? Is it about the money he borrowed from me?'

'Amongst other things. Has he paid it back?'

'No.' There was a catch in her throat. 'I've not seen him at all.'

Gillard feared she was about to cry. 'Ellen, do you have a work address for him?'

'Only a phone number. He's self-employed. Something in tech, travels all the time.' She passed it over. It was a mobile number. 'Why are you asking about him?'

'Gabriel was due to come with you to a dinner party here, but couldn't come. That's right, isn't it?'

'Yes.'

'But you had given him this address?'

'Yes, he said he might be a little late so would come independently.'

Gillard wrote down a few more questions as they occurred to him.

'How did you meet him? Was it online?'

'No. His car broke down just outside my house, and he knocked on the door for help.'

'When was that?'

'Sunday, 12 January.' The precision of her response showed what a significant moment it was in her life. Gillard felt sorry for her, but didn't have the time to indulge it.

'What kind of car did he have?'

'A black Range Rover. But it wasn't his only one.'

'What was the other vehicle?'

She blew a long sigh. 'I don't know. It was big and green, though. We went out in it for one of our early dates.' She thought for a moment. 'It had a little funnel thing on it, that stuck up like a chimney.'

The Warrior? Gillard's mind reeled. 'That's a snorkel, for deep water use. Did it have an open pick-up back?'

'Yes.'

'I don't suppose you know the registration numbers?'

'Sorry.'

'Ellen, do you have any pictures of him?'

'I did. He hated having his photo taken, because he had this scar. He forbade me to show anyone, he said that people were after him.'

'Can you email me the pictures?'

He could hear her voice dissolving now. 'No, no I can't. I deleted them both when he dumped me. And now I wish I hadn't.' Her voice tailed off into a full blown bout of crying.

I wish you hadn't, too. 'Ellen, I need you to bring your phone to a police station for forensic examination. We have people who may be able to retrieve the deleted photographs. You have to do this immediately, do you understand? I'm really sorry to have to ask this, but it's extremely important.' He asked her where her nearest police station was, and he made a note to get an NCA officer over there immediately with a portable data extraction kiosk. Finally, he had the momentous decision to make over whether to let her listen to the phone message he had just received. Any hope of keeping the nature of the crime secret would go, but if she recognised his voice, it would crack the case right open.

'Okay, Ellen. I'm going to let you in on the secret.' He held his mobile next to the answer machine and pressed play.

> 'Craig. You are being rather dim. It's gone five in the afternoon, and I'm here with Sam.'

He attempted to click stop on the machine at this point, but the buttons were tiny and for some reason it ran on and took two more attempts. So she also heard: '*I can't put her on the line, because she's gagged. In fact she is rather trussed up altogether. I've been enjoying her again, Craig, in a variety of ways, but—'*

Ellen's scream of betrayal drowned out the rest.

Chapter Sixteen

It was DI Claire Mulholland's bad luck that she was in the first car responding to the location tracked by the NCA team. Sat in the back, she was hanging on for grim death as the BMW touched eighty along winding country lanes heading for Westmeare. In front of her, two long-haired leather jacket-clad detectives called Worrell and Blunt seemed to think they were starring in a Netflix drama series. Blunt's extravagant revving and gear changing almost seemed designed to attract attention. He kept up a banter with Worrell at a low enough volume not to be heard in the back, and largely ignored her. She may have been senior to both, but they clearly regarded her as extraneous baggage. Just a local plod along for the ride.

'It's not very far,' Worrell said, looking down at the iPad on which the short trace of the burner phone was illustrated against a Google map. 'Down here somewhere,' he said to Blunt. The phone had been turned off within a minute of leaving a voicemail message at Gillard's, and had been on for only a couple of minutes beforehand.

They shot past the Westmeare bus stop, the last place where Beatrice Ulbricht, at least the real Beatrice Ulbricht, had been seen. 'Stop here,' Claire said. 'This will be the place.'

Blunt ignored her and instead took an instruction from Worrell to turn right, with a G-force that would have thrown Claire across the car had she not been belted in. Adrian Singer's cottage flashed past at missile speed.

'Blunt!' bellowed Claire. 'Stop the fucking car, that's an order.'

She saw his eyes slide to Worrell and a slight smile before he jammed the brake on so hard that Claire almost joined them in the front. The BMW slid sideways, tyres smoking, clipping a hedge until Blunt, steering into the skid, straightened it up, then whipped the vehicle round 180 degrees.

'Stop being such a little wanker, detective constable,' she said.

He tugged a generous forelock towards her. 'Yes, ma'am.' He managed to make even that sound insubordinate.

'Give me the iPad. I think you'll find the message was sent from the bus stop.'

Worrell tossed the device over his shoulder without looking at her. She caught it, got out of the car and walked the hundred yards back to the bus stop. It was a precise match for the location. She looked around the bus shelter and noticed that on the wooden seat was a pair of women's knickers. Basic M&S cotton jobs.

A message, no doubt. She took a small plastic evidence bag from her shoulder bag, and carefully picked up the item. The BMW was idling on the other side of the road, and she crossed over and resumed her position in the back seat.

'Find anything, ma'am?'

'A pair of women's knickers.'

Their heads swivelled to look at her in precise symmetry. 'Let's have a decko,' Worrell said, with a bit more than professional enthusiasm.

'Use your imagination. I'm sure you have plenty of stock images stored there.' She rang the incident room to report her find. Otara was put on the line.

'We have a dashcam ANPR camera just two hundred yards away,' he said. 'Bracketing vehicle movements five minutes either side of the message time, we got a quite manageable seventeen hits that we are currently processing. Stay in position.' He hung up.

Claire relayed the message to Worrell and Blunt. She looked out of the window and saw on the side road Adrian Singer walking down the road towards them. It didn't look like a planned walk on such a chilly spring day because he was in a lightweight jumper, shorts and Crocs. He looked up and down the road, and rubbed his arms for warmth, before walking over to the BMW.

Claire lowered the rear window and said: 'Hello. Remember me?'

'Yes. There were some boy racers going up and down the road just a few minutes ago. I could hear them even from the back of the house,' he said.

'I'll keep an eye out,' she replied.

'So what are you doing?'

At this point Blunt slid down his window and forcefully told the man to return immediately to his home. Singer recoiled at the directness of the order, and radiated indignation as he retraced his steps.

'…and Blunt by nature,' Claire said archly.

'He could blow our cover, ma'am.'

'Detective Constable Blunt, I fear it is your adolescent driving that is responsible for that.'

—

'I can't believe it! This was the man who said he had never loved anyone like he loved me. This was the man who made me go to the gym before work, who threw away and burned half my wardrobe because it was too frumpy, the man who went through my phone deleting the phone numbers of any male friends, the man who deleted all friend requests on Facebook. He claimed to be so besotted with me, the new slimmed-down me, that he couldn't ever look at anybody else.' Ellen's sobbing tirade poured out.

'I know he exploited you terribly, but if I may—'

'Do you know, Craig, what he did for me on the night of my birthday?'

'Ellen, please.' Gillard had the tricky task of trying to coax this scorned and deeply wounded woman away from her pain, and to focus on the here and now. He had very little time and needed to get from her every piece of information that might save Sam.

'Gabriel made me a beautiful birthday cake, cherries and icing and everything. All gluten-free too. I don't know how he found the time. He must have loved me, mustn't he?'

'I don't know, Ellen, people do strange things.'

It took another five minutes to calm her down, and as long again to get his questions answered. However it was already clear how little Ellen really knew about the man she had loved. Gillard rounded off the call by once again pledging her to secrecy, and reminding her to take her phone in to the nearest police station. 'Your prompt action could save Sam's life,' he said.

He ended the call gently, then rang Otara with all the information he had acquired.

'Gabriel Hallam is the man we should be looking for. Ellen Bramley recognised his voice very clearly.' Gillard said. 'I think it was he who stole the Mitsubishi Warrior. I think you also need to get a victim liaison officer to Ms Bramley. She is not only emotionally vulnerable, but she may need protecting if Hallam comes back.'

'Okay, we'll do that.' He told Gillard about the women's underwear and the call made from the bus stop. 'We've got some promising ANPR hits too, that we're currently analysing. None on the vehicles of interest list, and not surprisingly no sign of the Warrior. If our suspect drives through even the tiniest back lane in Westmeare, one of our mobile units will certainly have captured the registration number.'

'What if he walked?' Gillard said.

There was a short silence at the other end. 'Well, that hasn't fitted his M.O. so far, has it?'

'Who knows? He's devious enough.'

'If so, one of our officers will spot him,' Otara said, then hung up.

'But you don't really know what he looks like do you?' Gillard muttered to himself as he looked down at his jotter.

Gabriel Hallam. Gary Harrison. G and H. It made a lot of sense. Harrison must have groomed Ellen to get close to Sam, to find out where she lived. The cold, controlling strategy, played for the long-term, was chilling. And that meant Harrison was the thief who had stolen the Warrior.

The biggish bloke in a car coat, identified by the owner who had rushed out to save his car.

A frown crossed Gillard's face. He rang Ellen Bramley back, but the landline she had called him from went unanswered. Of course, he had just insisted she rush off to the police station.

Damn. He really needed to ask her a couple more questions and he didn't have her mobile number. She had told him that Gabriel Hallam had driven the Warrior on one of their early dates. But from what he half-remembered Sam telling him, Ellen had been going out with Gabriel for months. He re-read his notes. That's right, since January. But the Warrior had been stolen less than two weeks ago. If Ellen's recollection was correct, and this was the same green Mitsubishi Warrior, then Gary Harrison wasn't just Gabriel Hallam.

He was also Kyle Halliday.

Because that early date with Bramley must have occurred *before* the Warrior was stolen. Who else could have been driving it but Halliday? Unless he was in the habit of lending his car out.

Gillard held his head in his hands. The new explanation didn't make any more sense than the old one. Because as every member of the CID had seen, in the 'case of the flying slipper', someone really had stolen the car from Halliday. He couldn't have stolen it from himself, because there was CCTV showing him running out to stop the car. And CCTV doesn't lie.

Moreover, some big bloke in a car coat and ski mask had used the vehicle to try to run him down. And that was well after it was stolen. At a time when Kyle Halliday was still on crutches. Either way, there must now be a big question mark over Halliday's witness account.

The detective felt his brain was going to explode. Worst of all, none of this conjecture seemed to bring him any closer to finding Sam.

–

John Perry had been off duty from six. No longer the detective inspector, he could get back to his freelance operation. He was sitting in his VW Polo just down the road from 16 Wensleydale Walk. At 6.42 p.m. the same athletic-looking, dark-haired man he had seen before exited the house, got into the black Range Rover and drove off. Perry was tempted to follow him, but there would be other opportunities for that. He had seen a woman's face at the window, and thought it might be a good opportunity to speak to her. Angela Wright, thirty-three, a company director at AWL Property. He'd found out quite a lot about her from LinkedIn. Perry wondered if she knew what her partner's 'hobbies' were. He had the perfect excuse to get a little closer.

He waited a few minutes and then went up and rang the doorbell.

The woman who answered was tall and arrestingly attractive, seemingly dressed for a night out.

'Detective Inspector John Perry,' he said, showing his card.

'Is it about the stolen car? Because if it is, Kyle's just gone. He'll be away in Madrid on business for a couple of days.'

'I just need to double-check a few details with you.'

She sighed and rolled her deep blue eyes before showing him in. She had long wavy dark hair, one of those lacy black blouses that hint at the underwear beneath, and a grey knee-length pleated skirt. With the high heels she had at least four inches on him. Perry was juggling with unfamiliar emotions. His years as a schoolteacher, seeing in pupils the damage caused by self-image worries, had stopped him judging women by their appearance. After leaving education and joining the police he had been shocked by the outdated attitude amongst male colleagues, whose treatment of women was often, to put it mildly, Neanderthal. But right now, his own testosterone was surfacing. This long dormant part of him wanted to try to seduce this woman, to treat her like Kyle Halliday had treated Mel. He caught a glimpse of himself in the hall mirror, and common sense intervened. A thinning-haired, paunchy forty-two-year-old with a hangdog expression who was, he had recently been assured, under-equipped to please any woman. Ugly, but definitely angry.

The woman introduced herself as Angie. 'I'm due out in half an hour,' she said, clacking round the kitchen in her heels. 'So I hope I can answer your questions quickly.'

Perry had not really planned in detail what he was going to ask, and, feeling rather nervous, asked her to describe what she had heard on the night of the car theft. 'Well, I didn't hear too much at first; it was just when Kyle woke up and ran downstairs.'

He made notes and then asked: 'I understand you are a company director?'

'Yes, industrial property company. Bits and pieces really, all over Surrey and on the other side of the M4.'

'What does your partner do?'

'He's a self-employed international telecoms consultant.'

'Where is he based?'

'All over. He works a lot on the move, or from his home office here. But he is actually one of my own tenants as well.' She trotted out an address. 'He was kind enough to take one of the most unsaleable dumps I have, up near Pirbright. I think he keeps his jet ski there.' She looked at her watch anxiously, and said. 'So overall, has there been any progress on recovering the Warrior?'

'No. But we're trying to tie this crime in with others.' Perry really wanted to ask permission to take a look around, but he could see that the woman was worried about the time. There would always be another opportunity, and in the meantime he had an address to work with. She showed him out, and closed the door behind him. He waited a few seconds, standing between the two large planters that framed the doorway, then reached into his pocket for a roll of insulation tape that he'd had the presence of mind to bring with him. He knew from watching the CCTV of the car theft that he was standing in the blind spot of the camera mounted two feet above the front door. With his teeth he tore off a small strip, Íthen stepped up and carefully balanced himself on one of the planters so he could reach it. He stuck the strip over the camera lens.

Blanking out the CCTV would be essential for when he came back later that night.

–

Like Perry, PC Lynne Fairbanks was also off duty on Saturday night. She was waiting with a certain sense of anticipation on a bar stool in the cocktail bar of the Gilded

Swan, an exclusive eatery at Walton-on-Thames. Her date for the evening was running a little late, but had apparently called ahead and got them to serve her a bottle of chilled champagne. Now *that* was style. By contrast, the last time her boyfriend Michael had deigned to take her out, they had shared a mediocre pizza while she listened to him whining about money the whole time. Michael thought she was working the overnight shift helping on the Ulbricht murder case.

As she sipped her drink at the bar, the ice bucket at her elbow, she saw Kyle Halliday making his way across the crowded room. A big smile, the open-necked mauve shirt over that V-shaped physique, and his tight jeans.

'Hello, you sexy beast,' she said, watching his eyes as they were drawn down to the low-cut blouse she had deliberately worn. She stroked the slight silvery scar which ran down along his jawline.

'I've been thinking about you, Lynne. I hope you're enjoying the bubbles.' He topped up her glass, poured one for himself and toasted her, leaning in between her thighs against the bar stool, and kissing her delicately on the forehead. Already she could feel the heat of him down there, and eased forward on the bar stool to make contact.

The excitement of their tryst just a few days ago was still fresh in her mind; indeed, she'd hardly been able to think about anything else than what Kyle had done to her while she sat on his kitchen worktop. It was hard to believe he had ever needed a crutch to get about, given the athleticism and sheer stamina he had shown. The fact that he had booked a room for them both upstairs for tonight seemed to hint at a repeat performance.

She wasn't a fool. Kyle might be a beautiful man, but she was fully aware he was a bit out of her league. It wasn't her job to go barging into his relationship, trying to take ownership. The occasional exciting night would be enough.

As they sat down he said, 'I want to know all about you, Lynne, how such a lovely sensitive woman fought her way through as a cop. I imagine you need fairly sharp elbows given what a male organisation the police is.'

She smiled. 'It's not as bad as it used to be, but there are still plenty of old-fashioned attitudes. Funnily enough it's supposed to be easier for women once you start getting promoted. There are loads of female chief constables now, and they've proved themselves as tough as the men.'

He let her talk, asking intelligent questions, and seemed to be listening to everything she said.

'When I first got your message,' she said. 'I just thought you wanted to persuade me to prioritise the theft investigation. But I realised I misjudged you.'

He laughed, an infectious chuckle that seemed to dissolve his face. 'Well, don't get me wrong. I do want to know that you're all working flat out on it, but like your bullying colleague said, it's probably in bits in a crate on its way abroad.'

'My bullying colleague?'

'Yes. DC Hoskins. I watched him. He talked over you, rolled his eyes at me when you were giving your theory, and generally treated you like a doormat. I hope you don't mind me saying?'

Lynne was taken aback. 'I'm just impressed you noticed. Most men wouldn't.'

'Can't stand that kind of behaviour,' he said, rotating the stem of his champagne glass as he stared into the drink. 'Of course, once upon a time…' He shook his head, as if at a painful memory. 'Look. I'm different from how I used to be. I was once a paratrooper, did a tour of duty in Helmand, and actually realised I wasn't mentally tough enough for some of the things I saw.' He described seeing a couple of colleagues terribly wounded by road-side bombs. 'I lay on my bunk shivering. I thought I'd become a coward or something, but I just couldn't face it. I was diagnosed with PTSD, and ended up coming home.'

She stroked his face again. 'No one would ever guess about your vulnerable side.' Now she wanted to know about his wife, to find out how damaged the marriage was, but he seemed to read her mind.

'You don't want to worry about Angie. We've been more like friends for nearly two years now. It's the nature of my work that destroyed our relationship, and I do feel guilty about it. Don't get me wrong, I do care about her, particularly her being alone so many nights now we got broken into, but we go our own way a lot of the time.'

Kyle talked about his American-born sister, stuck in an expensive Colorado hospital since breaking her spine in a ski-ing accident a year ago. 'She'd just broken up with her bastard of a husband, a big real estate guy, and wasn't covered for most of the treatment she needed on his health plan. I've been trying to raise the cash she needs for co-payments, but you know how outrageous the sums are that they charge over there. I've had to mortgage the house, and I keep hoping we can shift her back here, but the immigration paperwork is terrible, and there are always more bills.'

'Kyle, that's so good of you. Looking after her like that.'

He shrugged it off. 'Someone's got to do it. She's the only sister I've got.'

To Lynne, the next hour seemed to melt away into a buzz of pleasure with wonderful food and a man who held her gaze throughout, never once reaching for his phone. She had never been made to feel so important. She was seriously reconsidering whether to limit this to a one-night stand. She watched as Kyle joked with the waiter and deprecated his own knowledge of wine, one of many subjects he said he couldn't pretend to master. Almost every woman that passed the table glanced at him.

With the champagne finished, they were just about to order dessert when she made the whispered suggestion. 'Kyle, let's forget about the crème brûlée. I want you now. Let's go to the room.'

'You horny little minx,' he whispered, his hand on her bottom. They tiptoed up the narrow wooden staircase arm-in-arm. Leaning on him she made her tipsy way around the Tudor gallery, past suits of pewter armour and stern paintings of Elizabethan nobleman, and climbed the thickly carpeted steps to the honeymoon suite. In the doorway they embraced, she shamelessly caressing the sizeable bulge in the front of his trousers, her other arm around his neck. Her imagination was running riot. She could not remember ever having been so aroused. She had really fallen for this man, and literally could not wait.

Once inside the room, she took in the king-size four-poster, the mullioned windows, the chintzy curtains, and the gigantic red plastic suitcase he had presumably already brought up when checking in.

'Ha, it looks like you're moving in for a year,' she said.

'Yes, it does, doesn't it?' he replied. She had no idea that by morning, after he'd had his fill of her, he would squeeze her slender neck while making love to her until she had been utterly deprived of air. That he would ransack her mobile phone for information about the murder inquiry. Her lifeless body would fit snugly inside the suitcase, and after a leisurely breakfast, he would slide her into the back of his Range Rover to be disposed of at a later date.

Chapter Seventeen

Perry drove back to his own home, unable to defer the inevitable any longer. Mel wasn't in, but had sent him a rather terse text message asking if he'd heard from their daughter. Vanessa was a law unto herself, often staying a night or two at her boyfriend's place on the other side of Woking, or with female friends. He looked through his phone and saw that the last message from her was three days ago, on Wednesday, in reply to his request to know if she was actually going to honour them with a visit over the weekend. It simply said: *Stop hassling me, ok?*

He parked on the front drive, leaving room for Mel's Audi. He let himself in, and hunted through the fridge for some food that might be ready to eat. There were some leftovers, and in the freezer a couple of ready meals. He pulled one out. Thai vegetarian, as it turned out. He was surprised that Vanessa hadn't nabbed that one, it was just the kind of food she enjoyed. He was microwaving it when the landline rang. The caller ID identified Becky, Vanessa's best friend. Perry decided to let it go to the answer machine rather than end up involved in the thankless task of ferrying meaningless messages between teenagers.

'Hi Van? Where are you babe? You were going to come over this afternoon remember? Can't get you on your mobile, nothing on Facebook or WhatsApp. Hope you're not freezing me out because—'

He snatched up the phone. 'Hi Becky, it's John, Vanessa's dad.'

'Oh hi.' Becky's tone indicated she would rather undergo root canal surgery than continue the conversation with him.

'Wasn't she at your place two nights ago?' he asked.

'Supposed to be.'

'And?'

'She never showed. I messaged Steve, but he's up in Scotland and she's not with him. I've not seen her at college either.'

Steve was Vanessa's boyfriend. A big outdoors type, all biceps and brooding silence, he was often camping and hiking in Scotland or Wales in all weathers. It wasn't Vanessa's thing at all. Perry was suddenly concerned. 'Becky, she's not been here for days. Her mother has been looking for her. If you see her can you ask her to ring home ASAP?'

Becky agreed, then rang off.

Perry shook his head. It was probably nothing. After all, he'd been through this before, when at fifteen Vanessa announced she was 'divorcing' her family and going to live in a tepee in Wales. He had only just started at Surrey Police, but using their resources to trace her phone had quickly managed to establish that Vanessa was in Brighton, not Wales. When he found her, she was indeed living in a tent, one erected inside the second floor of a historic building. She and a dozen other squatters had taken over the place and were, she told him, 'Going to start a world revolution.' This was when she had first illegally acquired tattoos, and according to Mel, some kind of intimate piercing. When he went to fetch her, she had grudgingly agreed to come back home, on condition that she did not have to apologise, and that her father agreed to read the manifesto that she and her friends had cooked up. He had been so relieved to find her alive that he would have agreed to anything.

He picked up a photograph of her from the sideboard, taken when she was fifteen. She was wearing a pullover, jeans and wellingtons, and sticking her tongue out at him, the photographer. She was standing, with ill-disguised boredom, on some hillside in Derbyshire during one of the many weekends away that he and Mel had tried to use to bond her back into the family. Her blonde, naturally wavy hair and her precocious curves made her look much more grown-up than the little girl he had always so adored. Evidence of her love for him, such as it was, took almost archaeological skills to unearth. One time when he had found her unexpectedly in the kitchen for breakfast with a female friend, he had ruffled her hair and said that he loved her. She had ducked away, responding with an angry: 'Fuck *off*!' Once her friend had gone, he had then had to endure a lecture about how he was 'destroying her credibility'. So much for parental love. Vanessa's disrespectful and dismissive tone towards both him and Mel was so ingrained and so pervasive that she barely looked up from her phone when dishing out a wounding comment. Her favourite way of noticing him was: 'Hey John, you *really* are short.' Always John, not dad, since she was fourteen. And it was true, she had half an inch on him even in bare feet. His biggest mistake, a year ago and never repeated, had been to remind her that five foot seven was not actually short for a man, merely the low end of average. Her uncontrollable laughter, which actually required her to hold onto him for stability, had cut him to the quick.

Yet, very occasionally, Perry had noticed hints of daughterly affection: a warm glance, an affectionate dig in the ribs while he was shaving with a wet razor, an attempt to trip him up as they passed in the hallway, even an arm briefly draped around his neck while she was texting somebody else. Was this all the validation a parent was expected to subsist upon? In exchange for the worry, the expense and the endless time of bringing her up? He sometimes felt like an astrophysicist, examining the faintest pulse of radio waves from a far-distant galaxy for signs of meaning, for traces of significance, hoping for evidence of love.

Mel's last message to him seemed to indicate that Vanessa had been home on Tuesday, because of the great pile of dirty clothes dumped in the laundry basket on that day, and the disappearance of all the fresh vegetables from the fridge. The physicist again: Vanessa was dark matter, and invisible. Her existence could only be deduced by the gravitational disturbance of objects around her as she swung past on an undetectable orbit. Finding her would not be easy, but if she was still missing by tomorrow night, he would report her missing. That would bring the sky down, all round.

–

Angie Wright had given Perry an address for Halliday's storage unit at Shildon, not far from Pirbright, halfway between Woking and Farnborough. The light was failing by the time he got there, and he only just spotted the turn-off, an anonymous right turn on the B3400 just before a railway bridge. The detective steered his VW down the long, bumpy and descending private road alongside the main London to Basingstoke railway, which gradually rose above him to the left. The access road was lined with dozens of 1930s industrial units which backed on to the embankment of the busy line. Perry guessed that they had been originally owned by the army, from their curved hangar-like roofs and because in many cases they still bore the flaking remnants of olive drab paint on doors and windows. They now hosted low-rent businesses, from car repair, windscreen replacement and marine engineering through to skip hire and party supplies. Most entrances were hedged in by vertical sheets of corrugated iron, crowned with barbed wire, and the gates padlocked. Many had no signs at all. The largest was a scrap metal yard whose chained Alsatians barked as Perry drove slowly by. The road dipped gradually, and turning left through an arch under the railway line reappeared in the man-made canyon between two diverging train tracks. This crescent-shaped piece of land boasted a dozen businesses under the railway arches to left and right, with the gravel apron between them gradually widening as the two railway lines diverged, until it ended at a disused spur of a canal. Hall-iday's place, unit K, was right at the end, nearly on the canal, separated from the towpath by a high barbed wire fence, through which nettles, ragwort and a variety of other weeds grew in profusion. A mini skip sat outside.

Although the brickwork of all these units looked neglected, and was dotted with buddleia at the higher levels, there were signs of care. Perry spotted two modern CCTV cameras with night vision capability over Halliday's place. The white cabling looked fairly new, as did the roller door, which was secured by a series of new, shiny and very hefty padlocks.

Perry stroked his chin. There was no one here, and it didn't make a whole lot of sense to go digging around under this kind of surveillance. There were easier ways to get back at the man. He stepped out of the car, and walked over to the skip. There were bits of timber, a bag of plaster, and some old electrical kit. Shining his torch in, he spotted a sheaf of soggy papers. One or two were business letters to Kyle Halliday at this address. He hauled them out, and stuck them in a bin bag to examine later, once he had dried them out.

He had one more piece of theft to do before the night was out.

–

Perry had only ever seen cops going through bins on TV dramas. It was the sort of thing that private detectives did, sneaking in for a dig through the rubbish. But having heard that Halliday was away on business, and his wife out for the evening, he had a golden opportunity. He had studied the CCTV of the car theft from the same address, and knew that the only motion sensor light was on the house to the right, as you faced it. Fortunately the wheelie bins were on the left, next to the garage. It was the recycling he was after. Any incriminating paperwork would be in there. It had to be done before Monday morning, when the bins were emptied at the same time as his own.

Ideally he would have waited until the middle of the night, but in some ways any noise at that time would be more incriminating. If Angie Wright heard any kind of disturbance, given that they'd already had a car stolen, she would be sure to ring the police. Instead, he drove up at 9.15 p.m. and reversed the Polo right up the drive, almost to the front door. Neither the Range Rover nor the white Merc were there. He got out, wearing an old high-vis jacket, boots and a woollen hat pulled low. He quietly flipped open the blue lid of the recycling bin, saw it was satisfyingly full of paperwork, and laid the bin gently on its side. He fitted a black bin bag over the mouth of the bin, and tipped it. He scrunched up the mouth of the bag, checked the bin was empty, tossed the bin bag in the boot of his car, and then drove away to his own home.

Anxious to avoid being disturbed, he took the bin bag to his shed. Mel and Vanessa avoided this spider-infested place, which suited him just fine. He used a bundle of old newspapers to dry the correspondence he had found in the skip. Among these he found a jiffy bag, in which were a series of handwritten envelopes addressed to Halliday's address at the unit. The writing was familiar. It looked a bit like Mel's. He pulled out a Valentine's card. When he saw what was inside, he gasped.

No, it couldn't be.

This was too cruel. He couldn't bear it.

Chapter Eighteen

Dearest Kyle,

It is only a few months since we met, when you so sweetly gave me a lift in the rain after my bike had a puncture. I still recall that dark cold January evening, in which your lovely hazel eyes and that huge handsome smile were the only warmth. How you took me out for coffee, how you ran your fingers through my damp hair. There is something so nurturing and caring about you, which makes me so happy to give my heart and body to you. You have taken me to places that I didn't know existed, done things to me that I didn't know could be done to a woman. My body was just fizzing with happiness all day afterwards! You told me not to worry that you are married, and when I hear how she has treated you, I understand. I know that I am much younger, but I think I understand you in the way that she doesn't. I can give you the care and the love that she won't. I'm so grateful that you came into my life and together we can change the world.

God, I can't wait to see you! Until Friday!
Van xxx

The next card he picked up was earlier, dated 30 January.

Dearest Kyle,

I do understand why you don't want me to text or ring you. I hope you don't mind me saying but your wife sounds like an absolute witch. I would have thought you could get a secret phone, where I could ring you as you travel, but if it's too risky, I accept that. You're the telecoms expert, after all. And for me, it's really great to actually sit in the college library writing love letters to you just like people did fifty years ago. By the way, I have never mentioned you to my parents (obviously), but my mum mentioned your name. You did a really good job on her phone. Really good customer service, apparently. Small world!

All my love
Van xxxx

The final card was the first, dated 14 January, and was the soggiest, the words smeared where the rain had got to the ink. It actually looked like tear tracks across the thick card.

Dearest Kyle,

Thank you so much for yesterday, I've never eaten oysters before! I thought they'd be slimy but they were nice. And champagne too! I've never stayed in a posh hotel before, my dad is far too tight to ever pay for such luxury. And what we did in that huge supersoft bed, my God! It is wonderful to be with a real man, someone who knows how to please a woman. You can rely on me always. When I finally get my A-levels and leave college, I want to be with you. Always. Always, always. I

have wanted to change the world, ever since I was
fourteen. To break the rules, not enforce them like
my dad (he hates anyone knowing he's a cop! I
don't think he is much of one to be honest). Only
two days to wait until I see you again. I wish you
didn't have to travel so much, the absences tear me
apart. I love you. I really, really love you.
    Van xxx

Perry's hands were shaking. The enormity of the trans-
gression by this hateful man. Taking his wife *and* his
daughter, one thirty-eight years old and the other just
seventeen. Halliday didn't even value them, tossing aside
the testaments of Vanessa's love into a skip to be destroyed
by the rain. Vanessa, his own child, who had not even
written him a birthday card this year, was completely
in thrall to this monster. Fantasies of revenge uncoiled
in his mind. Of murder, torture and dismemberment.
His rational physicist's brain was helpless to extinguish
the mediaeval furnace of rage which consumed him. He
squeezed his eyes shut, fighting for mental balance, for
sanity, but in the poorly lit, rough wood confines of
that garden shed, surrounded by tools and rusting garden
implements, he had discovered a personal dungeon of hell.

What have you done with my daughter? Where was she?
Were there any clues he had missed? He picked up a
garden fork, and stabbed at the wooden floor of the shed
with it again and again and again, crying with anger and
fury, until the screeching pain in his shoulder, unused to
such activity, forced him to stop. Panting, sweating, his
eyes wild, he tried to reach for rationality.

He put the cards aside and turned to the bin bag full
of stolen recycling. Peering inside, he fished out pieces of

paper, leaving the drinks and food cans. There was a great mass of shredded material, which was disappointing. What was left was largely old correspondence relating to Angie Wright's property business, AWL Ltd. He only spent five minutes on it. There was nothing of any interest there.

A light from the kitchen alerted him to Mel's arrival. Through the shed window, he watched her pacing about in the kitchen, putting on the kettle, getting a cup down from a cupboard. Estrangement perfectly described his feelings for her. He had thought he knew almost everything there was to know about this intelligent, petite, well-turned-out career woman, running her own wellness shop, with an MBA and a glowing self-confidence that put his to shame. But now he looked at her as if he was seeing her for the first time. As a stranger. For she had concealed something so cosmically enormous within their marriage. He was staggered never to have had a clue about it.

Did he hate her? Certainly tendrils of hatred had coiled around his heart, but it was no longer the dominant feeling. The most powerful emotion was one of being expelled from the household that he had thought he headed, like a piece of waste. For the last few days since their monumental row, he and Mel had avoided each other. Him tiptoeing, her slamming. It really should have been the other way round. Wasn't he the innocent party? Wasn't it him that had been wronged?

He had in his shed just the weapon to bring Mel to her senses. The temptation to march into the kitchen and toss Vanessa's cards onto the kitchen table would undoubtedly bring Mel's affair with Halliday to a crashing end. But he retained just enough sense to know that his wife would not thank him for bringing her this terrible news.

She would hate him all the more for it. Shooting the messenger. And in all this, he knew that he didn't want there to be any more hatred between them. Despite her infidelity and her cruelty, despite everything, Perry still loved her. He wanted nothing more than to fall asleep and wake up to find that Halliday's emotional carpet bombing of his family had all been a nightmare.

So when he walked into the kitchen at 10.45 p.m. he said nothing about his discovery. He simply gave a neutral greeting and then asked: 'Have you heard from Vanessa?'

'No.'

'I'm thinking we should report her missing,' he said.

She looked at him, and raised the cup of camomile tea to her lips. 'You're doing this deliberately, aren't you? You know she's been away this long before, and always comes back. But if you bring in all your mates from the police station, you're back in control, aren't you? Detective Inspector John bloody Perry.'

'Mel, they won't put me in charge of the case. I would have thought you would have welcomed this.'

'The bloody press will be on it, though, won't they? A policeman's daughter gone missing. Let's dig into the family. Let's see who's got the big secret. My love life will be in the tabloids.'

He looked at her with fresh eyes. 'I never realised how selfish you were.'

She stared levelly at him. 'It's about her, not me, you idiot. We'll lose her forever, don't you see? You don't begin to understand our daughter. She's got some of my streak of independence, and dragging her back home when she is not ready—'

'Mel! None of her friends have seen her either. Not Becky, not Steve. When she went off on one of her grand disappearances in the past, at least one of her friends knew where she was.'

'Well, maybe she's got a new exciting boyfriend,' Mel said, one eyebrow raised provocatively.

Perry shook his head. *If only you knew.*

Claire Mulholland watched DCS Rajinder Otara set up the incident room meeting for one a.m. in Mount Browne's biggest conference room. On three separate whiteboards he had written up everything they knew about the four interlinked crimes: the abduction and murder of Beatrice Ulbricht, the discovery of the body of Jane Morris, the attack on Trish Gibson, found bludgeoned in her car, and finally the abduction of Samantha Gillard. On a fifth board, at the centre of the room, he had written everything that they knew about the abductor. The one thing they were missing was a decent photo. Research specialists had dug up some old photos of Gary Harrison, when he was in the army, and later amongst a row of cooks in a South London college. Nothing recent. They were now trying to find his old army pals to see if they had any. It was a slow process, even with their resources, and they just didn't have any time.

When Otara was ready, he called in the entire night-shift team. That included a dozen NCA plainclothes officers as well as various technical specialists who were looking at the electronic and forensic evidence. Surrey's team included DI Claire Mulholland, plus DC Carl Hoskins, who was concentrating on the murder of

Gillard's aunt, and a handful of uniformed officers. Claire looked around at all the experts and specialists, and knew that Gillard would have loved to have been there.

Otara called them to order. For a man who had been continuously on duty for thirty-six hours, he looked remarkably fresh. Clear-eyed, trimmed beard, crisply ironed shirt. It all projected competence.

'I just want you to hear the latest, for those who have been stuck in their own silos for the last five or six hours. One, is that the women's underwear recovered from the bus stop in Westmeare produced a DNA match with Sam Gillard. The last message to Craig Gillard, from her phone, was made from the same bus stop. So we can be sure that the messages Gillard has received on his home phone are indeed from the abductor. Two, we made very quick progress on the phone number provided by Ellen Bramley.'

'Sorry, can you just remind me who she is?' asked a sleepy-looking male officer.

'She's an old friend of Mrs Gillard, a former colleague from her days training as a PCSO, who had been dating a man called Gabriel Hallam.' The DCS pointed to one of the whiteboards where the name had been written in marker pen at the centre of a web of arrows and question marks. 'She got in touch with Craig Gillard when she heard on the grapevine that her friend Sam had been abducted.'

'Oh yes, now I remember.' Sleepy rubbed his five o'clock shadow.

Otara continued. 'She contacted Craig yesterday evening, and following his advice surrendered her phone at Bedford Police Station, and we were immediately able to analyse it. We are now working on the assumption that Gabriel Hallam is a pseudonym, because we cannot find any banking, residential or location data for this name, apart from this one burner phone which is currently switched off.' He looked over at the two female officers who had worked through the night to try to track down this information, and they nodded.

'His name seems to exist only on social media,' said one of them. 'We believe this woman was deliberately groomed by the abductor in order to piggyback on her connection to Mrs Gillard. That's how he found her home, and learned details about her movements and those of her husband.'

Otara turned to a male officer, DS Stephen Dodd. 'What is the latest on the mobile ANPR trawl, Steve?'

'We got more than a dozen hits around the bus stop at about the time the message was sent. None match any vehicles of interest, as of now. The Warrior seems to have disappeared. We've managed to eliminate three or four local Westmeare residents from those hits, after house-to-house visits. The best connection we have is a black Range Rover, registered to an address in Telford, Shropshire, to a Mrs Sophie Harris.'

'That's no good. It's a hundred and fifty miles away,' Hoskins said. 'Could it be a cloned plate?'

'Maybe,' Dodd said. 'Anyway, this vehicle was picked up four times on our back roads network.' He turned to a female officer across the room. 'Sally, have you managed to overlay the Range Rover's movements onto a cell site analysis for the Hallam phone?'

'I have.' Research Intelligence Officer Sally Rickard asked for the lights to be dimmed so she could project a map from her laptop. 'As you can see, we cover everywhere from Woking and Lacey Dutton in the west of the county, right the way across to Chipstead, near Gillard's home, and Caterham in the east. Unfortunately, we only have a very few data points. The red dots are the ANPR hits, and the blue squiggles are the cell site paths for the phone. The question we have to ask ourselves is this: what is the probability that this phone was in the vehicle? Now apart from the Westmeare bus stop, which is an almost exact coincidence of the two colours in time and place, all the others have a time and geography disconnect. The good news is that there is not a single impossibility.'

A hand went up at the back. 'Sorry to be dim but—'

'Right, let me explain,' Rickard said. 'If we had a cell site flash in Woking at, say, noon, and an ANPR hit forty miles away in Caterham five minutes later, I think we can all agree that would be an impossibility. So all of our observations show the phone may have been in the vehicle we've identified. We'd need many more observations to prove the thesis, but it is the most likely.'

'That is all very impressive,' said Otara, who was sitting on a desk close to one of the whiteboards. 'But the working assumption of this analysis is that the phone remains with the vehicle.'

'That's implicit,' Rickard said.

'But if you cast your mind back to the earliest events, and the tracking of Beatrice Ulbricht, we know the phone was separated from the individual for long enough to waste a week of police time looking in London for her, when she was actually here in Surrey.'

'But unlike that case, I don't think our suspect knows we have this phone trace,' Rickard said.

'Don't bet on it,' Otara replied. 'He's smart.' He turned back to the other officers. 'What's the latest on the cold case?'

Rainy Macintosh put up her hand. 'I'm waiting for DI Perry to forward me some historic documents. He's off tonight—'

'Off? Why now of all days?' Otara asked.

'It's compassionate leave, family trouble, apparently. DCS Dobbs said it was okay, because this is the least urgent part of the case.'

'Speaking of which, where *is* Dobbs?' Otara asked.

'Och, I think he's tucked up in bed,' Macintosh replied.

–

Perry had agreed to stay out of the marital bedroom, and he certainly wasn't going to sleep in his daughter's room knowing what had gone on in *that* bed. The sofa downstairs was comfortable, but he had a sudden image of Halliday making use of it with Vanessa. He swore softly to himself as he padded about, realising that Halliday had not only screwed everybody in the Perry family bar him, but may well have used every piece of soft furniture to do it on. That left the futon in the box room, which also doubled as his study. Seeing as it was too cramped for sleep, it was an unlikely choice for sex. That's where he would lie.

Sleep eluded him. He had a huge workload that he was paying far too little attention to, and his personal life was falling to pieces. After three or four hours thinking about it, tossing and turning, he put on a bathrobe and tiptoed to his daughter's room. There must be some clues in there to her whereabouts. He eased open the handle, and closed the door behind him before putting on the light. Going back to first principles, he'd know how far she could have got if he knew which of her possessions were missing. The room had been tidied up since he'd last seen it. The mattress was made up with fresh sheets and pillow cases. The bin had been emptied. There was a small metal chest of drawers by the window, which had a certain household notoriety. Stick-on 'no entry' signs were all over it, the drawers locked. There would be answers in there for sure, but he would leave that until last. He peered into her wardrobe, standing on tiptoe to examine the top shelf. There were women's magazines, blouses, skirts, jeans, a few hats and a collection of bags.

The trouble was that he had never noticed her clothing, luggage or even her phone. He had no idea what might be missing. Mel had claimed, after helping him yet again to find his reading specs, that he was so unobservant that it was a joke him becoming a detective. Mel was the opposite. She would know which were Vanessa's favourite clothes and bags, but as they barely cooperated about sharing the same kettle, doing an exact inventory of their daughter's possessions would be a big step. While lying awake, he had conceded some of Mel's points about the dangers of officially reporting her missing, particularly the involvement of the press. There *was* a middle way. He could trace her phone and her bank cards on the quiet. That could provide reassurance without a huge fuss. Better still, he should get a colleague to do it. It wouldn't do to be discovered working on a personal project when he had a double murder to investigate, though heaven knew Radar Dobbs was a pretty slack boss.

He knew just the person who could help them. Not his kind of policeman, but a known quantity. DC Carl Hoskins. He'd ring him first thing.

Newly enthusiastic about finding his daughter, DI John Perry set about using a nail file to pick the locks on the chest of drawers. The bottom drawer gave in easily. Inside were various bits of make-up, some pills he didn't recognise in a foil packet, and a small plastic bag with a dozen mauve tablets in it. Certainly illegal. He blinked at the foolishness of youth. The top drawer took longer but eventually relented, though he was sure it would never be able to be locked again. There were two large packets of condoms and various feminine hygiene items. The second drawer held firm, and he was forced to retreat to the kitchen in search of a screwdriver. When he finally broke the lock, at 4.37 a.m., he found the drawer contained only one thing, a bulky plastic bag. Inside it was a brown curly wig.

Why did his daughter, with her gorgeous blonde wavy hair, need a wig?

He jumped back as the realisation hit him. He went back to the wardrobe, on tiptoe again and pulled out from the back of the top shelf a brimmed hat, a fedora. Holding it out in proper light he could see it was mauve. Maybe Mel was right. He hadn't clocked it when he first looked.

Vanessa had Beatrice Ulbricht's hat.

Everything now made sense.

All that exhaustive work to identify the girl on the train, and the answer was so incredibly close to home. It was Vanessa, disguised in a wig. Which meant that Kyle Halliday wasn't just an immoral wrecker of marriages. He was a murderer. Perry's own daughter was in love with him, and had helped to foil the investigation of a missing woman.

-

Gillard hadn't been sleeping well himself, and had been working the phones until one a.m. To be woken now by a call at 4.45 a.m. made him leap from the bed. At this time it was either going to be very good news about Sam, or very bad news.

When he heard it was Perry on the line, he was unsure which way it would go. 'Craig, my daughter is missing, and I've just discovered a wig and a mauve fedora in her room.'

The detective chief inspector listened with incredulity as the details and implications of Perry's discovery poured out. 'Hell, I'd been thinking about Kyle Halliday on and off for days. But now it all makes sense. He's the man we're looking for, he's been sitting there right at the centre of this web of intrigue, and we keep missing him.'

'I'm so worried about Vanessa. My wife always assumes she can look after herself, but this is something else.' His voice sounded shaky.

'All right, John. I'm coming over right now to your home. I'll be there in less than an hour. In the meantime, call in the details to the incident room. I think Rainy Macintosh is on duty tonight. We are going to need warrant applications for Halliday's home address, Hallam's address in Fleet, and the industrial unit. You start the process and I'll follow up with Rainy on the hands-free to make sure we've got everything we need.'

Gillard was already dressing at top speed before he cut the call. Perry had sounded decidedly shaky, which was hardly surprising if you've just realised your daughter is in cahoots with one of the most devious and dangerous murderers ever known. They didn't even dare discuss the awful possibility that she too may have become a victim once she had outlived her usefulness to him.

That put Perry and him in the same boat. Halliday had them both by the short and curlies. In Sam's case, she had just twelve hours to live unless he could find her.

Chapter Nineteen

Sunday morning

The GCHQ technical boffin arrived at Surrey Police headquarters at dawn, as suddenly as if materialising from another planet. DI Claire Mulholland was just finishing her overnighter on the Sam Gillard abduction, when someone from reception buzzed up to say a Dr Chris Steele was there to see DCS Otara. Claire looked out of the window into the car park. The visitor section was darkened and empty, and she knew most of the vehicles in the staff car park, which was dominated by the new red SUV of Chief Constable Alison Rigby. Intrigued, Claire decided to put aside the paperwork and go down herself rather than try to find Otara.

Claire won her bet with herself. The only person in reception was in his early twenties, had short hair, meticulously parted, thick glasses and a worn suit. On his lap was a hefty silver box, like that used by photographers. She walked over and said: 'Dr Chris Steele? I'm DI Mulholland.'

The man look confused. 'No, I'm Brian Hutton, emergency bollard replacement...'

Claire became aware of a figure at her shoulder, and turned. 'I'm Chris,' said a woman in her late thirties. 'I was in the loo,' she said, faced with Claire's perplexed expression. Dr Steele looked every inch the high-flying businesswoman, power dressed in houndstooth skirt and square shouldered jacket, heels and understated pearl earrings. Her eyes were feline and pale green.

Claire made her apologies to the bollard man and led Steele upstairs, where they were joined by Alison Rigby, dressed down in white blouse and black slacks, who ushered them into a secure but rather gloomy windowless conference room. Already seated there were DCS Raj Otara and Rob Townsend. Claire was surprised that everyone but her seemed to know this was happening. Indeed, the chief constable seem to be visibly excited by the presence of a spook, especially a glamorous female one. Another glass ceiling smashed, perhaps.

'There are now three mobile phones we need you to look at,' Otara said. 'The first, which we already told you about, was used to leave a message from a bus stop in Westmeare yesterday afternoon. The second was used by the suspect to ring his former girlfriend Ellen Bramley on a number of occasions in the last few months. That device has been switched off for two weeks. The third, which we've only heard about an hour ago, is an iPhone belonging to Vanessa Perry, who is believed to have been assisting the suspect, Kyle Halliday, evade capture. None of the devices are on at the moment.'

Dr Steele nodded. 'We've identified device one as a cheap Samsung running Android. The exact technical spec is here.' She passed across to Otara a technical looking sheet, which he then passed on to Townsend. 'Let me get HQ to examine the others. What exactly are your requirements for the first device?'

'Basically we need it turned on, and the GPS activated in order to locate it,' Otara said. 'We've already pre-set a monitoring system on the switch, so should get an identifiable location in less than ten seconds. The suspect has at least one and possibly two women hostage, one of them the wife of a serving officer, who he is threatening to kill at five p.m. today.'

'You can see why we wanted you involved,' Rigby said, smiling.

'Absolutely,' said Steele. 'We can get video too on the Android device, which should allow us to hear what is going on, even if the phone is in a pocket. If you need to make contact with the kidnapper I can also remotely turn on the speakerphone. That I'm sure will give him quite a shock.'

She opened her briefcase and slid out quite the thinnest laptop that Claire had ever seen. It was matt black and had not a single logo visible. It seemed to exude a penetrating pale blue light from underneath. After a few keystrokes, she looked up, the reflected light of the screen giving her eyes an almost sci-fi luminosity. 'I've got the secure connection that we need. I have authorised the activation, which will be undertaken from our base in Cheltenham.'

'I'm amazed that you can take an electronic device that is off, and turn it on,' said the chief constable, batting her eyelashes at the woman. My God, she's flirting, thought Claire.

Dr Steele's green eyes widened further. 'When a human is asleep, the heart still beats, the breath continues and the circadian rhythms still operate. Likewise, the concepts of on and off in telecommunication devices are a little mutable at the margin. We just whisper a few significant words into their sleeping ears.'

'Fantastic.' Rigby's shoulders eased back, as if the woman had caressed her with this poetic simile. The chief constable was playing with the chain at her neck, her eyes radiating their most powerful blue. Claire caught Rob Townsend's eye across the table, expecting to share a knowing glance, but as chief office nerd he seemed oblivious to the chemistry being stirred up in this darkened room. Instead he absent-mindedly scratched his ear.

Chris Steele returned to her laptop, tucking a hank of hair behind her ear as she did so. The gentle clack of keys continued. 'The target device is now awake, the firmware under our control. The GPS chip is being bootstrapped; the next pass from the satellite transponder may take a few seconds, but it will give us the information you need.' She looked across at Townsend, whose own laptop was open. 'I'll make you my slave, for the data,' she said, reaching across and connecting the two laptops' USB ports with a cable. 'You'll get an exact copy in real-time. This phone is a slave to an emulator constructed by my colleague on Taurus, our computer at Cheltenham. Sadly, Edward Snowden revealed a lot of our techniques back in 2015, though we have developed many more since then.'

Rigby leaned over Townsend, ostensibly to see the screen better, but also giving both Claire and the spook the benefit of some cleavage. Claire eyed the intelligence officer to see whether her transponders had been lit by the chief constable's all-frequency broadcast. The woman was such a cyborg it was impossible to tell.

'I've got the map,' Townsend said excitedly. 'The phone is travelling west of Woking towards Basingstoke.'

'You want the video?' Steele asked.

'Yes, let's try to see what's going on,' Rigby said.

Townsend's screen remained blank, and the only noises were a deep rumbling. 'He's in a car with a phone in a pocket, or possibly in a case,' he said.

'But we still know where,' Rigby said.

Otara was on his own phone. 'I want two vehicles on the B3400,' he said. 'Target has just left Pirbright, heading west. Can we get one to intercept from the Basingstoke end?'

Claire interrupted with information that Perry had called in just an hour previously. 'Halliday might well be driving a black Range Rover.' She read out the number plate.

She had already awoken the duty magistrate, a rather grumpy fellow in Norwich who clearly thought it unnecessary to be pulled out of bed at six o'clock on a Sunday morning. The warrants approved, two NCA cars plus a people carrier full of uniforms had been dispatched ten minutes ago. One to the address in Fleet that Gabriel Hallam, a.k.a. Kyle Halliday, had told Ellen Bramley was his own, and the other to the industrial unit at Shildon.

'Unit one ETA Shildon twenty-five minutes,' Otara announced. 'Unit two will be at Fleet in five minutes.'

The DCI looked up from a clipboard on his desk. 'Where the hell is PC Lynne Fairbanks? She was due on at six.'

A sergeant at the far end of the room raised his hand. 'I rang her home number, sir, and there is no reply. I assume she is on her way.'

Slack, Claire thought. Biggest case for a decade and the woman has probably overslept.

DCs Worrell and Blunt raced into Fleet, and turned off the siren five minutes before reaching the address at 7.15 a.m. The house they had been directed to was an anonymous three-bedroom redbrick semi in a row of similar 1980s homes. An old red Fiat was parked outside. They cruised up and parked quietly. The two disreputable-looking leather-jacketed individuals sprinted up to the door. While Blunt rang the bell and peered through the reeded glass door, Worrell eased his way over the back garden fence and noticed there was a sliding rear door. He stood next to it with his back to the wall, just like he'd seen cops do on TV.

'Police, open up!' Blunt shouted, as he banged on the glass UPVC door. A shape coalesced behind, and the door opened. A teenage girl in fleecy pyjamas and puppy-headed slippers with a mass of dishevelled wavy blonde hair stared at them in alarm.

'Where's Kyle Halliday?' Blunt yelled as he forced his way in, waving a lanyard vaguely in her direction.

'Moved out two months ago,' the girl said. 'My parents are renting it now, but they're on holiday in Crete.'

'Nothing personal, darling, but we've got a bit of legal paper which allows us to take a look around anyway,' Blunt said, racing up the stairs and banging from one room into another. Worrell pushed past too, into the lounge and kitchen. There was nobody there. While Blunt made some notes, Worrell returned to the doorway, where the girl had now donned a bathrobe and was sitting on the stairs.

'What's your name, love?' he asked.

'Becky Keene. My dad is Gerald and my mum is Mary. I hope you didn't hurt my rabbits,' she pouted.

'Your rabbits are fine,' Worrell said, not having noticed any. 'You're a bit young to be in the house on your own.'

'I'm nearly fourteen,' she said indignantly, running her hand through her hair.

Worrell suppressed his amazement, but not his wandering eyes. While Blunt called in news of the failed raid, Worrell apologised for waking her up, but added that she could expect a call later in the day from uniformed officers who might take a statement and do some paperwork. 'We're too busy for all that,' he said.

Back in the car, Blunt left rubber on the road as they pulled away from the house.

'Christ,' Worrell said. 'Did you see the body on that? Fucking thirteen, I can hardly believe it.'

Blunt laughed. 'Jailbait. Gets worse every year. If she'd had make-up, she could have passed for twenty.'

–

Vanessa Perry stood at the doorway and watched the police car head off. It had been a close thing. But her natural acting skills, the ones that Kyle had praised, had carried her through, helped by borrowing her best friend's name. This time she hadn't needed to don a wig or carry a violin. She hadn't even needed to pad out a coat, to hide her figure, like she had when impersonating the German girl. Quite the reverse. The two cops were a couple of dim pervs.

The most difficult role had been the first one, the Monday afternoon spent with Kyle on a lonely country road, learning how to drive his big green four-wheel-drive. She'd only passed her test four months previously, and learning how to do a fast getaway had taken her several attempts. Then he'd produced two thick extra jumpers, two pairs of gloves and a big man's car coat for her to wear, and made her do it again. Finally she had to learn how to do it wearing a ski mask. Doing the getaway for real at night had all been enormously exciting, and she drove the vehicle with verve and enthusiasm just as if she were a real car thief. When she saw that she had dragged Kyle over, indeed almost run him down, she had wanted to go back and see if he was all right. But he had previously made clear to her that no matter what she was to park the Warrior in his workshop by the railway arches, and pick up the Fiat that was already there to drive to Fleet.

She had worried at first about the extraordinary things he had asked her to do for him. But the almost incredible story he had told her, about who the German girl really was, and how Kyle was being pursued by the British state, had convinced her. Not many people ever get a chance to really make a difference, and here she was just seventeen striking a blow against the big state.

Vanessa checked the new iPhone that Kyle had given her, in exchange for her old one. She should have left half an hour ago, to pick him up at the church at Long Stainton. She'd overslept. She changed into jogging gear, grabbed the duffel bag she had already packed and the car keys, got into the Fiat and drove away. She had only been going two minutes when three police cars packed with uniformed officers raced past in the other direction sirens blaring. It was just like Kyle had predicted. She was so excited that she was going to see him again.

Perry was gripping the dashboard with both hands, his knuckles white. He had never endured such a ride before. Gillard had broken all blue-lighting records, picking him up in Woking just after seven a.m., and then racing off to get to the industrial unit at Shildon before it was properly light. They had been listening to the traffic on a police network, and had just got news of the failed raid in Fleet. It seemed that Hallam/Halliday/Harrison had given Ellen Bramley an old address, now rented to someone else. No surprises there. However there was considerable excitement about some unspecified trace on the location of the black Range Rover.

'Tell me about the warehouse unit,' Gillard said, as he overtook an articulated lorry at about ninety miles an hour.

'It's at the junction of two railway lines, where the Southampton track separates from the Basingstoke line, and crosses over the old spur of the Basingstoke canal. They are almost all small units, many of them arches underneath the viaduct.'

'A bridge?'

'Not exactly.' Perry's scientific precision wouldn't allow him to classify the embankment and railway viaduct as a bridge, except perhaps at the very end where the canal was crossed.

Gillard reminded him of the riddle.

Under the bridge/ That's where you'll find her/ cold, with the fishes/ drowned by your own hand

'Was there a fishmonger's or anything similar?'

'Not that I saw. Scrapyards, car repair outfits, that kind of thing.'

Gillard shook his head. 'It still could be the place. I've personally checked a dozen bridges in the last two days, but of course I've concentrated on those over rivers or canals. I haven't got round to anything to do with the railways.'

At Perry's instruction, they turned off right into the industrial estate, still doing sixty. The unmarked Vauxhall hit the first road hump with a bone-shaking impact that had it airborne for the next two seconds. Gillard skilfully dodged the worst of the potholes on the crumbling tarmac, and brought the car back under control as he passed under the viaduct, slewing the vehicle to a halt outside unit K.

'We're ahead of them,' Gillard said, jumping out of the car and going to the boot where he habitually left a toolbox. 'They'll be here in two minutes. Now, let's get this door open.'

'We don't have the warrant,' Perry said, hurrying along behind the DCI.

'John, I overheard on the radio that a warrant has been issued. It doesn't have to be in my own sweaty paws to be effective.' Gillard went up to the roller door, which was running with moisture. He took off his glove and touched it with his bare hand.

'It's freezing! It's bloody freezing.' He turned to Perry. 'This is the place. She must be in here!'

He flipped open the toolbox and, like a man possessed, tossed out various tools, trying to find something hefty enough for the job. Three fist-sized die-cast steel padlocks secured the shutter to a thick cast iron loop, part of a thirty-foot-wide baseplate that ran the full width of the unit. The best he could find was a very large screwdriver, but it was obvious it would make little impression.

John Perry raised his head, and looked behind him.

The sound of sirens, many of them, in the distance.

–

Three police squad cars and two vans screamed through the tunnel under the viaduct and up into the tarmacked apron. Uniformed officers piled out of their vehicles. The final van had a locksmith's logo on the side.

DCS Raj Otara spotted Gillard and said: 'Craig, you're not supposed to be here.'

'My wife is in there!' Gillard retorted, jerking his thumb over his shoulder.

'And maybe my daughter too,' Perry added.

Otara sighed. 'All right, I'm not that cruel, just stay out of the way.'

The locksmith, a skinny guy in his sixties, came up to them. 'With these locks, you're talking a good ninety minutes to cut them. The easiest way in is actually to cut along the base of the shutter, that'll have you inside in ten minutes.'

Otara sucked his teeth. 'Okay, go for it.'

The locksmith pulled out the back of his van the biggest set of bolt croppers Gillard had ever seen. He took them and a big metal box of tools up to the left-hand edge of the roller door.

'So what about the Range Rover you were tailing,' Gillard asked Otara. 'Wasn't it heading in this direction?'

'It was, but it's been found ablaze in the village of Long Stainton. The fire service got on to it almost immediately, so let's just hope there's enough evidence left when CSI finally get to give it the once over.'

'So Halliday has got himself yet another vehicle?' Perry said.

'Looks that way,' Otara said.

The sound of drilling, and then grinding blotted out their words. The locksmith was gradually snipping his way across the shutter about two feet off the ground.

DC Carl Hoskins was helping PC Tony Tunnicliffe, one of the biggest cops in the county, to try to wrench out the bottom flap, but the locksmith told him to stop. 'If you jam the mechanism, we won't be able to wind it up, and then you'll all have to go in and out the rabbit hole.'

'It stinks of fish,' Hoskins said.

Tunnicliffe had his hands resting against the metal of the door. 'That must be why it's so bloody cold,' he said.

'"Cold, with the fishes", that's part of the rhyme,' Otara said, glancing at Gillard. The detective chief inspector was clenching and unclenching his fists, staring at the shutter as if he could laser his way in with his eyes.

The locksmith, sensing their impatience, cut two parallel snips in the roller door down to the ground, and kicked out a three-foot-by-two slot. Hoskins lay on his side to get an early view, and was met with a fog of freezing air that drifted out. He shone his torch through. It was clear the place had originally been a car repair joint: metal-lidded inspection pits, a broken hoist at the far end amid piles of tyres. Everyone outside heard his soft cursing at whatever it was he'd seen.

'We found the Mitsubishi Warrior and Sam's Renault.'

Gillard dropped next to Hoskins to peer inside. Before anyone could react, he had grabbed Hoskins' torch, and wriggled under the shutter into the unit.

'Gillard!' Otara yelled, 'I told you. Come out of there, now.'

He didn't reply. The place was only lit by the control lights of two banks of vertical chillers, six in all, blasting out freezing air towards the vehicle. It took Gillard a moment to find the light switch, and the strip lighting flashed on. The Warrior stood glistening in the centre of the concrete space, so frost-covered it looked like it had been dipped in icing sugar. On either side were two supermarket-style glass topped freezers, and beyond them, deep in the recess of the vaulted space, Sam's black Renault. It was more mildly frosted.

Hoskins now squeezed through the gap, followed by the locksmith, who was intent on finding a way to get the shutter raised. Gillard flipped off the chillers so they could hear themselves speak, as two or three of the uniformed officers made their way laboriously inside.

Gillard pulled open the doors and then boot of the Renault. Empty. He turned back to the Warrior.

'The car's full of ice,' Hoskins said, scraping away the surface frost of one of the double cab's windows. 'That's not just on the outside. It's been filled with water and frozen solid.' He scratched away at the driver-side window, and then pressed his face to the glass. 'Jesus Christ Almighty, someone's frozen in there. A woman. I can see hair, long dark hair.'

Gillard let out a groan.

'Definitely dark?' Perry asked.

'Yes, dark,' Hoskins said.

Perry gasped with relief. *Thank God! It's not Vanessa.* His heart went out to Gillard, losing this roll of the cosmic dice.

'For fuck's sake, what are you all waiting for, let's get her out of there!' Gillard was working the controls of the freezers.

'What are you doing?' Otara called. He was on the ground outside staring through the gap, just as the roller door, finally cut right across, was being hauled up manually.

'I'm reversing these to defrost,' Gillard replied. 'We've got to heat this place up. Now you lot, get some tools, break the windows. Let's get hacking at the ice.' He stared disconsolately at the huge SUV, not only the double cab full of ice, but the truck bed too, a good foot deep. 'Can you open this car?' he asked the locksmith.

'Not till the locks are unfrozen. But I've got a blow-torch in the van.' He sprinted off to fetch it.

'Come on, let's have some initiative,' Gillard said, punching his fist into his open hand. 'She could still be alive in there.'

As if to emphasise his words, there was a bang of some kind from the vehicle.

'Is that ice cracking?' Hoskins asked.

'Shh,' said Gillard. They all listened for a few seconds, but could hear nothing.

The big industrial chillers were already now pumping out a huge amount of heat. 'Wind the roller door down again,' Gillard said. 'Retain the heat. We've got to get the temperature in here way up.'

Tunnicliffe had taken his jacket off, and had found a rusty metal crowbar. He smashed at the passenger-side window, which exploded like a bomb, showering glittering diamonds on to the concrete. Hooking out the glass, he then laid into the ice beyond.

With the door now down again, the temperature in the vault rose rapidly, and the car began to sweat, water trickling down from the panels and the roof, dripping down onto the floor, puddling by the inspection pit and draining out under the roller shutter.

The locksmith came back with his blowtorch and set to work on the driver-side lock. He then handed the blowtorch to Hoskins while he used a set of delicate-looking instruments inside the Mitsubishi's lock. A clunk announced the unlock, but the door wouldn't open. Tunnicliffe lent his considerable size and weight to the effort with the crowbar. The driver-side window exploded, and the window frame bent under the big man's strength. Eventually the door creaked open, and more officers could get to work on the ice. From this angle they could see she was clothed, a dark shadow within the translucent ice, the top of her head and hair just six inches from the surface. The locksmith and Tunnicliffe worked on the passenger-side door, trying to wrench it open, while Hoskins used the blowtorch to carefully melt the ice around her.

Under the bridge/ That's where you'll find her/ cold, with the fishes/ drowned by your own hand

The verse played in Gillard's head as he chipped away at the ice, and watched the meltwater coursing down over the sills of the car and draining away into the inspection pit. A bang from somewhere low within the car reached their ears. They stopped and listened, the ping and click of the car's expansion echoing the drip drip drip of the melting ice. Another bang, and a splash, as the vehicle adjusted to the rising temperature.

One of the female PCs was hacking furiously away at the ice with a screwdriver, her hands mauve with cold. 'Keep going! She could still be alive, people can live for hours after being frozen,' she yelled.

Gillard could now feel some of Sam's hair, soaked, ice cold. He forced his hand through into the ice and touched flesh beneath the hair. As cold as a glacier. The ice so reluctantly surrendered its grip, merely weeping under the assault of the blowtorch, resisting every blow. There just seemed to be no way to speed up the process. It took a few more passes of the blowtorch before a great lump came off, and Gillard could get his fingers down a narrow gap, to feel further down the face. A nose, an open mouth. If she's alive, there will be warmth inside. He tried to slide a finger into the mouth, but it ran into more ice, so cold it almost welded his fingertip to her teeth.

'Any warmth?' Claire asked, softly.

Gillard shook his head. 'Cold as stone.' *She's dead.*

'Oh Craig,' she said, and reached out for his shoulder. There was a chorus of sympathetic noises from the other officers.

'Well, let's keep going to be sure,' Gillard said, squeezing his eyes shut, and fighting to control his emotions. *Sam can't be dead, she simply can't be.*

On the other side of the car Tunnicliffe levered off a huge lump of ice, and said: 'They can do miracles now with hypothermia, sir.'

Gillard made a fist of his now-frozen hand and it created a crack above her face, which with his other hand he pulled at. A dinner-plate-sized wedge cracked, and the face was revealed.

Not Sam. Someone he didn't recognise. 'It's not her!' he yelled.

'Who is she?' Otara asked.

'I don't know, another victim I suppose. But definitely not Sam.'

There was a rattle and a splash. 'Where was that from?' Hoskins asked.

Claire looked at him, and then at Gillard. 'It didn't sound like it was from the car.'

Gillard stared in at the body emerging from the ice. He pulled back, and stepped away from the car, a glazed look across his face.

'Oh God, now I understand.'

Drowned by your own hand.

'We've got to move this car,' Gillard shouted.

'Why?' Tunnicliffe asked.

'Because he's buried Sam in the inspection chamber underneath and we're drowning her in the meltwater,' he replied.

'It's impossible,' Hoskins said. 'We can't roll it. Everything round the handbrake is frozen solid.'

'There's a dozen of us, we could try bouncing it,' Tunnicliffe said.

They all gathered around the vehicle, needing only to move it three or four feet to the left. Tunnicliffe, a massive man built like a power lifter, got a careful grip under the front of the vehicle. They all heaved, but with the additional weight of the ice inside, on top of the 1.7 tonne basic weight of the Warrior, it was beyond them. With the hot air blowers going full pelt they were soon sweating. They didn't have time to keep doing it this way.

'Give me the blowtorch,' Gillard said. He crawled under the vehicle and was immediately drenched by the pouring meltwater. He quickly found the hydraulic brake cable, melted the ice and burnt through it. Sliding out, he said: 'Quick, push it further forward towards the exit. Let's hope it's not in gear.'

Sure enough, with Tunnicliffe's help, they were able to edge the vehicle forward enough for Gillard to get to the metal plate locked over the inspection chamber. There was a bang, and a splash, then another bang. It was definitely coming from the pit in the concrete. The locksmith, lying side-by-side with the detective, worked away on the padlock. It took a full minute, but seemed like an hour. Once it was freed, Gillard pulled back the two metal plates, to discover the pit was already almost full to the brim. A coffin-sized metal locker was floating, its top just two inches above the surface of the water.

'Sam, are you in there? Give me a kick.'

The response was a furious rattling and sloshing. The metal box was secured by yet another padlock, drawing another sigh from the locksmith. 'Let's get the whole thing out of here,' Gillard said. With the help of a tow rope from one of the police vehicles, and the strength of Tunnicliffe at one end, they managed to haul the box from the inspection pit. The water sloshing around inside made it almost impossible to keep level, but they slid it across the floor of the workshop until there was space to work on it. The locksmith had bad news: 'The lock's been superglued, we'll have to cut it off.'

'We can't use the blowtorch, it'll cook her,' Gillard said.

'Fire service two minutes away,' Hoskins said.

'Let me try,' Tunnicliffe said. The box was well made, with a flanged lid and no gap big enough for the tip of the crowbar. There was nowhere for the big man to get any purchase to lever up the lid.

'Quick, the electric drill,' Gillard said.

The locksmith obliged, drilling ten quick shallow holes low in the side of the box. Water jetted from within. The kicking and rattling continued.

'Sam, if you can hear me in there. You've just got to hang on. The water's being drained out.' He feared that she might die of exposure because of the freezing water, even if she didn't actually drown. He couldn't imagine any worse way to go than drowned in claustrophobic darkness. Buried alive, but worse.

Sound of sirens and air horns in the distance proclaimed the arrival of the fire service and an ambulance. Tunnicliffe manually hauled up the roller door again to see a young man sprinting past the many parked police vehicles blocking the access road. He had on a fire service brown jacket, and carried a toolbox.

Two minutes later, with the help of hydraulic cutters, the lid was opened. Sam was inside, drenched, bound almost head to foot in gaffer tape, only her nose clear, arms locked in front of her by cable ties. Gillard borrowed a Stanley knife from the locksmith, and carefully cut the tape from her face. The moment her mouth was free, sobbing began, and he hauled her out and into his arms.

For a long time she couldn't speak, but simply clung to him, her eyes squeezed shut against the unaccustomed light. Everyone else stood back to give them a little space. Her body was frozen, her fingers and toes blue with cold. He carried her over in front of the warm air blasting from the chillers, and let the paramedics do their job. For the next forty-five minutes he held her hand while she was wrapped in warm dry blankets and put inside an exposure bag. He stroked her hair and kissed her cheek.

Eventually, he stood back and watched her being taken into the ambulance. For a moment he watched his colleagues, many of whom were now working again on the ice. Perry, his daughter still missing, was working away at the slushy mass. 'Who is she?' said the female officer working at his side, sweat coursing down her brow as she wielded the screwdriver.

'Another victim. Yet another poor bloody victim,' Perry said.

Otara put his arm around Gillard's shoulder, and encouraged him to go with Sam to the hospital where she would have a check-up.

'I want to nail Harrison. For what he did to her.'

'We all do, Craig. But right now we have got to find out where John's daughter is.'

Gillard nodded and made his way out towards the emergency vehicles. He turned back to his colleagues, who were watching him, and particularly to Perry. 'John, I'll call you later.'

The detective inspector nodded grimly.

'We're going to find Vanessa, you know. Have faith.'

Chapter Twenty

At 16 Wensleydale Walk, Melanie Perry came to after a dreadful night. After John had left in the small hours, saying he was going to look for their daughter, she had suddenly felt a great rush of regret. He wouldn't say exactly why he now thought she was in so much danger. He merely told her to watch the phone, to monitor emails and to keep her eyes peeled. If Vanessa made any contact, she was to text him immediately.

She stayed up for two or three hours, then fell asleep at the kitchen table before awaking briefly with the dawn chorus in a zombie-like trance. Again and again she alternately dozed off then awoke with a shock to relive the horror of a missing daughter. It was still dark when she went up to Vanessa's room, which looked like it had been ransacked. Presumably by John. There must be something he wasn't telling her, and she had a horrible feeling about it. She tried to ring him, but her calls kept going to voicemail.

Mel stumbled back down into the kitchen and made some coffee, and then noticed that the shed light was still on. That was strange. She changed from slippers into Crocs, slipped an outdoor jacket over her T-shirt and joggers, and padded across in the chill first light of the morning. The shed, foreign territory, was unlocked.

It was the place John would always retreat to like an embattled crab when the domestic going got tough. She generally had no curiosity about this masculine cave. She opened the door and realised the fan heater was still on low. Cursing him for the waste of energy, she reached down to turn it off, and then glanced at what was spread across the worktop.

Letters and cards written by her daughter. She recognised the handwriting, so much like her own. Such a rare treasure trove, from a girl whose entire life seem to be online, who could hardly be bothered to send a single Christmas card.

She picked one at random, and squinted at it in the poor light. From the second word, her heart was in her mouth. And then the last two lines. They tore from her a ragged heartfelt cry.

> *Dearest Kyle,*
>
> *Thank you so much for yesterday, I'd never eaten oysters before! I thought they'd be slimy but they were nice. And champagne too! I've never stayed in a posh hotel before, my dad is far too tight to ever pay for such luxury. And what we did in that huge supersoft bed, my God! It is wonderful to be with a real man, someone who knows how to please a woman.*

She couldn't read the rest, for the tears that poured from her eyes. She stumbled blindly from the shed, wailing as she hauled opened the kitchen door and threw herself sobbing onto a chair at the kitchen table.

How *could* he? How dare he? With my daughter!

And from that anguish began to build a towering anger, a fury that in her entire life she had never experienced. Revenge, they say, is a dish best served cold.

Wrong.

She was cooking up a gigantic cauldron, which she intended to dish up before the day was out. In the next hour she showered, washed her hair, and dried it carefully. She applied a blood red lipstick and smoky eyeshadow, and dressed in a navy blue skirt short enough to make the best of her legs. She rolled on dark tights, chose a smart jacket to match the skirt and checked herself over in the mirror.

Going back downstairs, she put on her white Aquascutum raincoat and a pair of elegant high heels. There was one more thing to do. She went back into the kitchen, to the knife block, and drew out the longest knife that they possessed. It was a sushi blade, forged in one piece of steel. It was expensive, and so sharp it had originally come in its own black plastic sheath, covered in warning stickers. She dug through the kitchen drawers until she found the scabbard, and slid the knife in with a satisfying gritty sound. She spotted Vanessa's college bag, tipped out the contents on the kitchen table, and carefully put the sheathed weapon inside the leather backpack.

She took a quick look round.

'Goodbye, house,' she said. 'I don't know if I'll ever be back.'

—

Gillard held Sam close in his arms throughout the ambulance journey to hospital. She clung to him wordlessly, like a child recovering from a nightmare. The paramedics, after having checked her vital signs, stayed back. It was not until an hour later, when she had been given her first formal examination, that the registrar said she would like to keep Sam in overnight for observation. Only then did she begin to speak.

'I want to go home, Craig,' she whispered.

It was another ninety minutes before she was given official permission to go. Craig took her home in a taxi, her head resting on his shoulder almost the whole time. It was halfway through that journey home when she began to cry. Big, gulping sobs that shook her shoulders, tears that wet his face and neck. Her hands blindly delineated his face, feeling the wounds on his ear and along his cheek and the two-day-old stubble growing on his jaw.

Gillard looked out of the window at the bright morning, the meadows silvered in dew, and the trees in bud. He started to assess the physical and mental toll that the confinement, captivity and claustrophobia had weighed on his precious wife. He was pretty sure that she would never be the same again. And neither would he.

–

'I'm sorry to have to drag you in at this time on a Sunday, Ms Wright, but we're extremely anxious to trace your partner Kyle Halliday.' DI Claire Mulholland was sitting opposite Angie Wright in an interview room at Woking Police Station. A matronly female constable sat in with them. It was just before nine a.m. and the detective inspector had been up all night. 'We are urgently looking for him in connection with a series of murders and abductions across the Home Counties.'

The woman actually laughed. 'I think you've made a mistake.' She looked fresh as a daisy in a flowered top, yoga pants and pink glitter-covered trainers: a glossy carapace of self-confidence.

'He's in Madrid, I've already said. He's usually away overnight five, sometimes six nights a week, mostly in Europe, but occasionally in the US.'

Ms Wright's hair was thick and silky, her make-up subtle but effective, highlighting her exquisite cheekbones and clear blue eyes. There was a faint waft of some kind of expensive perfume too. It all looked annoyingly effortless, particularly for this time on a Sunday morning. Claire was needled, and found herself dropping a piece of information that she had intended to retain until the end of the interview. It would have floored almost anyone.

'Our information, Ms Wright, is that your partner is not abroad, but in the UK and travelling with a seventeen-year-old girl. Were you aware of this?'

Angie Wright looked utterly unperturbed. 'I would suggest your information is incorrect. Kyle rang me last night. He's staying at the Hotel Intercontinental, near Madrid airport. I really think you've got the wrong man. Perhaps you could show me a picture of the man you're looking for?'

'We can get you one a bit later.' Claire knew they didn't yet have a single up-to-date picture. The old pictures of Gary Harrison would just confuse the issue. The research intelligence team were working hard to retrieve the photographs of Gabriel Hallam that Ellen Bramley had deleted from her own phone, but that meant delving into the server of the service provider. Results were due any minute now.

'Well that's it then, you don't know who you're looking for,' she replied, retrieving her own iPhone from her white leather Versace shoulder bag. She swiped and tapped, and then showed Claire the phone. 'That's my Kyle.'

It was a picture of a tanned man reclining by the side of a pool in some sunkissed locale. The face, smiling and sunglassed, was only partially visible because of the deep shade of a sun umbrella, and a raised cocktail, but the toned body would have graced the cover of any glossy magazine.

'Have you another where I can see his face?' Claire asked.

'He's a bit shy,' she giggled, flicking through the phone before passing it across. 'Try this.'

The picture was a facial close-up, slightly blurred and clearly without the cooperation of the subject. The big smile, the hazel eyes and the rugged jaw proved it. Halliday was spectacularly handsome. The CCTV of the flying slipper incident had done him no justice. Even as she looked at the image, Claire could sense the interviewee's eager smile, as if she expected some kind of compliment on the hunk she had managed to snare.

'We'd like to borrow this phone, if we may,' Claire said. 'It won't take long, but will allow us to trace him.'

Angie looked outraged. 'No, it's not all right! Look, I've told you it's not him. He's in Madrid, you've got the wrong man. And this ridiculous suggestion that a man like this would choose, would even *need* to choose, a schoolgirl, as if he's some kind of paedophile. Kyle could have any woman he chose, and he chose me.' She tapped the middle of her chest. 'Anyway, you said yourself you don't even know what your suspect looks like.'

'I didn't say that.'

'You most certainly did.' Ms Wright had worked herself up into quite a lather, and held out a well-manicured hand, as if Claire was going to return the phone.

'Ms Wright, we do have a warrant. But it would be better if you cooperate. The phone can be back with you within an hour once we've extracted the data.'

'So I've got no choice.' She stood up, and ruffed out her hair.

Claire gave the nod to the female officer, who opened the door. 'You're free to leave, Ms Wright, but you cannot go home yet.'

'Why?'

Claire looked at her watch. 'Because fifteen minutes ago we obtained a warrant to search your house too. Officers will already have effected an entry, and will be searching for evidence. Anything taken will be receipted of course, and we will pay for any damage to locks.'

The woman stared at Claire for a long half minute. 'You're an ugly bitch. He wouldn't even look at you.'

'Given what he is capable of, that would be a huge relief,' Claire said.

The female officer escorted Angie out, and returned with a cup of coffee for Claire. 'Nasty piece of work, her,' she said, jabbing her thumb over her shoulder.

'It's understandable. We've just punctured her bubble of romantic perfection, so she's hitting back. She put a brave face on it, but she knows we're right.'

'It's not true, you know.'

Claire looked up from her paperwork. 'What?'

'You've got a lovely face. And you're nice on the inside too. Just saying.'

Claire smiled. 'Thank you.'

–

The pictures retrieved from Ellen Bramley's phone were if anything poorer quality than those from Angie Wright's. But as Claire Mulholland put them all up together on a screen, it became clear that Gabriel Hallam was Kyle Halliday. But Gary Harrison, Sam's old ex, had only a partial resemblance to either of them.

'Come and have a look at this, sir,' she called to DCS Raj Otara as he walked past her in the incident room. She pointed out the resemblance and then added, 'But Harrison looks like a brother or something. The teeth are completely different.'

Otara stroked his beard. 'There's a scar on the jawline of Hallam and Halliday, but not on Harrison.'

'Do you think he's had surgery?' she asked. 'Some kind of cosmetic procedure?'

'If he has it's pretty substantial, because the shape of his jaw is quite a lot more pronounced now.'

'Or perhaps they really aren't the same person?' Claire asked.

'No, I think they're the same,' Otara said.

'There's one person who will definitely be able to tell us, when she is better.'

'Sam Gillard?'

'Yes.'

That was the exact moment when Craig Gillard walked in. The detective chief inspector looked to have aged. His face was gaunt and an unruly stubble shadowed his features.

'You look awful, Craig,' Claire said. 'How's Sam?'

He blew a sigh. 'She's utterly traumatised. It's going to be a long road back.'

'Why are you even here?' Otara asked. 'You should be getting some sleep and looking after your wife.'

'Sam's parents arrived from Keswick this morning, and will be looking after her at our house. A caseworker from Victim Support has been assigned too. I've asked Rigby to put me back on the case, part-time, until we find Vanessa Perry. I'm hoping to persuade her that I have unique insight and information, so I'm going up to see her in a few minutes to see if she'll relent.'

'Craig,' Claire said, with exasperation. 'You only have one unique role that nobody else can do, and that's looking after Sam and helping her recuperate. She'll want you more than anybody. I think that's what you should be concentrating on.'

Gillard thrust his hands deep into the pockets of his bomber jacket. 'I will do that, but not until we have nailed Gary Harrison for good.'

'So take a look, Craig,' Otara said indicating the screen full of images of their suspect. 'Tell me – is it the same guy?'

Gillard took a look and shrugged. 'I wish I could tell you. I've never seen him face to face.'

–

DCS Raj Otara called an impromptu update for the incident room at midday. Only half the team were there, the rest being out in the field. Gillard, his request to go back on the case refused by the chief constable, had just departed to return to look after Sam. Claire Mulholland was there, along with DC Carl Hoskins and most of the NCA research crew.

'Okay everyone, some great work has been done today. First, we discovered the whereabouts of Samantha Gillard, and rescued her.' There was a round of applause across the room. 'We have also identified the dark-haired woman recovered from the Warrior. She is Yvonne Fairfield, nineteen, missing for almost four years.'

Claire nodded. 'It's solved what for me was a very difficult and under-resourced case. I'm going to see her mother this afternoon, to break the news.'

Otara continued. 'This is great news, but as you all know, we have more to do. DI Perry's daughter Vanessa is still missing, and we are increasingly concerned for her safety. We haven't yet managed to track down our suspect, although we have discovered a burned-out Range Rover near the village of Long Stainton, between Aldershot and Guildford.'

He turned to Research Intelligence Officer Sally Rickard. 'Sally, how is the trace going?'

'The phone we're still on is the one Gabriel Hallam, a.k.a. Kyle Halliday, used to ring Elaine Bramley. It's been off most of the time, but has lit a few cell towers going west past Aldershot. Clearly it is not in the same vehicle anymore, though the speed of movement shows that it is still in a vehicle of some sort. If we are lucky we may get an ANPR hit while the phone is still on, which might allow us to narrow down the range of possibilities.'

'That's good. We've also managed to get a proper mugshot from the DVLA of Kyle Halliday's driving licence, which is still registered to the address in Fleet where apparently he no longer lives. Just to remind you we're still under newspaper and press blackout.'

A phone rang on the edge of the incident room. Hoskins answered it, and began making notes. His alarmed tone was picked up by others sitting nearby, especially when he started looking around.

'What is it?' Otara asked.

'Perry isn't here, is he?' Hoskins looked around the room.

'No. He's gone home to work on the Jane Morris case. I've sent a family liaison officer with him, in case of bad news.'

Hoskins nodded. 'Good. Because they've just found a young woman's body, near the village of Long Stainton.'

–

Detective Inspector John Perry arrived at the crime scene only a few minutes after CSI had erected the tent. The liaison officer had sensibly decided to come with him. Perry spotted the distinctive Tesla of Home Office forensic pathologist Dr David Delahaye, and managed to button-hole the man himself as he emerged grim-faced from the tent, wearing a Tyvek suit and blue latex gloves.

'Is it my daughter?' Perry asked. 'Is it Vanessa?'

A uniformed constable prevented Perry from following the pathologist back to his car, and seemed unaware that he was actually a detective, until the liaison woman explained. Perry's eyes followed the pathologist as he rooted about in the boot of his car and returned with a black briefcase.

'How old is your daughter?' Delahaye asked, as he prepared to duck back into the small tent that had been set up at the edge of a hedge.

'Seventeen,' breathed Perry.

Delahaye permitted himself a small smile. 'It's not her, then. The victim is in her mid-twenties I would say.'

'Thank God.' It was only the intervention of the two uniformed officers that prevented Perry falling to his knees. The liaison officer put her arm around Perry, and led him to her car. He clung on to her like a child, sobbing with relief.

'We'll find her soon, John, don't you worry.'

His next utterance, choked with tears, took her a while to understand. *Five dead already. What chance does she have?*

She shushed him, and stroked his back. Over his shoulder she could see a large red plastic suitcase being removed from the tent in a clear plastic bag.

Chapter Twenty-one

Two hours earlier

There was no satnav in the Fiat and Vanessa Perry wasn't very good with maps. Two police cars screamed past her in the opposite direction just before she got to the turn-off for the village of Long Stainton. She had only gone a hundred yards down the narrow country lane when Kyle ducked out from behind a hedge and flagged her down. He pulled open the driver-side door and seized her by the hair, dragging her out. 'Where have you been, you stupid bitch?' He cuffed her round the head, three times: forehand backhand forehand. It made her ears ring. It was only the second time he had ever hit her, not counting when they had sex.

'Ow, I'm sorry I'm sorry I'm sorry.' She fought back tears, not of pain, but of anxiety that having let him down, he might go off her.

'Did you bring the petrol can?'

'Yes, it's in the boot. I filled it up yesterday.'

'Get it.' He dragged her out of the driver's seat, and pushed her towards the back. 'There's matches and wadding – run to the Range Rover, it's just a quarter of a mile on the right. Burn it. I'll text you the rest of the instructions.'

Vanessa opened the boot and pulled out the canvas bag which contained all the arsonist's tools she needed. She was just about to return to the passenger seat when Kyle said, 'Close the boot, idiot.'

She did so, and she watched in amazement as Kyle reversed the Fiat, almost knocking her down. 'Aren't you going to give me a lift?' she shouted through the open window, as she ran after the car. 'My clothes are in there, in my bag.'

'No time,' he bellowed, pointing to his wristwatch. 'Remember what I said? Make the rendezvous. Don't put your phone on until eleven, understand? Don't go home or contact anyone else.'

Vanessa blew him a kiss as he reversed away from her down the lane towards the main road. He didn't see her, because he had his arm over the passenger seat, and was looking behind him.

'I love you,' she whispered. 'Looking forward to seeing you tonight.'

After the car had disappeared and its engine note dwindled to nothing, she shouldered the heavy canvas bag and turned on her heels, slogging down the lane away from the main road. Crows were cawing in the still-bare trees. It felt lonely here, and sad. A few hundred yards on, sure enough, the black Range Rover was there, in a muddy passing place on the quiet twisty lane. The car was unlocked, and the keys in the ignition. There was an enormous red plastic suitcase in the boot. He hadn't mentioned that to her. Maybe it was something important that he had forgotten.

In the months that she had known this wonderful, exciting man, he had told her many tales of working for

British military intelligence in Afghanistan. How there had been cover-ups of terrible crimes against civilians by American forces, crimes Kyle had witnessed, and that was why he now had to live under a pseudonym. The British government always did what it was told by the Americans, which is why the British police were after him. It had all made sense when he'd explained. Kyle had built this dossier on a datastick that he kept with him at all times in his silver briefcase. One day soon, when the data was complete, he would reveal it to WikiLeaks.

But things had gone wrong.

The German violinist girl had some vital information which he needed to prove his case, and had come all the way to Britain to give it to him, but at their rendezvous told him she had been poisoned at a London hotel. She gave him the information he needed but died in the back seat of the big green car. He took her body to his workshop under the arches.

Vanessa had found it all very difficult to believe, until he showed her the body in the freezer. She was stunned to see the poor poisoned woman. That's when she knew Kyle couldn't be lying. She had cried for the poor girl, living undercover as a musician, working for the underground opposition. Kyle had explained that he wanted to goad the authorities, to convince them Beatrice was still alive, which would force them to show their hand with a huge police operation. He had told Vanessa to expect the British state would kill more people, and try to blame it on him. The newspapers would be proof. In the end he was proved right. Kyle had such a difficult life to live. Even his partner, the awful Angie, didn't know who he really was, and the terrible secrets he was holding.

Vanessa was very excited, even though she was dizzy from where he had hit her. She quickly realised it must just have been the stress of the situation. She could feel the big roll of cash in her pocket, all her savings that he had asked her to withdraw, because his accounts were being monitored. Once she had burned the car, all she had to do was find her way to Manchester Airport. He would meet her there, in departures by the Thai Airways desk, this evening for the 20.50 flight to Bangkok. It was so romantic. She had been so excited about this that she could hardly sleep.

The one thing he had not explained was how to burn a car.

She assumed that if she just sloshed the petrol around on the seats, and tossed in a match, that would do the trick. But what about the suitcase? If that was all his stuff for their trip, clothes he had forgotten in his haste, he would be furious if she set it on fire. She thought about messaging him, but remembered how angry he'd been before when she disobeyed him. She lifted the rear hatch and tried to open the case. It was locked, and there was also a surprisingly big padlock with a combination on it. Clearly there was something important in there, and there was no way he would want her to burn it. She tugged it towards the edge of the boot, and tried to lift it down. It must've weighed almost as much as she did, but she managed. Why didn't it have wheels? Vanessa slid, pushed and shoved the case into the base of the hedge, next to the car. She covered it with a branch so it couldn't be seen so easily, but then realised it might catch fire when she burnt the vehicle. What was she to do? She thought for a moment and then realised that driving the car a short way would avoid the problem. Then if Kyle needed the suitcase he could come back and pick it up. Although he had been so stressed with her, she thought he would be pleased that she had shown this piece of initiative. She climbed into the car, started the engine, and set off further down the lane. She found a layby midway between two bungalows. She leaned over to the passenger seat and unscrewed the can of petrol. The stink of the fuel filled her lungs, and she tipped it out onto the passenger seat. A sudden coldness on her thigh made her realise she had splashed her leggings. She would have to be really careful. Opening the door and easing her way out of the driver's seat, she took the box of matches and a single match, holding it away from her, and struck it against the side of the box. It flared, and she immediately tossed it inside the vehicle.

It went up like a bomb, and the blast of heat forced her back.

She ran for twenty yards, then turned back to look. The Range Rover had been transformed into the biggest bonfire she had ever seen. She wasn't sure which way the church was. Instead, she saw a footpath sign, and decided that this would be the best way to avoid being spotted. It looked like a sunny day, and the first rays that lit her face made her think of Bangkok, and the new life that awaited her there.

–

Melanie Perry pulled up at the traffic lights, revving the engine in her eagerness to get on the trail of the man she now hated. 'You really thought you were going to get away with this, didn't you?' She didn't normally talk to herself, but now she was shouting over Classic FM, which she had put on hoping it would calm her. 'I trusted you, bastard. I gave you everything. I bailed you out with thousands that I could ill afford. When I think that I remortgaged my own house, sweet Jesus, what was I thinking? Now I don't even know whether to believe that you really have a sick sister in Colorado with some expensive medical bills. But, Christ, didn't I fall for it?'

She arrived at the head office of AWL Properties, a small modern office next to a car dealership on the edge of Woking. Kyle rented at least two if not more of the AWL properties. 'Ah yes, Angie bloody Wright,' Mel shouted at no one in particular. 'I bet he fooled you too.' It was a Sunday, and AWL's office was closed, but the car showroom was just opening.

Mel had dressed up purely for this part of the operation, and marched into the showroom. A young man of perhaps twenty-five in a suit and slicked back hair offered her a broad grin as he came out to greet her. 'Hello madam.' His wholesome display of insincerity reminded her of Kyle, and for a moment she imagined whipping out the sushi knife, and neatly beheading him. She shocked herself with the lucidity of her imagination, the spray of red over the shiny bonnet of the white BMW he stood next to, his perfectly coiffed head bouncing and clattering to the floor. The chiselled features not his but Kyle's.

'You can save your patter. I'm Mel Perry, head of sales at AWL. I need the spare office keys, which I know you keep in that filing cabinet.' She pointed behind him through the internal glass window into the dealership office. She remembered. It was almost exactly two years ago that Kyle had brought her there and tried exactly the same stunt one evening, in order to get in. Once they had managed to get into the AWL office, he tore her clothes off and they had had passionate, in fact almost unbelievable, sex on the client settee. He had grabbed her throat and told her that she had been too noisy. But with him she never knew how to be quiet.

The young man blinked. For a moment she felt that he could read her mind, and felt her cheeks flush.

'Okay. You'll have to sign them out,' he said. 'You could have warned us.'

'It's okay, I'll only be five minutes.'

With the keys in hand, Mel let herself in. The secretary's in-tray showed an up-to-the-minute listing of which AWL properties were taken. Perfect. She had already driven past three of them before coming here. In each case the lights were off, so she assumed he wasn't there. That left only five to do. She'd do the furthest property first. It was a secluded rural barn, just the place he'd take Vanessa to avoid being disturbed. Mel laughed. *I'm going to disturb you alright.*

She dropped the keys back with the salesman, and drove off at a ferocious speed.

–

Programming the satnav, Mel drove over the M4 and into Wiltshire. It was forty minutes later when the female voice told her to take a rural side road, which eventually became a track between two arable farms. In the distance she saw the building she was aiming for. The sales sheet said it was a charming nineteenth-century barn, with satellite Internet, wifi and all mod cons. But she had been there once before, briefly, and could testify that it was dirty and ill-kempt, with pigeon shit everywhere. They had been on their way out for a night at a country hotel while John was away on the nightshift at Mount Browne. Kyle had shown her the internal office, like a portable ticket booth, that he had created within the barn from flatpacks. He had also pointed out the barn had an illegal blue asbestos-lined roof. Completely impossible to lease, and it would cost tens of thousands to renovate. Kyle had been scathing, saying it was the most obscure and useless bit of Angie's entire industrial property portfolio. She had come out of her divorce with the worst end of the deal. She had supposedly been awarded half the value, but her ex-husband must have bribed the surveyors to over-value all these semi-derelict buildings, and not to notice the asbestos on this one. They had both laughed about Angie being duped. Already by then Mel had become enmeshed in scorning a woman she didn't even know, simply because she was a rival.

'I used not to be like that,' she shouted, over Bach's 'Air on the G string'. 'I used to be nice. He's made me greedy, selfish and bitchy. I'm clingy and shallow. And jealous, even of my own daughter.'

There was a red Fiat that she didn't recognise outside the barn. She hoped that she had not made a mistake and that it really would be him that was there, not some other tenant who had been given informal access. There was no window for him to see her from, but she was aware that the rough track would create tyre noise. She knew too that she must not underestimate him. She had no idea whether there was CCTV fitted on the barn. It would be typical of him to have done that. He was meticulous. Always meticulous.

She slid the car into a gap by a hedge, 300 yards away from the barn. She shrugged off the formal jacket and went to the boot. She slipped on John's stab vest, then his thick outdoor coat and over trousers which she had grabbed from his home office on her way out. She could have taken his formal cap too, had she been so minded. Finally she took off her high heels, and slid on John's wellingtons. There are some advantages to having a short, slightly built husband. For the first time in many days she felt a slight twinge of affection for the poor sod.

Finally, she donned Vanessa's leather backpack with its deadly blade within, then trudged towards her target.

–

Picking her way around puddles and noisy gravel, Mel approached the barn. At ten yards it was clear there was no CCTV camera, just a satellite dish. She could see the building's hardwood doors were closed. She rested her ear against them but could hear no sounds within. She also knew that with the internal office, which did have windows, there was no way she could surprise him. Was it really just a question of waiting for him to come out? It was only noon, and he could be in there all day. She made her way carefully around the perimeter of the building, noting that there was a lean-to shed at the back, with a cracked window and a rotten door. It seemed to be full of discarded timber, old window frames and builders' rubble.

She reached the door handle and, as she pulled, it let out a grinding noise. There was a great clattering of wings as a flock of pigeons exploded from the top of the barn. She jumped inside the shed, close the door and waited. After a minute she heard the creak of the barn door opening and footsteps. She held her breath as the crunch of feet came closer and then went past. She saw the shadow of him pass across the window. She took a deep breath, slid the knife from its scabbard and burst out of the door.

He was just turning away, his craggy profile catching the light. She knew what she must do. She had surprise on her side, but must use it quickly, and decisively. If she hesitated she was dead. But she was a woman and violence did not come easily. The prospect of taking a life terrified her, especially that of a man who for the last three years had been the secret joy of her world and her reason for living. And that was why she hesitated. She hesitated because she wanted answers.

'Why wasn't I enough? She's my *daughter*, you bastard!'

'Mel!—' Surprise flew across his face on spotting the blade, and instinctively he crossed his arms to protect his chest. Her first downward slash bit deep red exclamation marks into the outer edges of both his hands, even as one snaked out for her throat, his favourite target. He caught her on the windpipe even as she ducked, but not before she thrust deep and low, her entire right shoulder behind it, pushing, pushing until her fist connected with his solar plexus, and the deep-buried blade jarred against bone. His screech of agony as he keeled over backwards was an octave higher than she had ever heard from him, and was accompanied by a spray of blood that spattered them both.

But she wasn't finished with Kyle.

In fact she had hardly begun.

Chapter Twenty-two

Vanessa Perry was fizzing with excitement. It was five p.m. and she was standing by the Thai Airways check-in desk at Manchester Airport. It had been an epic journey to get there, by taxi and several trains, and had made a hefty dent in her cash. She had picked up all the clothing he had ordered for her from John Lewis in Manchester, including the big white suitcase with her wedding dress in. She could hardly keep still, even though the flight didn't leave until 20.50. She had dutifully messaged him at eleven, once she was on the train to Manchester. He had messaged her back quickly, but did not respond to her subsequent texts. She had been shocked when he had struck her earlier that day, but having thought it through it was simply a measure of the depth of his passion for her, and his disappointment that she could not quite match his standards of organisation and planning. She would just have to try harder. Even what he did to her in sex, when he liked to press her throat hard with both hands until she almost fainted, she realised was just another form of love. When she had first mentioned it to Becky, her friend had said that it was supposed to make the pleasure more intense, and porn stars did it all the time. It must be normal, so she would just have to get used to it, to surrender to his power.

She cleared her mind of these minor worries. Just a few hours and she would be in his arms again. From her new Louis Vuitton handbag, she took out the small jewellery box, and slid off the tight-fitting lid. She stared at the beautiful ring within, the big sparkly diamond he had bought her, much larger than the measly thing her dad had given Mel. Surely it would do no harm to put the ring on now? Kyle wouldn't mind. She slid out the ring and carefully placed it on her engagement finger.

Feeling like a different woman, and full of the joy of love, she looked around the busy check-in desks for signs of her lover approaching. He'd told her he'd booked them both business class tickets, which had presumably cost loads. She could hardly wait to get her glass of champagne, the proper meal with cloth napkins and the real cutlery that someone who travels in style should feel entitled to. Her dreams really were coming true.

She was still standing there at six o'clock. None of her texts had been answered, and the queue for economy had begun to form. She smiled away her anxiety, telling herself that there was still plenty of time. He was busy, obviously, a bit under stress. The papers were full of stories about dead bodies, and then this evening's *Manchester Evening News* had mentioned his name in connection with the inquiry. She had no idea how anyone could deal with the kind of cloak and dagger life that he had to live. She passed the time by looking at her ring from various angles, watching it sparkle, and thinking about the life in Thailand that they would have together. But as the minutes passed, and Kyle didn't show, she began to rehearse various disappointment scenarios: *He's annoyed with me over the late arrival with the car. He's upset because I keep messaging him. He's not managed to find the big red suitcase. He's been arrested by the police or MI5.* That would be awful, but for her it was not the worst fear. That was a much more personal one:

He's met somebody else and abandoned me.

That was always the biggest worry, and never far from her thoughts.

Just before seven o'clock, and now feeling decidedly anxious, she walked up to the business class check-in clerk. 'My fiancé has our passports and booked the tickets, I just want to check my big suitcase in to save some time.'

The woman smiled and said, 'What name is it please?'

'His name is Kyle Halliday.'

She worked the terminal and looked puzzled. She asked Vanessa to spell the name, and after another minute said. 'Hmm. No booking in that name. Can I have your name?'

'It's all right,' she said hurriedly. 'He'll probably be here in a minute.' She realised that the police might be looking for her too, and using her own name would be stupid. Kyle had arranged the passports, and of course they would have to be false names. Hers too. Silly not to realise that.

For half an hour she wandered around the terminal, looking at the other check-in desks, peering into shops, but always with a view of the approach routes to the Thai Airways desk. The economy passengers queued up and were gradually dealt with, luggage checked in, boarding passes dispensed, all ready to pass through security. The check-in area gradually emptied out, just the odd passenger now hurrying in to business class. But no sign of Kyle. At eight o'clock, with still no sign of him, she began to cry. A few people came up to her and asked her if they could help, but each time she shook her head.

Vanessa kept telling herself that she had to be brave. What he had asked her to do was very little compared to all of the work he had done. At five past eight, having tried to ring him and text him another dozen times, she went back to the business class check-in. The clerk double-checked for a Halliday booking, and then shook her head. 'I'm really sorry. All of our business class passengers are already checked in,' she said.

Vanessa twisted her ring desperately. 'He might have left a ticket for me,' she sobbed. 'I'm Vanessa Perry, Mrs Halliday-to-be.'

An immediate look of pity crossed the kindly face of the check-in lady. 'I'm so sorry,' she said. 'Let me check again, perhaps the tickets are for seats in economy.' As she worked the keyboard, her expression subtly changed, a crease of concern in her brow. 'Just one moment, please,' she said, and picked up a phone, and stared over Vanessa's shoulder. She spoke quietly to someone and then said, 'Okay, that's fine. No, she's right in front of me.'

'Is everything all right?'

'Yes, everything is just fine.' The smile this time was more formal, colder. Vanessa looked over her shoulder, and saw two uniformed security men approaching her.

'Vanessa Perry?' asked one.

'Yes?'

'Everybody has been very worried about you.'

'Why?'

'I think you need to come with us.'

–

Detective Inspector John Perry got two calls in quick succession. The first was to tell him his wife had rung

999 to announce that she had killed the man who had abducted their daughter. The second was while Gillard was driving him to that crime scene in Wiltshire. It was Greater Manchester Police, with news that Vanessa had been found safe and well at Manchester Airport. For a good half hour after that, Perry had sat with his eyes closed, breathing deeply. Gillard left him to it.

'What I don't get,' Perry eventually said to Gillard, 'is how Halliday managed to get his own Mitsubishi Warrior stolen, yet still have it to run you down a few days later.'

The DCI accelerated hard to pass a slow lorry. 'My guess is that he arranged for your daughter to steal it, in disguise. Then in his witness statement, which of course nobody would challenge, and the CCTV kind of confirmed, he described seeing some bloke driving it off.'

'But what on earth is the point of something so elaborate?'

'All right, imagine he just picked up Beatrice Ulbricht at the bus stop on Sunday, attacked her in the Warrior, maybe made some kind of mess in the car, blood, semen whatever. All the forensic leads are going to point back to him, right? He's sharp enough to know that even if he scrubs it well, there are going to be traces. So his best protection is to have a fallback position in case the car is identified, and that fallback position is that yes, the vehicle is his, but it was stolen from him before Beatrice was killed. So of course it's got his DNA in it. It's kind of brilliant really, making himself the victim. Because his is the only description we have, and it is one we are going to trust. After all, we've all seen him fall on his arse in the road.'

'Well, it did look real.'

'I'm sure it was. I can't imagine he expected Vanessa to pull him off his feet like that, though I'm guessing that he exaggerated the extent and duration of his injuries.'

'Vanessa passed her test first time four months ago, but she'd have needed coaching on a big truck like that.' Perry thought for a moment. 'Look, I used to be a physics teacher. There's no point arranging to have his Warrior stolen on the Monday, say, if he killed Beatrice on Sunday. He can't go back in time and fix it.'

'Yes, but the marvellous service that Vanessa provided for him on the train was to make Beatrice appear to be still alive two days after she actually died. It's a kind of timeshift.'

Gillard looked at Perry, who was staring out of the window. It was clear he wasn't thinking straight, but that was hardly surprising. His whole life had been turned upside down. Not many people could recover from that.

The next day

An early morning incident room meeting saw DCS Rajinder Otara reveal the results of the CSI investigation of Kyle Halliday's lair under the railway arches. Gillard was aware of most of the main points: that Yvonne Fairfield's body, already frozen for some years, had been the decoy inside the Mitsubishi Warrior, with Sam bound and gagged inside a locked metal box in the inspection chamber underneath. But some details had eluded him.

'Here is the Japanese tuna freezer,' Otara said, pointing to a photograph of a very large cabinet freezer. 'It's in this, we are convinced, that the bodies first of Jane Morris, then Yvonne Fairfield and later of Beatrice Ulbricht, were stored. By the time CSI got to look at it, it was clear this freezer had stopped working.'

'Presumably that is why he got rid of the bodies into the river,' Gillard said. 'The freezer he had been relying on for decades finally packed up, soon after he dumped Beatrice into it.'

'That's right,' Otara responded. 'We think there was a power surge during the thunderstorm on Sunday. Halliday was able to monitor the electricity from an app, and must have realised immediately, and driven over to try to rectify the situation.'

'But what about the other bits of chiller kit there?' Gillard asked. 'There was enough to freeze the car.'

'My guess is that he saw a problem and an opportunity,' Otara said. 'Once he realised the extent of the flooding, he saw that it was a chance to dispose of a couple of the bodies in circumstances that might not draw attention to him. Stowing them inside the Allegro put someone else in the frame. If the bodies had been lost in the water for, say, another three or four days, they would have been much harder to identify, particularly Jane Morris.'

Rainy Macintosh put up her hand. 'We know from credit card activity that Halliday had ordered another big industrial freezer, but there was a week-long delay in delivery,' she said. 'He would have been left with three decomposing bodies in the meantime. He only got the big chillers delivered a couple of days after, and they would never have been a long-term solution.'

'That's all beginning to make sense,' Gillard said. 'But what strikes me now is that it was only because he was trying to get revenge on me that he kept Sam alive.

Otherwise she'd have been killed and then frozen with the others.'

A hush descended on the incident room, as all eyes turned to Gillard.

Otara addressed him directly. 'You can take great solace in having cracked the riddle so quickly. Even another minute in that inspection pit and she would have drowned.'

–

After the meeting finished Gillard and DI John Perry remained in the incident room while DCs Rainy Macintosh and Rob Townsend showed them Kyle Halliday's silver briefcase, found yesterday at the barn. 'What we've got here is his complete box of tricks,' Rainy said. She opened the lid to reveal a foam insert, in which a small laptop and six mobile phones were embedded. There were spaces for half a dozen more. 'Each mobile phone is used only for one woman. The social media, the photographs, text messages and so on only correspond to a particular relationship.'

Rob Townsend meanwhile had broken into Halliday's laptop, and opened up a large spreadsheet with colour-coded columns, each headed with a woman's name, and a series of dates marked on the rows. 'This is the master spreadsheet, which details exactly who he's seeing, when, and which particular set of lies he has told them. He has written and presumably memorised everything he learned about their families and life history, so he doesn't get mixed up.'

'Incredible,' Gillard said.

'Aye, our Mr Halliday made a note of the wedding anniversary of Ellen Bramley's parents, even though he only dated her for a few months,' Rainy said. 'Whereas my ex, bless his cotton socks, was married to me for a decade and couldn't even remember *my* birthday.'

Perry looked closer, and saw that his wife's name was on the second column, and his daughter's on the ninth. 'Good grief, how many women were there?'

'Aha,' said Rainy. 'We are not yet sure. We have just found in here a wee set of bank cards relating to somebody called Geraint Harris, of Telford, Shropshire, someone we hadn't heard about, who had been buying the freezers and chillers. We traced the address and rang Geraint's wife, Sophie, who isn't even on this sheet. She hasn't seen her husband for more than a week. We haven't broken the news to her yet, not until we're absolutely sure he's the same person. Mrs Harris may have been targeted originally because she had a significant lottery win eight years ago. She turns out not to have seen her husband for over a week. She thought he was visiting his sick sister in Colorado, where she is undergoing expensive medical treatment.'

'That's a lie he told to many of the women,' Gillard said.

Rainy smiled. 'It's clever because it provides not only a motive for being a bottomless money pit, but it proves what a wee angel he was, looking after his sister. In fact there is no sister. The photos he used to back up this lie, of him sitting at her bedside, are actually of a paralysed woman called Valerie Turner, who lived in Nottingham but died in 2017. It's at an early stage, but Nottinghamshire Police is already investigating whether she was defrauded of her half million accident compensation two years before her death.'

'What a bastard,' Perry said.

'So Geraint Harris was in Telford? That's where the black Range Rover is registered to,' Townsend said.

Gillard smiled. 'We had assumed it was a cloned plate. Still, Gary Harrison, Gabriel Hallam, Geraint Harris. There's a certain pattern here.'

'Until we come to Kyle Halliday,' Rainy said. 'He is the central pivot of the whole spiderweb of lies and fantasy, because of the property he leased from Angie Wright, which enabled the entire seduction operation. Claire Mulholland and I interviewed her again this morning. Her ladyship is being a lot more cooperative now, though she's still defending Halliday and is reluctant to see him for the piece of scum that he was. He first leased the railway arches from her husband twelve years ago to store the big freezers in, but after a while wormed his wee way into her marriage. Her husband divorced her in 2011, and gave her the crappy end of the property portfolio. Our love rat then leased three or four additional out-of-the-way places from her, which he used mainly for sleeping with other women.'

'I don't know how he had the time,' Perry said. 'Just being in one relationship is hard enough work.'

'The answer is that he didn't have a job,' Rainy said. 'Years ago he was a telecoms engineer, repairing handsets, and later a chef at a college. He got some basic qualifications soon after leaving the army, but presumably found defrauding women was an easier life. The international telecoms consultancy is a fiction, just like the sick sister fable, and the even more preposterous story about being an undercover agent in Afghanistan, which according to the spreadsheet is one that he told your daughter.'

Perry shook his head in disbelief.

'Halliday wasn't a husband or a dad, and wasn't involved in providing for or supporting anyone but himself,' Rainy said. 'He seems to have lived entirely on money cadged, borrowed or stolen from the various women in his life, who he moved between on a rota that was set down on his spreadsheet. That was his career, and it was pretty much full time. We know about the fourteen grand he took from Ellen Bramley, and we can see from the Geraint Harris accounts that he has had over a hundred and fifty grand from his wife in the last year. There was a lot of money coming in, but just as much going out. The numerous cars, the jet ski, and so on. He regularly booked himself escorts too, according to the Geraint Harris cards.'

Gillard turned to look at Perry, who shook his head ruefully. 'I don't think Mel would have given him anything. She is pretty shrewd.'

The other detectives looked meaningfully at each other but said nothing.

'Sam had always told me what a fragile ego Gary Harrison had,' Gillard said. 'Charming at first, paying lip-service to women's rights and equality, but it was always to an end. She felt used by him, as if he owned her.'

'Until you turned up,' Rainy said. 'I've been giving this some thought. I'm sure that's why you were targeted. He'd probably never lost a woman to another man before, and even though it was years before, he couldnae handle it. I'm sure that's the motive for targeting you and Sam. He was after revenge.'

'And any woman who resisted, got murdered,' Perry said.

Rainy snorted in disagreement. 'You didn't even have to resist. Valerie Turner died a year after her compensation was paid. It seemed like natural causes, but there's an incriminating note on the spreadsheet giving a "termination day" for her.'

'Rainy, that's great work you've done,' Gillard said.

'Well, he seemed to write everything down, so once we cracked the access code with Rob's help, this whole Pandora's box of crime just opened up on the laptop. According to both Ellen Bramley and Angie Wright, they never knew when he was due to arrive. But he was careful to be considerate and charming,' Rainy said, her eyebrows raised in bemusement. 'Let me read you something from Valentine's Day this year, when our wee love rat was as busy as a blue-arsed fly. "Posted roses for Ellen, Sophie and Vanessa. Massage (!) with Mel 11.40 a.m. at Wholebods, lunch after at Creighton Hotel…"'

'The absolute bastard!' Perry exclaimed. 'I'd got Valentine's Day off, but Mel turned down *my* offer of lunch because she insisted she had a client who booked in months ago!' He stood up, his face flushed.

'Och, I'm sorry, John.'

'It was a bit thoughtless, Rainy,' Gillard said, as he watched Perry storm off.

'I'll just finish this wee bit while he is not here. "Dinner with Angie (bring jewellery) at Gilded Swan, room booked. Two a.m. slipped out for Vanessa: ten-minute BJ in back of car".'

Gillard looked over his shoulder where Perry was no longer visible. 'I'm sure he wouldn't want to have heard that either.'

'The guy was a machine,' Townsend said softly, with a hint of admiration.

Gillard retorted: 'Well before you start getting envious, young man, let's recall that he was a multiple murderer, a kidnapper and rapist.' He turned his focus to the laptop. 'What have you got for the date that Beatrice Ulbricht died?'

'Ah yes, we've got something on this.' Townsend moved the cursor across to Angie Wright's column, and a large comment box opened up for the day in question. '"Argument with AW", which I assume is Angie Wright. "Arranged to meet call girl at Excelsior. No show. Driving back saw enticing girl in hat at bus stop. Offered her a lift. Quite a bit of resistance, bitch squirted pepper spray. Lost my temper and squeezed too hard, so sadly she's got to join Mum".'

'In the freezer,' muttered Gillard.

'There's something else that I wouldnae let John know,' Rainy said. 'There's a so-called termination date for Vanessa on the spreadsheet. It was to be tomorrow.'

–

Rainy Macintosh eventually tracked Perry down in the canteen to apologise for her crass insensitivity. 'I'm really sorry,' she said. 'Maybe you shouldn't have sat in on that part of the investigation.'

The detective inspector shrugged. 'It's just so humiliating.'

'Well, maybe I've got something to cheer you up. It looks like your hunch was correct that the murderer was related to Jane Morris. He calls her Mum in his own spreadsheet, and we now have some science to prove it. The familial DNA test you asked for came in a wee while ago. Halliday has got a forty-four per cent match to her, which is within the range of mother–son connection. We should follow it up with a mitochondrial test to be sure.'

He emitted a small smile, but the rest of his face remained dour.

'I also looked in more detail at the register of births around the time that Jane Morris disappeared. A child was registered as Graeme Garrison in Wandsworth, parents given as Linda and Harold Garrison, six months before wee Jane vanished. That presumably was the child in the pram. Graeme left school at sixteen, and that's the last trace of him. I think that must be when he changed his name to Gary Harrison. There is no trace of it, because as I've discovered you don't have to formally notify anybody unless you do it by deed poll. I reckon he took a couple of years to shake off the family association, and then he joined the army under the same Gary Harrison name.'

Perry nodded. He'd seen close up that Halliday was a man who gave women what they wanted. Yet in the end, he took each of them for all the money that they had. He turned honest women into liars, clever women into fools, and independent women into helpless supplicants.

He went home to meet his daughter, pushing his way through a crowd of reporters that had gathered in Romney Crook now that the press blackout had been lifted. Vanessa was there with family liaison officer Gabby Underwood. She was snuggled up under a blanket on the settee, and without make-up looked lost and innocent, the little girl he always pictured in his mind. There were tears in her eyes and as he smiled at her, she put out her arms to him.

'Dad,' she said. 'I am so sorry.'

He sat next to her and embraced her, the prodigal daughter finally back at home.

–

Later that week, Gillard found himself accompanying the chief constable to RAF Brize Norton in Oxfordshire. A private flight had been laid on to take the body of Beatrice Ulbricht back to Germany for burial. The two police officers stood on the chilly windswept apron by a small jet, alongside a group of Beatrice's closest British friends and colleagues. Among them were the three remaining members of the Lysander String Quartet. In the distance, a sleek hearse led a cortège of vehicles towards them. The polished black Jaguar came to a halt and four uniformed pallbearers got out and slid the coffin from the back. Beatrice's parents emerged from a following vehicle. As they did so, the sound of a solo violin soared above the distant traffic.

Karl-Otto Ulbricht put an arm around his wife. They watched the coffin being gently slid onto the conveyor which took it almost silently into the belly of the aircraft. As the ramp withdrew, and then closed like a giant mouth, many of those watching embraced each other, and quietly cried. Gillard blinked too, his vision smearing. This was not only sympathy with those close to her but also a measure of guilt for his own failure to apprehend the killer before he had struck several more times. It was only yesterday when he had met the parents of PC Lynne Fairbanks, still struggling to come to terms with the death of their daughter. Her funeral would come next week, along with that of Yvonne Fairfield and of Jane Morris. His own aunt had narrowly avoided that fate, still in a coma, her condition stable.

Claire Mulholland had told him that after three years Yvonne's mother had ceased the daily emails beseeching her to think about her missing daughter. She had rung Claire yesterday and thanked her for giving her the peace of knowledge.

'There is some kind of closure now,' she had said.

Epilogue

Melanie Perry was charged with murder, but admitted the lesser charge of manslaughter on the grounds of diminished responsibility. The trial created a huge public debate. In the middle of the judge's summing up someone shouted out from the public gallery: 'She shouldn't go to jail, she should get a bloody medal!' This didn't just sum up the public mood but that of the jury too, who, ignoring the comprehensive evidence of premeditation, acquitted her. For manslaughter, she was sentenced to three years.

Sam Gillard was slow to recover from her horrific confinement of more than thirty-six hours in the steel box. The sensory deprivation, the panic-inducing claus-trophobia and the feeling of freezing water mounting slowly towards her gagged mouth reappeared nightly in horrific dreams for many months. Counselling and therapy helped, and she was eventually able to describe her ordeal.

One of Sam's first trips out of the house in those difficult early months was a trip with Gillard to visit John Perry and his daughter Vanessa, who were also rebuilding their lives. Later Sam would go to visit Melanie Perry at HMP Bronzefield women's prison, partly to thank her, but also to share her experiences of being a victim of the same devious criminal.

–

On a beautiful spring day towards the end of May, Sam Gillard sat with her husband in the garden of the Royal Oak pub not too far from where they lived. The first parasol-like leaves of the horse chestnut trees had emerged, fresh and green and fragrant. The psychotherapist said she was making excellent progress, and most nights she no longer suffered nightmares. Despite that, she had been advised not to try to return to work too early. The chief constable had given Craig generous compassionate leave, and more to the point had insisted he take all of it.

Sam sipped her gin and tonic, and eyed the man who had saved her from being drowned in darkness. 'Okay Craig,' she said. 'I'm ready to hear the details.'

He had promised to fill her in on the various bits of the investigation which had not been made public but wanted to wait until she felt she could hear it without becoming upset. Today, finally, she did feel ready.

Her husband took her hand and stroked it gently. 'As far as we can work out,' he said, 'Graeme Garrison became Gary Harrison at eighteen, and Geraint Harris six years ago. That was the first proper false ID, when he started to get all the utility bills with his name on in Telford, that subsequently allowed him to get a passport under that name.'

Sam shook her head. 'So even in the year or so that I went out with him, he was already married to Mrs Harris under another name?'

'I guess so,' Gillard said. 'And he was dating others. He'd already destroyed the marriage of Angie Wright, and was siphoning off money from a disabled woman in Nottingham. The family and two kids in Croydon, which he had mentioned when he was working at the college in Bromley, turned out not to exist.'

'Sophie Harris was the first, then?'

'Yes. He must have read about her and the lottery win. The story she tells is that he fell off his racing bike in front of her car, just as she was pulling out of a minor road one evening. She felt terribly guilty and gave him a lift to hospital. He must have played up his injuries, because she offered him money not to report the accident. She'd been drinking, and already had plenty of points on her licence. She said he was utterly charming about it and gradually worked his way into her affections. She was flattered, because she's at least fifteen years older than him, and at first he didn't seem interested in her money.'

'Typical Gary, all charm at first.'

'Like all the others, she just accepted that he would be away several nights a week. Sophie Harris said that he had gone to Miami for jaw surgery in 2018, which is where he got his teeth changed so radically. I think she paid for it.'

'And the woman in the suitcase?'

'PC Lynne Fairbanks. I think he might have been a bit disappointed how at little knowledge he could get out of her about the state of the investigation.'

Sam took another sip. 'He was obsessed with getting back at you, Craig. He asked me a lot of questions when I was captive in that awful garage, about you and about the state of the investigation. I don't think he ever wanted me for who I am, but just couldn't bear the idea that I'd chosen you over him.'

Gillard gave a wan smile. 'It just showed he'd never grown up. He had such a big inferiority complex that he could only feed it by trying to sleep with as many women as possible.'

'I do remember,' Sam said, 'that he hated his family and never wanted anything to do with them because they were brutal to him as a child. Only in the army did he ever feel that he belonged. I'm surprised he ever left.'

'He got a dishonourable discharge after only a few months, that's why,' he said. 'A sexual offence of some kind, unsurprisingly.'

'There was something else I heard when I was held captive. It was about Beatrice Ulbricht. He'd had some kind of row with Angie on the Sunday evening, and had gone out to meet an escort at a hotel, but she didn't show. On his way home he saw Beatrice at a bus stop where he gave her a lift. Of course being Gary he thinks women will just melt at the first thing he says. But when she refused his advances she fought back like crazy apparently, kicking and punching and using pepper spray. He complained that it got sprayed all over the car, and wouldn't come off. I think that's why he dreamt up this elaborate plot to have the vehicle stolen from him.'

'And of course helped by Vanessa, who worshipped the ground on which he walked,' Gillard said. 'When we talked to her, she said that they practised the theft manoeuvre for half an hour on an old airfield until she got the feeling of the vehicle.'

After lunch, they finished their drinks and drove off for an afternoon together in the warm sunshine. They found themselves at the pleasant riverside village of Lacey Dutton. They walked over the Loxcombe Bridge, now fully repaired, and strolled along the embankment where inquisitive ducks gathered at the water's edge hoping to be fed.

–

At that same exact moment, in Croydon crematorium, a private funeral service was taking place. The celebrant, an experienced sixty-seven-year-old called Michael Noonan, looked out at the almost empty benches of those who had gathered to witness the life of a man christened Graeme Garrison. Noonan always tried to speak to the friends and relatives before a funeral service. Often it was impossible because of the numbers. But in this case the task had been simple, because they were so few. In the front row, the redoubtable grandmother, Betty, was there with a couple of elderly neighbours from her care home. And there were also two elegant and well turned out women, Angie and Sophie, who were sitting at the opposite ends of the rear bench. Each had described themselves as Graeme's partner.

Noonan knew exactly who it was who would be cremated. He had done his homework, and knew the press had wanted to attend. There had also been many email enquiries by members of the public, and plenty of trolling. The most surprising was an official letter from HMP Bronzefield, requesting a CD copy of the service to be supplied. The crematorium had the facilities for live streaming for those relatives who were unable to attend a ceremony, and they could keep copies. But he had never before heard of a prisoner being able to request one. If the prison authorities were prepared to allow it he could see no reason to refuse. The grandmother had requested no hymns nor prayers, no eulogy nor description of the life of this mysterious man. That left him with most of the allotted forty-five minutes of the service to fill. He decided that he would have time for most of Fauré's Requiem and a full committal. In the middle, however, he had to say something. He was saved by a letter, received the day before, which just had a few lines.

> *My love,*
>
> *I don't have a name for you now that I'm sure about, but I do have many wonderful memories. I knew you just a few months, and despite all your faults and many deceits your touch upon me will be indelible.*
>
> *Ellen xx*

Afterword

I have taken some liberties with the geography of Surrey for the purposes of the plot. There are no sizeable railway embankments near Pirbright, and the villages of Shildon and Westmeare are fictitious. Lacey Dutton, a village which first appeared in *The Body on the Shore*, reappears here in its full and charming glory. If it existed I'm sure I wouldn't be able to afford a house there. The new development of Shepherd's Rest near Woking is also fictitious, though obviously similar to many that actually exist.

I would like to thank Home Office forensic pathologist Dr Stuart Hamilton for carefully checking my forensic and post-mortem scenes, and retired Detective Inspector Kim Booth for his insight and knowledge. I was also helped by Simon Thomas, crew manager at Lincolnshire Fire and Rescue, on the river rescue scenes. Thanks also to Mark Buckle, to the media relations team at British Transport Police, Duncan Claber at South Western Railway, and Kiat Huang for his knowledge of mobile phones. Any mistakes remaining are my own.

Michael Bhaskar and the Canelo team as always were enthusiastic backers of the book. Miranda Ward did an excellent editing job. Tim Cary, Cheryl Cullingford and Sara Wescott, my readers' circle, made invaluable suggestions. Above all is my wife and first reader, Louise, to whom this book is dedicated.

ⓒ **CANELO**CRIME

Do you love crime fiction and are always on the lookout for brilliant authors?

Canelo Crime is home to some of the most exciting novels around. Thousands of readers are already enjoying our compulsive stories. Are you ready to find your new favourite writer?

Find out more and sign up to our newsletter at canelocrime.com

Lost Cause
Rachel Lynch

DI Kelly Porter has solved some of the Lake District's most gruesome murders but nothing has prepared her for the monster she's about to meet. The answers may lie with a local oddball – is he a victim, or a killer?

Lies to Tell
Marion Todd

Since she joined the St Andrews force, DI Clare Mackay has uncovered many secrets lurking in the picturesque Scottish town. When there is a critical security breach inside Police Scotland, she realises she may have put her faith in the wrong person – will it be a deadly mistake?

The Body Under the Bridge
Nick Louth

DCI Craig Gillard has spent his career hunting criminals. When a missing person case reveals itself to be far more than a routine disappearance, it isn't long before the perpetrator has another target: DCI Gillard himself. Suddenly the detective isn't just running the case – he's part of it.

A Front Page Affair
Radha Vastal

Capability 'Kitty' Weeks is determined to prove her worth as a journalist. Headlines about the Great War are splashed across the front pages, but Kitty is stuck writing about society gossip – until a man is murdered on her beat and she is plunged into a story that threatens the life she has always known.

When the Past Kills
M J Lee

The Beast of Manchester was the case that defined DI Thomas Ridpath's career, but the wrong person was convicted and only later was the true culprit put away. Now, those connected to the case are being targeted. Someone is desperate for revenge, and Ridpath risks losing more than he can stand.

Small Mercies
Alex Walters

DI Annie Delamere is off duty and enjoying a walk in the Peak District when she comes across a mutilated corpse. As the body count increases, Annie is under intense pressure to solve the case. But are the crimes the work of a deranged mind – or a cover for something even more chilling?

Home Fires Burn
Lisa Hartley

DS Catherine Bishop is dealing with the aftermath of the most brutal case of her career. Her small team is overwhelmed by an arsonist, and a new murder case provides far more questions than answers. The pieces finally fall into place, but have Catherine's demons already won?

When the Dead Speak
Sheila Bugler

Eastbourne journalist Dee Doran is investigating a woman's disappearance when the body of another is found. There are startling similarities between the dead woman and one who was killed sixty years previously. Dee is determined to uncover the connection, but sometimes the only thing more dangerous than secrets is the truth…